Mounted

E. H. Reinhard

AUTHOR'S NOTE

This book is a work of fiction by E. H. Reinhard. Names, characters, and incidents are products of the author's imagination or are used fictitiously. Any resemblance to actual events or persons, living or dead, is entirely coincidental. Locations used vary from real streets, locations, and public buildings to fictitious residences and businesses.

CHAPTER ONE

William Allen David sat in a gray cloth recliner in the largest of four rooms on the lower level of his home. His feet were perched on a leather ottoman. The basement of the single-story home was partially finished and contained the living room he was sitting in—complete with fireplace—another finished room that the previous owner had made into a den, and two additional rooms—one for storage and one for laundry. He'd recently purchased the home and relocated to that part of the country for a new job, one he'd been terminated from after two days. In his right hand, he clutched a remote control. A large flat-screen television was affixed to the wall beside the mantel of the fireplace, which was an odd placement for the television but one that would serve his needs. William clicked the button on the remote to rewind the DVD that had been playing on a loop—he played the recording again and paused the screen at two minutes and twenty-six seconds—his favorite part of the recorded telecast—where the female sports anchor fumbled for her words.

William set the remote control on the end table beside

him and lifted his glass of scotch from its coaster. He tucked the glass under his thick, overgrown mustache and took a long, slow drink as he stared at the image paused on the television screen.

A sound caught his ear from over his left shoulder. He set his drink back down on the end table and pushed himself from his seat. William walked to a closed door at the back of the room, near the stairwell leading up, and opened it.

Inside was the storage room, with the laundry room off to his left. The left, right, and back walls in the storage room were white-painted cinder blocks though they weren't visible. Plastic sheeting hung from the ceiling to the floor and draped over the chest freezers butted up against the left and right walls. In the center of the room was a large table, which was also covered in plastic—a couple of items sat on the table's surface.

William stood in the doorway and stared at his guest standing near the back wall. The woman's name was Katelyn Willard, and she was a twenty-two-year-old brunette. William had followed her from a restaurant back to her apartment and had picked her up in the parking lot. William took in her body once more. Katelyn had a thin face with big brown eyes—they'd need to be changed. Her skin was flawless, the same tone as what he sought. Katelyn's long, straight hair hung inches past her shoulders. The hair color and style wasn't right, but William could easily take care of that with a trim and some hair dye.

He walked over to the table and picked up an old camera. He hung it by its cord around his neck and stepped directly before her. The woman was standing with her back against the cinder-block wall. Her arms were outstretched at her sides, her wrists shackled. The cables that extended from the shackles, four feet in length each, went up to bolts through an I-beam that supported the floor above. Katelyn's ankles were also shackled in a similar fashion though the cables restraining her were connected to anchors sunk into the concrete floor. Katelyn wore a ball gag in her mouth—nothing else.

William gently took her face in his hand—she yanked her head back from his touch. He rubbed the wetness from her teary cheeks across his brown-and-red flannel shirt. He lifted the camera and put his eye to the viewfinder, centering her head in the window. Katelyn turned away from him.

"Look at me," William said. "They need to see what you look like while you're alive."

His words must have caught her off guard, for she looked directly at him. William caught her look of fear in his viewfinder as he focused on her.

"There we go," he said and snapped the photo. "That one is going to look real nice."

Katelyn mumbled something again.

"I didn't catch that," William said. He pulled the camera from around his neck and set it back on the table, from which he picked up a large hunting knife, and walked back to Katelyn. William held the knife before her so she could get a look. He spoke inches from her face. "Sorry, I'm going to have to kill you now. I need more practice."

She screamed into the gag and ripped her body back and forth.

William tapped the blade of the knife against the ball in her mouth. "You know what they say: practice makes perfect. I need it to be perfect."

Katelyn screamed again into the gag.

"Let's get that thing out of your mouth."

William reached behind her head and undid the ball gag's straps. He pulled it from her mouth and let it drop to the ground. Before the plastic-and-leather gag made contact with the floor, Katelyn was screaming for help.

"Shh," William said. "You're wasting your breath. No one is going to hear you. I was just keeping that thing in your mouth so your noise wouldn't interrupt my television. I had some sports to catch up on—recorded most of it." He leaned in closer to her and filled his lungs through his nose. "That smell. You smell just like her."

William pressed his body against hers, pinning her against the cinder-block wall. Katelyn screamed at the side of his head. He could hear her teeth snapping together as she bit at the air, trying to get a bite of his ear or face or anything she could.

William kept his weight against her while he pressed his left fingertips hard against her chest above her left breast.

"Someone help!" she shouted. She tried to pull herself away from his touch.

"Just let me find the soft spot," William said. He pressed his fingertips harder against the ribs of her upper chest. Then he found his spot and stopped moving his hand. He pressed the knife tip to the area. He looked Katelyn square in her blue eyes as he applied pressure.

"Don't kill me," she said.

"It's required."

Katelyn screamed for help again, to no avail.

William applied more pressure to the blade and felt it sink into her chest cavity. He slowly pushed the blade into her chest until it bottomed out on the knife's guard. Her screaming, like the others before her, went silent as soon as the knife entered her. He watched her facial expressions change from fear, to shock, to panic before her eyelids went heavy and the life left her body. William backed away from her, leaving the knife in her chest. Katelyn's screams still echoed in his head. Her body hung from her arms, her knees were buckled, and her feet no longer supported her. William watched the blood roll down her naked body and pool in the plastic beneath her left foot.

William fished his hand in his pants pocket and removed the key for the shackles. He walked back to her, knelt, and freed her dead body from the restraints. After taking Katelyn's body in his arms, he lay her across the table, positioning her head so it was just off the table's edge. He confirmed that she was arranged the way he liked and went to the far corner, where he pulled the plastic from the wall and exposed some metal shelving filled with supplies. He grabbed a pair of clear safety goggles and strapped them around his head. William stripped off all his clothing and tucked it away behind the plastic sheeting. Wearing only the safety goggles, William crossed the plastic-lined floor for his reciprocating saw. He took it in both hands and squeezed the trigger multiple times—the long, thin saw blade flapped back and forth in the air as he did.

CHAPTER TWO

"I have to run, babe." I knelt and said my good-byes to Porkchop then grabbed the Jeep keys from the kitchen table. "I'll probably be back in a few hours."

"Hold on." Karen walked up to me and wrapped her arms around my neck. "Ball didn't say what he needed you guys in for?"

"He just sent the message last night to show up this morning. I'm guessing we probably have an investigation. I doubt he'd ask us in on a Sunday if it wasn't something like that."

"Okay." Karen didn't let go of my neck but stared at me and smiled.

"All right. I'll be back in a bit. Then we'll go do this brunch or whatever."

She still didn't let go—just stared at me.

"What?" I asked.

"Nothing."

"Can I go to work?"

"I guess," she said but didn't let me go, continuing to smile at me.

"What's with you this morning?"

"Nothing."

"Mmm hmm. Something is up with you," I said.

"What makes you think that?"

"My job is to notice when things don't add up. You, since last night and especially this morning, don't add up. And we never do brunch. What's the occasion?"

Karen chuckled and scratched at the side of her head through her dark hair. "Whatever. You think you're so smart."

"So, I'm right is what you're saying?"

"I guess you'll find out when you get back."

"Right," I said.

Karen dropped her arms from my neck and followed me to the door. She saw me out and waved as I pulled out of the driveway—both of which weren't normal.

I pulled up to the Manassas building a couple minutes after eight thirty and walked into our empty office ten minutes later. As I walked toward my desk, I spotted Beth and Ball sitting in the meeting room. Ball waved me in.

I popped the door open and stuck my head inside. "Morning. I assume the Sunday meeting means that we have something." I entered the room and swung the door closed at my back.

"We do," Ball said. "Come in. Grab a seat."

I did and noticed Ball had a couple files sitting before him.

He ran a hand through his gray hair and leaned back in his chair. "This is ugly," he said.

I shrugged. "I've seen ugly before."

"Not like this," Ball said.

"Okay," I said. "So it's that kind of bad? What are we dealing with?"

"All right." Ball let out a puff of air. "The *Louisville Press-Gazette* received a roll of film and a letter in a package last Wednesday. There is a copy of the typed letter in these files. The film contained the images that are in these files—four deceased women. The letter states that he plans to kill more until his process is perfected. The original film and letter, as well as the package that they came in, are with our local office there."

"Process perfected?" I asked.

"Yeah, you'll see what that entails inside here." Ball tapped on the files before him.

"Are you going to let us look at those?" I asked.

"Here." Ball slid one file toward me and another toward Beth. "You're going to Kentucky. Tomorrow morning."

I took the file and flipped the cover open. The number on the cover page told me it was a new investigation. "When did this come in?" I asked.

"I got the call late last night, just before I sent you guys the messages to come in this morning," Ball said. "The locals have been on it for a few days already. I looked over everything before I went to bed, which probably wasn't the smartest thing to do. I didn't sleep worth a shit."

I turned the page and stared at the sheet before me, which showed photographs of four women's driver's licenses—all Kentucky issued. At a quick glance, the women all appeared in their early twenties. I looked at the names: Kelly Paige,

Jennifer Pasco, Trisha Floyd, and April Backer. The fact that I was looking at actual photos of the driver's licenses themselves, as opposed to copies of the licenses, was odd.

"What's with the photos of the DLs?" I asked.

"The images of the driver's licenses were processed from the film that was sent. The guy wanted the identities of his victims known."

Ball motioned for me to flip the page. The next page was four more photographs. Each woman had a ball gag in her mouth—each was alive. I could see fear on their faces. Their foreheads were marked, in what looked like Sharpie ink, with the numbers one through four. A couple of the women had noticeable eyeliner streaks down their cheeks where tears had washed it from their eyes.

"Do we know if these women are in fact the ones that the DLs belong to?" Beth asked.

"Yeah," Ball said. "Here comes the bad part." Ball motioned for us to continue into the file.

I turned the page and looked. "What the hell?"

"Geez." Beth groaned.

I rubbed my eyes and stared at the four photos. Each photo was once again of each woman's head—severed from the body at the base of the neck and lying on a plastic-covered table.

Ball rubbed at the back of his neck. "Unfortunately, it still gets worse."

I flipped another page and rolled my head back on the headrest of my chair. "Come on." I shook my head and held up my palms. "Who in the hell does this shit?"

"That's what you guys need to find out," Ball said.

I looked back down at the page. Each head was mounted by the neck on wood—similar in fashion to a deer-head mount. The mounts looked gruesome and macabre—completely unnatural, as if they had a freak-show air to them. The necks of the women were craned so the heads looked forward. Below each woman's head was her hands, mounted at the wrists, and fixed as though they were supposed to be holding something. Something immediately struck me as off.

"Their hair has been changed—different color and style," I said.

"He's apparently trying to make them look the same," Ball said.

"To look like who, though?" Beth asked.

"Also something we'll need to figure out," Ball said.

"What do we know about the women?" I asked. "Any way to connect them?"

"The local office has been contacting friends and the families of the victims, and honestly, I have no idea what the hell they could have said to them. Anyway, from everything that came through, they can't connect the women. The only thing we have is that they live in the same area geographically—about a seventy-five-mile radius or so."

"What the hell is wrong with people?" Beth asked. "I mean, who even thinks to do this kind of stuff and then actually follows through with it?"

I grumbled, rubbed my eyes again, and looked back down at the photos. Each woman's mount was positioned the same. The numbers written on their foreheads were still visible on the completed mounts.

"These women's bodies?" I asked. "Have they been found?"

Ball shook his head. "No, never found."

"When did they go missing?" Beth asked.

"All four within the last three weeks, and all from the Louisville area. None of the women were taken from the same locations, though," Ball said.

"The locations and the way they were taken?" I asked. "What do we know there?"

"Seemed they were all alone, at night. Opportunity, I guess. Two women…" Ball looked through his file, "Kelly Paige and Trisha Floyd, were last seen at bars—vehicles found nearby, where they'd parked, we assume. Jennifer Pasco was last seen leaving a party and walking back to her residence. The last and most recent, April Backer, we don't know. She lived alone and disappeared sometime between when she got off of work at a restaurant and when she was to report to work the next day. Her vehicle was found on the side of the road with a flat. No other information there."

"Tell me about the flat," I said. "A legit flat tire or punctured?"

"That's as much as I know," Ball said. "There are some files from the missing-persons divisions that were handling these girls when they went missing—the papers are in the backs of your file folders there," Ball said. "You might want to touch with them on that."

I nodded and flipped the page in the file. The letter from

the killer came next—as Ball had said, it was typed. I took a minute and read it over. The gist of it was that he'd killed four women and planned to continue killing women until he perfected his method—a few a week, he said. The reasoning behind him sending the photos to the newspaper was to let their families know that the women were dead and that they shouldn't waste any more time searching or hoping for their return. He said he'd send another package when he was ready. The bottom of the letter was signed The Sportsman.

"The Sportsman?" I asked.

Ball shrugged. "He named himself, apparently."

"Any record of the name in anything we have?" Beth asked.

"No. The closest thing we had was some nut back in the eighties that the media had dubbed The Trapper, on account of his occupation as a fur trapper," Ball said. "The guy is still alive, albeit in prison with another hundred years or so remaining on his sentence. The guy operated out of the St. Louis area. He kidnapped a couple of young women and then killed them after hanging onto them for a month or so. He dumped their bodies in the river a few miles from his house. There isn't anything to tie this guy to what we're looking at here."

"No kids, family—nothing on this Trapper guy?" Beth asked.

Ball shook his head. "Nope. No children or siblings. He was only in his twenties when he was apprehended. The guy has spent more years in prison than he ever had out in the world. Aside from the name the press gave him being remotely close, nothing else ties the two."

"Okay," I said. "Any leads with anything that was sent? The film, packaging, letter?"

"No prints, but there were signs that everything was handled with latex gloves. The film roll was expired by a few years, meaning it was a few years older than the expiration date. I don't think we'll have much luck with that. The package used regular postage, enough to cover the charges, and looks like it was dropped in a random mailbox."

"How do we know that?" I asked.

"The package was tracked back to the post office that it was scanned in at. Obviously, no return label, but the mailman—or woman in this case—remembered where she picked it up from. Local agents went to the house. Seems no one was home, and the post office had a 'stop delivery' listed at the address for a week. They got in touch with the family that resides at the home, who are out of the state on vacation, which checked out."

"So our killer knew that this family was out of town?" I asked. "Suggests he knows who they are or is local enough to know when someone isn't around."

"Or just got lucky in that regard, but it needs to be looked into," Ball said, "which the local office is already doing."

"Did they try to print the mailbox?" I asked.

"They found nothing," Ball said.

"The numbering of the women?" I asked. "What are the thoughts there?"

"I was kicking that around last night. I'd have to think the numbers represent which victim came first."

"He says in the letter that he's trying to perfect his method. Maybe the numbering goes along with that," Beth said. "I mean if you're experimenting with something, you keep a log of your results, change methods, see what works and what doesn't, that kind of thing. The numbers could be so he can track his progress."

"What's the goal, though?" I asked. "Trying to make a perfect mount?"

"Could be," Ball said.

"What are we thinking here?" Beth asked. "Taxidermist? I mean…" She paused and brought the photos of the mounted heads near her face. "The facial features are a little off, like they've been monkeyed with, and the eyes are reflecting back. They look like glass. Hold on." Beth shuffled back through the file to the women's driver's license photos. "Says here we have brown eyes on the DLs for three of these women." She flipped back to the photo of the mounted heads. "Each of these women now has green eyes to go along with the changed hair, and it looks kind of like higher cheekbones."

"I saw that," Ball said. "Like I said, he's trying to make them all look like someone."

"Him trying to make everyone look the same strikes me that he may be trying to perfect the method to do this to a certain someone, you know," I said.

"Could very well be," Ball said. "But then there's the question of who he is practicing this for."

"Okay, so we find taxidermists in the local area that we can connect either geographically or another way to the home that the package was mailed from, and we have our guy." I slapped my hands together. "Easy as it gets. Which leads me to wonder why we're being sent out."

"Well, it's not that easy. There's only fifteen or so taxidermists located within the area we believe our killer resides. The local office has been on anyone in that line of work since the paper received the package. Aside from everyone checking out, it seems that none of them believe whoever did this was a skilled taxidermist."

"Why is that?" Beth asked.

"Aside from the general unprofessional look of the mounts, human skin being removed and mounted doesn't work very well, we were told. One of the taxidermists had a look at the photos. Skin discolors when tanned, which the skin on these photos is not. He went on to say that human skin would stretch too much and is far too thin to be suitable. The taxidermist seemed to think that, within a week or two, the skins from these women's faces would be decomposing, rotting, and falling off of the mounts. Which, thinking about it, is even more horrible than if they didn't."

"Yeah, there's a nice visual image that I probably didn't need," I said.

"Jim is going to come in after a bit and get you guys all set for your travel. He'll e-mail you guys the details later this afternoon."

I flipped my folder closed and stood. Beth did the same with hers.

"Give me a ring tomorrow when you get out there," Ball said.

“Will do.” I started for the door when a thought bubbled up in my head. I stopped and looked back at Ball pushing himself away from the table and standing. “Have there been any other women reported missing since the last known victim?” I asked.

Ball shook his head. “Not yet, but that doesn’t mean that our killer doesn’t already have someone or more than one.”

I scratched at my cheek, nodded, and walked from the room.

CHAPTER THREE

Beth and I touched down at the Louisville airport a few minutes after one o'clock. Though we sat business class, my flight was filled with a constant machine-gunning back massage from the five-year-old girl seated behind me kicking my seat. I looked back at her once or twice, at which she smiled, stopped kicking, and then resumed shortly after. Her mother, seated beside her, didn't seem to be too concerned with her daughter's airplane behavior—only administering a brief scolding once when the little girl let out a bloodcurdling shriek.

Beth and I trekked through the concourse and made our way down to the baggage claim. She stood at my shoulder, tapping away at the screen of her phone. I glanced over, saw she was sending a text message with a number of exclamation marks at the end, and took my eyes from what she was doing.

Beth dropped her phone into the pocket of her black blazer. "Done."

"Done, what?"

"With Scott. That's enough."

"Did you just break up with him through a text message?" I asked.

"It was more of a finalization. We had it out pretty good yesterday. I told him I was heading out of town on an investigation, and he threw a little-kid fit, like normal. As soon as he started in, I grabbed my things and left his condo. So he calls and calls and calls. When I finally answered, he started right back up. We argued on the phone for a bit, and I told him that I was done trying and that it was over."

"How did that go?" I asked.

"Well, he reverted to his usual offense of trying to make me feel guilty, but I stuck to my guns. I'm not happy with him, so enough is enough. The text I just sent was in response to him asking if I'd come to my senses. My response was, 'Yes, I have, finally; we're through; and I'd like you to get your things out of my place while I'm out of town.'"

"If not being together is going to make you happier in the long run than being together, it was the right move," I said.

Beth nodded. "So how was your brunch yesterday?"

"Huh?"

"Yesterday, brunch? Before we left the office, you said that you and Karen were going to have brunch out in Fairfax."

"Oh, yeah, it was good. We went to a little place in the downtown strip of Fairfax—sat and ate. Karen told me that we'd been approved for adoption. I guess the home studies went well enough."

Beth swatted my shoulder. "That's awesome news, Hank. Why didn't you tell me that right away this morning?"

I shrugged. "I don't know. It's just kind of another step.

Karen was pretty happy about it, though. Apparently the parties involved believe that we're an acceptable family for a child, so I guess that's something."

"Yeah, that's something. Congrats. So now what?"

"We wait."

"How long?" Beth asked.

"I don't know. There's some things that Karen and I have to discuss there. We'll see. Longer wait if we go one route, shorter wait on another. We've kicked around a couple of options, but we really need to get into it. I guess I'd like to adopt a child in need of a good family, anywhere from about five to ten years old. Karen wants an infant, which would make the wait years, and by then, an infant when we're well into our forties doesn't seem like the best idea, I guess. Like I said, we need to continue the discussion."

"Either way," Beth said. "I'm sure you guys will be great parents. I'm happy for you. Tell Karen I said congratulations."

"Appreciate the vote of confidence. And I'll make sure I tell the missus."

"Any new news on the house hunting?"

"A bit," I said. "Apparently, a place that we looked at a few weeks ago and actually liked came back on the market. So now, Karen is all hot on that again. We'll see. I told her we'd talk about it when I got back."

"When is your lease up on the townhouse?"

"A couple months. I'm not against staying there, but Karen has this vision of us being settled into a nice house and welcoming in a child. If I know my wife, which I do, I'm guessing she'll really start pushing the house thing any time now. Which makes me think that I should call our finance guy for preparation."

Beth smiled.

After a couple of thumps and squeaks, the track on the baggage carousel started spinning.

"So, Agent Duffield is who we'll be looking for when we get over there?" Beth asked.

"Yup." I pulled back my suit-jacket sleeve and took a look at my watch. "When I talked to him on my way to the airport this morning, I said we'd be over around three. Figure we should have enough time to get checked into our hotel and get over there."

"And the hotel is downtown?" Beth asked.

"Yeah, didn't you get everything from Jim?" I asked.

"I did, but I just glanced at it. Like I said, I had a pretty full day and night of dealing with Scott," Beth said.

"Okay. Hotel is north from here—downtown about ten minutes. Bureau office is east about twenty."

"Got it."

The luggage carousel started kicking bags out a moment later. Beth and I grabbed our suitcases and picked up our cars from the rental counter. After a quick drive, I pulled up to our big, brown fifteen-or-so-story hotel, smack in the middle of downtown Louisville. Red awnings hung over the shop windows of the businesses to the sides of the main entrance—a larger red awning hung out from the front of the hotel over the valet area. The sides and front of the awning at the front entrance read The Brown. The navigation running on my phone told me to round the building for the parking structure behind it, which I did.

As I waited to pull into the building's parking structure, I caught a view of Beth in her rental car behind me in the rearview mirror. She was waving her hands and looked as though she was yelling into the mouthpiece of her phone. I pulled into the parking area and found a couple of free spots a few levels up. I stepped from the car and went to the trunk. Beth parked beside me, opened her car door, barked a few profanities into the phone, and jabbed her finger at the screen.

She looked over at me but said nothing. We wheeled our bags toward the bridge connecting the hotel and the parking structure.

Beth's phone chirped in her pocket. She didn't answer it or bother to look to see who was calling. We crossed the bridge, entered the hotel, and walked down a flight of stairs to the lobby. I glanced at the ceiling of the place and took everything in.

"Some place," I said. "Looks kind of like the Drake Hotel we stayed in while we were in Chicago." I regretted mentioning it the second the words left my mouth—Beth and her now-ex-husband had been married in that hotel, and I was sure a few thoughts were stirring in her head. "Sorry."

"No, don't be. Here, hold on. I need to take care of something quick." Beth wheeled her suitcase up to the back of a black leather love seat, one of about ten sitting in the lobby, and pulled her phone from her pocket. She clicked a few buttons on the screen, let out a breath, and put her phone away. "There. He's on the autoreject list until further notice. I don't need him bothering me while I'm trying to work."

I didn't respond, choosing instead to stare up at the giant gold-and-crystal chandeliers, three stories above—the ceiling the chandeliers hung from was ornate, painted plaster. I looked up and to the left. A long hallway behind an iron railing looked down onto the lobby from inside painted decorative archways.

"This place is gorgeous, hey?" Beth asked.

"Fancy. Jim is trying to suck up to us again. I actually kind of wonder what his reasoning is as to where he gets us rooms."

"You don't know?" Beth asked.

I looked at her. "No. Does he actually have some kind of method?"

Beth smiled. "Sure. Ball says either 'put them somewhere nice,' or 'just get them a hotel.' Then Jim goes into his office and pulls up a search for hotels. He'll literally search the words *nice hotel* and the city and pretty much just book whatever comes up if it's within a certain area."

"So Ball is the key?" I asked.

"Yup," she said.

"Good to know. When is his birthday?"

Beth snapped her fingers. "You just missed it."

"Damn."

"Come on, let's go check in." Beth pointed across the lobby at the front desk. We stopped at the desk, checked in, and got the keys for our rooms on the seventh floor. Then we headed to the elevators and rode up.

"We probably have a half hour or so until we should head out," I said.

"I really only need to drop my things and splash a little water on my face. I'll be ready in five. Maybe we can hit a drive-through or something on the way over there. I'm starving."

"Yeah, that will work," I said.

The elevator let us off, and we walked toward our rooms. I stopped at my door, and Beth's room was directly across the hall.

"I'm going to give Ball a ring quick," I said. "Just pop over when you're ready, and we can take off."

"Okay." Beth disappeared into her room.

I slid the card in the door and pushed it open. The room, not unlike the Drake hotel, where Beth and I had stayed months prior, was classically designed. The wallpaper in the room was a pattern of gold, which matched the bed and had a striking resemblance to the carpet. A wingback chair, also matching in color and with walnut-stained legs, stood next to a big wooden armoire that held the television. I wheeled my suitcase between the bed and armoire to the office chair and desk near the windows. I set my things down and pulled open the curtains. My view consisted mostly of an old stone-colored high-rise directly across the street. I looked down at the street below and saw the red awning over the valet area at the front of the hotel.

I scooted the office chair out, sat, and dialed Ball.

He picked up at his desk right away. "Ball."

"Hey, it's Hank. We're here. We're going to head over to

the local field office in a few minutes."

"Sure. Did you make contact with Agent Duffield yet?"

"Just briefly this morning. Basically, an introduction and I'd see him this afternoon."

"Did he say that they had anything new?" Ball asked.

"No. I don't think he was even in the office yet. It was fairly early when I called."

"Okay. Why don't you or Beth give me a ring tonight when you're through for the day? Let me know what, if anything, you come up with."

"Sure," I said. "Hopefully, there is something to report."

"Right. We'll talk later."

I clicked off and stood. A knock came at the door a moment later, so I opened the door for Beth, and we left for the bureau office.

CHAPTER FOUR

William sat in his studio, as he liked to call it. He'd converted his home's master bedroom into his workplace for creating his mounts. Before him, Katelyn Willard's skull was bolted to the framework he'd attached to a walnut mount—he'd removed the skin and brain and had boiled the skull the night prior. William reached out and ran the tip of his thumb along the modeling clay he'd applied to recreate facial muscles. The glass eyes had already been set, and the fiberglass resin and cloth to form the neck area that extended down to the mount had dried. William lifted the skull on its mount and walked to the table nearest the bedroom's window, looking out over the grass of the backyard. He slid out the chair at the table, had a seat, and placed the mount before him. Across the table were various spools of waxed string, threading needles, cans of adhesives, and women's makeup. William looked down to his right at the skin from her face, which he'd prepared earlier.

His process for removing the skin from the skull was fairly straightforward—William ran a razor from the base of the neck, where he severed the head, up through the back of the hair on the scalp and stopped just before the hairline met the forehead. From there, he carefully peeled it away.

William lifted the facial skin from the table and gently turned it inside out in his hand. He reached over, grabbed a can of spray adhesive from the corner of the table and sprayed the inside of the skin. When the total area was covered, he draped it over the skull and positioned it, running his hands over the face and applying light pressure to smooth the skin to the clay and bone beneath and allow the adhesive to make contact and set.

He let his hands drop to his lap. His shoulders sank as he let out a long breath. "Better, but still not quite right," he said.

William shook his head while staring at the face. He grumbled to himself and spun the head so he could stitch it up in the back. After that, he was ready to apply the makeup, seal the face with a spray lacquer, and then work on her hands.

CHAPTER FIVE

Driving, Beth made a right down the street that bent around toward the Louisville FBI office. The building came into view as Beth slowed for a four-way stop.

I stared through the windshield, across the grass, and over at the main Bureau building set behind a concrete-and-metal fence. The office building looked older—thirty or forty years was my guess. The red-brick main building was three stories and set partially into a small hill. At the building's front, facing the street, was what I figured to be the main entrance. A big, rounded, gray overhang stuck off the building, supported by pillars. An American, an FBI, and a Kentucky flag flicked in the breeze on large poles stemming up from the landscaping. Beyond the flags was a break in the fence and what looked like the blacktop of a parking lot.

"I think the parking lot is to the right over there." I pointed.

Beth clicked on her turn signal and proceeded up the small incline to the entrance. She pulled in and found us a spot in the mostly empty lot.

"It looks like we have to walk through the guard building

there to get into the facility." Beth motioned toward a square building with fencing protruding from its sides.

I nodded and stepped out of the car, taking my bag with the investigation files from the back. We headed into the security office and stood in a small room with a white floor. To our left was a bulletproof-glass window—dead ahead, a security door that led us back outside for the walk to the complex. A pair of benches lined the right wall below a large FBI insignia.

I stepped to the window, where a thirty-some-year-old man leaned back in a chair, wearing a blue T-shirt with "FBI" written in yellow across it.

I took out my credentials as Beth passed me hers. "Agents Hank Rawlings and Beth Harper from Manassas. We're here to see Agent Duffield in Serial Crimes."

The man leaned forward in his chair and slid out a metal tray from below the window without saying a word.

I dropped our credentials in, and he slid it back. I watched through the glass as he scanned both and sent them back through the slot at me.

"Just a second, Agents. I'll get you guys some badges made. You'll be able to use them to get into the security doors. The next time you come through, you'll be able to just swipe and enter. We also have a secured parking deck around the corner from the guest lot you guys used. If you're making return visits, you can just use that."

"Sure," I said.

Beth and I took seats on the bench and waited in silence for a couple of minutes before he had us set.

"Here you guys go." He sent the metal tray out toward us with two plastic key cards with our names and faces on them. "The bar code on the back will get you through the secured doors. Head into the main entrance and use the elevators on the left. You'll need to scan your card to access the elevator. Serial crimes is on three."

I scooped out the badges and passed Beth's to her. I thanked the man, and he sent us through into the grounds. I hung the badge on its cord around my neck as we walked toward the main building's entrance. We stepped through the doors into the building's lobby, which was far more modern than I had expected. My original thoughts about the age of the building diminished—the building was either newer yet meant to look old, or it had had an extensive remodel. The floors were patterned marble—the center darker with lighter triangles arranged in a checkerboard fashion. A couple of midcentury-modern leather chairs and sofas sat to our right. A large reception desk stood at the back of the lobby. Beth pointed left at a pair of stainless-steel elevators set into the wood-coffered wall, and we walked over. I hit the button to take us up and scanned my card under the reader. The doors opened a second later and took us in.

We stepped off on the third floor and walked down a long hallway. To our left was a solid wall, painted white with wood dividers every few feet sitting out a couple inches from the walls. The hallway wall on our right was all glass from the waist up to the ceiling, letting us see inside each room. A doorway was placed on our right every twenty or thirty feet, signifying what division of the bureau the nearby offices belonged to. Past a small cutout filled with a couple of vending machines and a stairwell, we found a large office. The interior of the room had smaller offices lining the walls and a center common area filled with individual desks. We approached the door and saw it was our serial crimes unit. I held the door for Beth, and we entered. A man in a suit approached, trying to get past us to exit the office.

"Do you know where we can find an Agent Duffield?" I asked.

"That office in that back corner is his." He turned back toward the room and pointed at the office at the back right.

"Thanks," I said.

He nodded and dipped past Beth to leave.

We headed through the walkway between the desks in the room and made our way to the office door. Seated at the desk inside was a man on the telephone—he looked to be in his forties, dressed in a white dress shirt and gray tie. The man, whom I assumed to be Agent Duffield, had short black-and-gray hair and a round clean-shaven face. I knocked. He looked up from his desk and held a finger up to ask for a second.

We waited a moment until he hung up the telephone. He wrote down a few things on a piece of paper before him and waved for us to enter.

I pushed open the door. "Agent Duffield?" I asked.

"Yeah. You must be Rawlings and Harper," he said.

"We are."

"Come on in."

Beth and I entered and shook Duffield's hand as he leaned forward across his desk.

"Matt Duffield," he said.

I pointed at myself and then at Beth. "Hank Rawlings. Beth Harper."

"Grab a seat," he said.

We did.

Duffield leaned back in his big office chair. "I've never seen anything quite like this in my time with the Bureau. I can't even really put it into words."

"Agreed," I said.

"Well, you guys have a hell of a timing. The call I was on was in regards to this, or I should say could be in regards to this investigation."

"Something new?" Beth asked.

"No way to know for certain at this point, but it could be. So here is what we did." Duffield paused and scooted himself closer to his desk. "When we got word that these women had been reported missing prior to us finding out their identities from the killer's photos, we alerted every law-enforcement agency and missing-persons department in about a hundred-mile radius. I wanted an alert the second a person was called in as missing. Well, that's what that call just was. A sheriff's station about a half hour from here just took a call."

"Does the missing fit?" Beth asked.

Duffield groaned quietly. "It's a twenty-two-year-old female, so it could."

"And this was the only one that has been reported?" I asked.

"It is. I put the word through that the second anyone even attempts to file a report, I want this office notified. We have no intentions of letting the proper time pass to file an official report. If someone calls and says, 'I think so-and-so might be missing,' we'll know. And that's basically what just occurred."

"Do we have the information from this latest report?" I asked.

"I just jotted a few things down from the phone call. The girl's name that's thought to be missing, cell-phone number, the roommate's name who called it in, and the sheriff's department it came from."

"Did anyone try to get a GPS location on her phone?" Beth asked.

"Her phone and purse were found in her vehicle at her apartment complex."

"Probably not a good sign," I said.

"I'm going to get someone on banking and cell records on the girl. The local department asked the roommate to come in as soon as she could. They're also trying to get a hold of the missing girl's parents, to get them in as well. They sent someone out to the vehicle to collect evidence, but even with the sheriff's office having the phone, a call or message could have been deleted, which is why I want to put in for the records. As soon as the chief deputy I spoke with has both parties in his building, he's going to give me a call. I was planning on going over there personally. Hopefully, by the time I go over there, we'll have some more information. Does that sound like something that you guys wanted to join me on?"

"Yes," Beth said. "But what are we going to tell them is the reason that we, as in the FBI, are there?"

"Just that we are looking into missing persons in the area," Duffield said.

"And if they ask why?"

"I'll field the questions on that."

"Okay," Beth said. "Any other developments in the investigation over the weekend?"

He shook his head. "We haven't come up with anything new."

"You know, I don't think I heard the story of how this newspaper actually got the package," I said. "I mean, I know it was mailed, but who was it sent to? Who opened it? Who viewed the contents? Who made the call to the authorities?"

"It's not in your file?" he asked.

I shook my head. "Our file is basically the contents of the evidence sent, photos, and the missing-person reports."

"Oh, all right. You guys must not have gotten what we'd put together over the weekend. We basically have some more detailed photos from the film—segments of the photographs blown up for a better look—and the statements from our interviews at the newspaper. There's nothing there that's really groundbreaking, but I'll make sure you get some copies of all of that. Um, the package wasn't addressed to anyone in particular. One of the mail-room guys opened it. He didn't do anything with the film but obviously read the letter. He took it to one of the higher-ups, who contacted the local authorities, which was Louisville Metro. They basically passed it off to us immediately after seeing what was on the film."

"I'm guessing the contents of the letter, combined with the photos, triggered something in the local law enforcement that they might be dealing with something beyond their scope," Beth said.

"Could have been," Duffield said.

"Where are we at with this in the press?" I asked.

"It's not," Duffield said. "The Louisville Metro Police Department basically told the newspaper that it was probably a hoax but they'd look into it. When they saw what was on the film, they contacted us right away. I don't think more than a handful of people at the PD even saw what was on the film."

"What about the families of the known victims we have? Who handled dealing with that, and what was said?" I asked.

"I dealt with it personally. They know what happened, and we asked them—as hard as it is going to be—to not spread the word about this while we are investigating."

I shook my head. "None of that is going to work. This will be all over the news in days, national by the end of the week. I worked local law enforcement. If someone sees something like that at a station, it won't be long before everyone inside the station knows about it—hell, I bet they already do. The families are another story. As soon as one person decides to talk, the whole keeping-it-under-wraps thing is over. We need to have something in place for when that happens because it's going to. There are too many people who know—someone leaking it is inevitable."

Duffield nodded in agreement but said nothing.

"The packaging, original letter, and film… Is all that in the building?" Beth asked.

"Yeah, everything is in the lab downstairs. Did you want to head down there and take a look while we wait to get this call back?"

"We do," Beth said.

"Any word on when the family that owns the house that the package was shipped from will be back in town?" I asked.

"Wednesday morning," Duffield said.

"Okay." I made a note of the day in my notepad.

Agent Duffield rose from his desk. "Okay. Let's head downstairs. I can pop in to our tech department and get someone going on this girl's information, and you guys can have a look at the package and contents." He took the piece of paper from his desk, and we followed him from his office.

CHAPTER SIX

We spent a half hour looking at a torn-open box, a letter in an evidence bag, and an old yellow roll of film before getting the call that the local sheriff's department had the missing woman's family and roommate at their building. The forensics team stated they'd found nothing on any of the items that could lead us in a direction, and as we were already aware, each item had trace evidence that latex gloves had been used for handling. We were still waiting to hear on banking and cell-phone records.

Beth and I followed Agent Duffield up Interstate 71 toward the town of La Grange, where the Oldham County Sheriff's Department was—a half-hour ride from the Louisville Bureau office. We exited the interstate and drove through the small town. Old houses mixed in with the older storefronts on the sides of the road. We stopped at the four-way stop sign at Main Street. I looked right and left to see angled parking at the fronts of hundred-plus-year-old brick buildings that made up the classic Midwestern downtown area. A handful of people were rummaging about, entering and exiting the mom-and-pop shops. Beth continued forward, following Duffield before he made a left at the next block. After Duffield's left turn, he slowed in the street and turned left into a small parking area beside an old two-story red-brick building with a white balcony attached to the front. Below the balcony and above the entry doors was a sign that read Oldham County Courthouse.

"I guess this is the place," Beth said.

"It looks like it."

Beth pulled into the small parking area and took an empty spot next to Duffield's four-door Toyota pickup. We stepped out.

"The sheriff's office is inside." Duffield pointed his chin toward the red-brick building. "We're going to be looking for Chief Deputy Patrick King."

I nodded. Beth and I followed Duffield toward the entrance. We entered the old building, told the woman at the front who we were looking for, and were escorted back to a small conference room. The woman that had led us back opened the door, poked her head inside, and after saying a few words, pulled the door open for us to enter.

I followed Agent Duffield and Beth into a gray-carpeted room with bare white walls. A projector screen sat on the back wall behind a small stage with a podium. The center of the room was taken up by a long conference table with about ten chairs lining each side. A man, dressed in a uniform consisting of a white shirt with a badge on the chest and starred shoulder epaulets, sat at the table's end. A thin black tie ran down the center of his shirt. To his sides were three women—the two on the left appeared to be mother and daughter—the older woman looked to be in her forties, the younger in her teens. The woman seated by herself must have been the roommate, looking to be in her early twenties. The three women and sheriff all stared at us. Duffield introduced our group, and we took chairs on both sides of the table.

I sat across from the two women, who Chief Deputy King confirmed as the mother and sister of the reported missing woman—we still hadn't caught their names. Both women had puffy red eyes from crying. I glanced right, toward the roommate, seated at my shoulder—she sniffed and stared down at the table.

"We were just going through the last time Katelyn was seen," Chief Deputy King said from the end of the table.

The mother stared at me and cleared her throat. "I didn't know that the FBI came in on missing-person reports," she said.

I glanced over at Beth, who was staring at Duffield. I had no intentions of telling the woman what we were actually investigating in the area, and I was pretty sure Beth had the same thought.

"This one, we'd like to be a part of, ma'am," Duffield said. "We're actively investigating missing persons in the area."

"Has, um, has there been a lot lately?" she asked.

"More than we'd like," Duffield said. "Just know that the Oldham County Sheriff's Office, as well as the local branch of the FBI, will be looking into this. Obviously, everything will be done, that can be, to locate your daughter."

I had mixed feelings about not being entirely truthful with the woman, but at the same time, telling a mother that a serial killer was murdering and mounting the heads of women that fit her daughter's profile wouldn't go over well—and we didn't know if her daughter was a victim or not. I sat quietly in thought, hoping the girl had decided to run away on vacation or to leave the area otherwise on her own accord. However, the car parked at the daughter's apartment, with her purse and phone inside, stirred a bad feeling in my gut.

"I just want her back," the mother said. "It's not like her to do this."

"Your name, ma'am?" Duffield asked.

"Patty Willard, Katelyn's mother. This is my daughter, June."

"Same last name?" he asked.

"Correct," she said.

I took the notepad from my pocket and wrote down the family members' names.

I looked over my right shoulder at the roommate. "Your name, miss?" I asked.

"Jessi Bromley."

I requested a spelling and wrote it down.

"Ms. Willard, when did you see or speak to your daughter last?" Duffield asked.

The mother dabbed at her eyes with the sleeve of her beige shirt. "Katelyn came over Saturday after work. She stayed until around nine o'clock at night and then left to go back to her apartment."

“Roughly nine o’clock is your best guess on time?” I asked.

“That’s going to be pretty close. It could have been a minute or two after. I record two shows that start at nine, which is kind of pointless if I’m home and in front of the television because my cable box can only record two at a time—it makes you watch one of the two programs while you’re recording. The television had just switched over to one of my shows.”

“Okay.” I wrote the time down.

“We have the apartment address, which I’ll give to you,” King told Duffield.

Duffield nodded. “Do you remember what she was wearing?” he asked.

“A pink hooded sweatshirt—it said *love* real big in black letters on the back—that and blue jeans. She changed out of her work clothes at the house. She still has me do her laundry. They have coin-operated at her apartment.”

I wrote down a description of the clothing.

“And you called in the report?” Beth asked, leaning forward and looking past me to the roommate, seated at my shoulder.

“I called, yeah,” she said. “Katelyn didn’t come home Saturday night. I just figured she stayed at her mom’s. I didn’t leave the apartment at all on Sunday. I called her a couple times and sent her a few text messages, but she never responded. I thought it was weird but wasn’t really worried about it or anything. But then this morning when I went to leave for work, I saw her car in the apartment complex’s parking lot. I walked over to it. The window was down, and her purse was inside. I called her phone, and it rang inside of the car. So I called her mom, who said she'd left to come home Saturday night."

"I told her to call the police, left work, and went to the apartment," Ms. Willard said.

"What time this morning?" King asked.

"Around nine in the morning," the roommate said.

"Okay." King made a note of the time.

"Does the apartment complex have video security?" I asked.

"They have cameras in the parking lot there," King said. "But we found out that they were inoperable when we got a hold of the landlord."

I tapped the tip of my pen on my notepad. "So no help there. Did Katelyn have a boyfriend or maybe a group of friends that she could have possibly decided to leave the area with? You know, just to get out of town for a few days." I thought it a pointless question, with the purse and phone having remained in the car, but it still needed to be asked—if only to get names of potentials to contact.

"She didn't have a boyfriend," the roommate said. "If she was going out of town for something, I would have known."

"You're sure of that?" Beth asked.

"Positive," the girl said.

"Maybe not a boyfriend per se but any male friends that could have picked her up? Something like that?" I asked.

The roommate shook her head. "She was too focused on school. The last boyfriend she had was last school year, and

I don't know if I would even call him a boyfriend. They only hung out for a month or two."

"His name?" Beth asked.

She gave it to us.

We went back and forth with the family and roommate for another half hour, distributed a couple of business cards to them, and left the room for the hallway. King followed us out.

I put my back to the wall of the hallway. "Where are you guys at on the investigation with this? Any leads?" I asked.

King shook his head. "We had a look through the apartment itself and the grounds of the complex—nothing out of the ordinary. We focused on the car and the surrounding area. We didn't see any signs of a struggle—nothing dropped, nothing that looked like it could have been from either Katelyn Willard or anyone else. Purse was filled with credit cards—some cash was still there. The keys for the vehicle were still in the ignition. The last I heard, they were moving the car back to our garages to start processing it in more detail. At her apartment complex, we door knocked every unit that would have had a visual of the area where her car was parked. We got nothing. If she was taken from there, it was a damn clean grab. We're going to look into this guy she was seeing last year and get his whereabouts for Sunday. We put in for her phone and banking records, but it takes us some time to acquire those things. Maybe you could assist us in speeding that up a bit?"

"We already put in for both banking and cell records," Duffield said. "I should have something today yet, and I'll forward it on to you as soon as I get it. Did you guys check the call log from the cell phone itself?"

"We did. The last call was earlier in the evening, prior to her even going to her mother's after work."

"Print the phone?" Beth asked.

"They're processing the prints lifted," King said. "Just one set, the last I heard—probably hers. I have to ask, what is the FBI's high level of interest in missing persons all about?"

"It's an open investigation," Duffield said.

"You're not going to give me anything other than that, are you?" King asked.

Duffield didn't respond.

King slowly nodded, seeming to accept the fact that he'd get no further information on the matter. "Are you guys done here, then?"

"I'm thinking so," Duffield said. "There isn't really anything we can do here." Duffield looked at Beth and me. "What are you guys thinking?"

"Yeah, we're set," I said.

"Okay." Duffield reached out and shook the chief deputy's hand. "I'll get that stuff to you in a little bit. Let us know if anything develops with the old boyfriend."

"Sure," King said.

We walked from the sheriff's office and stopped at the back of our rental with Duffield.

"What's going to be the plan of attack?" Duffield asked.

"I'd like to dig into the victims that we know we have," I said. "See the locations where they were taken from. Pound the pavement, knock on doors. Right now, we basically have nothing. There's no way that one person out there didn't see something."

"Agreed," Beth said. "Did we do the usuals? Try to pull traffic-cam footage from around where they were taken, look for cameras in the areas, talk to friends and families?"

"We did," Duffield said. "Dead end after dead end after dead end."

"Well, let's do it again," I said. "Start from the top. Visit the scenes where the grabs took place and meet with everyone involved. I also wouldn't mind stopping at this newspaper and getting a run-through of exactly how everything with this package transpired firsthand."

"Okay," Duffield said.

"Let's head back to the bureau office and get organized," Beth said. "We'll lay out how we want to proceed step by step—get our days set up."

"Sounds good," Duffield said. "Do you guys just want to follow me back?"

"Lead the way." Beth headed for the driver's door of our rental car.

CHAPTER SEVEN

William, tape measure in hand, measured down from the drop ceiling of the den and then out from the wall on his right. He placed his fingertip on his spot, let the tape measure drop to the cushions of the sofa he was standing on, and took the hammer from the loop on his tool belt. William removed the nail he was holding in his lips and hammered it into the wooden paneling of the den. He stepped from the couch and replaced the hammer in its loop.

"Wall time," William said. "Let's see how you hold up."

He scooped up Katelyn's completed mount, which was resting against the side of the chair in the room and stepped back up onto the couch cushions. He slid the wood-backed mount down the wall until the cable on its back caught the nail head. He let the wall take the weight of the mount and adjusted it until it was straight.

William stepped down and took her in, lined up next to the others. His eyes went from one to the next. From Katelyn to the first he'd hung, the skin of each woman's face seemed to droop more and more. He walked to the far side of the room and stood before the mount of Kelly Page, his first try.

The skin of her face sagged and hung from her chin line. The number one he'd written in marker on her forehead was barely visible. William could see bits of modeling clay and bone around her eye sockets, where the skin had shrunk and begun to pull back. William took the lamp from the end table that was directly beneath the mount, set it down on the floor, and stepped up onto the table to reach eye level with her. He examined her face and her skin from inches away. He sniffed and pulled his head back—her flesh was rotting. William reached out with his fingertips and touched her skin—it was squishy to the touch. The pressure of his fingers made more of her skin pull away from her eye, exposing an inch and a half more of her skull beneath.

"Dammit," William said.

He pulled her mount from the wall, crouched, and placed it on the floor beside the end table—the mount would have to be taken to the burning barrel in the backyard and disposed of.

William stood, and as his eyes went to the next woman's mount, his anger built, for around her eyes, he could see effects similar to those on the first mount. William stepped from the end table to the arm of the couch to get an up-close look at the woman he'd marked number two, Jennifer Pasco. He put his nose to the side of her face and took in a deep breath. The odor of rotting flesh filled his airways.

"Son of a bitch!" He ground his teeth together as his jaw muscles flexed.

William put his fingertips to the bottom of the walnut base of the mount and swatted upward, sending the mount off its hook. The wood of the mount hit William in the side of the face as it fell, bounced off the corner of the end table, and came to rest on the floor. His simmering anger immediately turned into rage.

William yanked the hammer from his tool belt and swung his arm back as he took a step on the couch toward the next mount. He brought the hammer down with everything he had into the side of the face of the next woman, Trisha Floyd—that mount flew from the wall, sending the next in line crashing to the ground with it.

"None of you are good enough!"

William took another two steps on the couch. He stood before Katelyn's mount, which he'd just hung. He swung the hammer back over his shoulder and delivered it squarely to her forehead. The impact sent her right glass eye sideways. William swung again, and the end of the hammer crunched through her skull. He ripped back on the hammer to pull it out, but it was lodged into her skull cavity and would not come free. Pulling the mount from the wall with both hands, he turned on the couch and slammed his creation to the ground below with everything he had. The mount smashed into pieces—the hands came from the mount and bounced across the floor—the skull broke away from the fiberglass neck area, ripping from the bolts securing it to the bracket, and Katelyn's head rolled across the floor.

William stared down at the floor of the room, littered with pieces of rotted flesh, hands, and broken chunks of the mounts. He stepped from the couch and let himself fall back into the beige cushions.

“They’re not right,” he said.

William took his finger-length hair at the top of his head in both of his hands and pulled. He shook his head, sitting in silence for minutes. He closed his eyes and rubbed at his temples.

“Think. Think, think. What can we do?” he said. “There has to be a good way.”

William opened his eyes and stared at the bits and pieces of debris covering the carpeting. His eyes focused on one object and then another and then another.

“The hands,” he said.

CHAPTER EIGHT

I sat over a plate of what was basically beef gnocchi though it had some spruced-up name when I'd ordered it. We'd gone back to the Louisville bureau office, spent a couple hours planning how we wanted to proceed on the investigation, and left for the evening. The time spent meeting with the mother and roommate of the latest missing woman, Katelyn Willard, in addition to plotting how we wanted to proceed in the coming days, had taken up most of the usable hours of our workday—the plan was to start bright and early the following day.

"So I'm on friends and family tomorrow, and you're on the grab locations?" Beth asked. She put a forkful of some kind of salad in her mouth, chewed, and awaited my response. She'd been mostly preoccupied with her phone over the course of our dinner.

"That's the plan," I said.

"What time are you going to take off in the morning?" she asked.

I glanced at my watch—a couple minutes before nine o'clock. "I'll probably be up by sixish, do my morning routine, and scoot out of here before seven. I took a look at how long it's going to take me to get to the first stop—looks like about forty minutes. I figure if I'm in the neighborhood knocking on doors by around eight, I can catch any nine-to-fivers before they leave for work for the day."

"Good idea," Beth said.

"Did you get some times set up to meet with friends and family?"

"A couple slots. I figure I can make some calls and try to get a couple more interviews set while I'm driving from location to location tomorrow. Any news from Ball?"

"No. I just checked in with him," I said. "I told him about the latest abduction and what our plans were, going forward. As far as back at the home office, nothing new going on there, other than what Bill and Scott were up to."

"The religious sect thing?"

"Yeah. I guess they're still poking around at it. They got some names."

Beth nodded but didn't respond. She set her fork down and took a drink of her wine.

"You know, I was thinking about something." I jabbed at a piece of braised beef and a piece of gnocchi with my fork tines.

"What's that?" she asked.

"Okay, so we have a good idea that this guy is not a taxidermist, right?" I stuck my fork in my mouth and pulled it out clean.

"Right," she said.

I paused to chew. "That doesn't mean that he didn't

purchase the things he needed from one locally. Or online. The green human glass eyes can't be that common. Plus, the wooden mounts were more than likely purchased from somewhere as well."

"Those could have been made."

"Could have, but I'd lean toward bought. There isn't a ton of the general population that are craftsman and could make something like that. I'm betting they could be had online for cheap, meaning it almost wouldn't be cost or time effective to make them. Especially if you're just experimenting with the girls."

"I'd have to think we'd have our best luck just focusing our efforts on trying to hunt down where the eyes came from," Beth said.

I took a sip of my gin and tonic, set it down, and pulled my notepad from my inner suit-jacket pocket. I wrote down *green glass eyes* and *find out where to get them.*

"What else is sticking out at you?" Beth asked.

"The mailbox that package was dropped into—too much of a coincidence that our killer just got lucky that they were out of town."

"Well, what do you think? The people who reside there checked out."

"That's all fine that they checked out," I said. "I just think our guy knew they were out of town."

"Okay. So spitball it. Who would know that they weren't home?"

"Friends, family, neighbors, coworkers."

"Duffield said they'd be back Wednesday?" Beth asked.

"Wednesday morning, he said. If we could meet with this family and ask them who all would know that they were gone, and get some names, we might be able to spin something into a lead." I tapped the tip of my pen on the notepad's page and wrote down *mailbox family leads.*

I looked back up at Beth. Her cell phone, sitting on the white tablecloth next to her salad bowl, was lit up. She grumbled and poked away at the screen.

"Scott will not leave me the hell alone," she said.

"I thought you blocked him."

"I did. Now he's sending messages through my messenger app. He just won't stop. Like he doesn't get the fact that I'm at work and I need to not be interrupted by him."

"He probably figures you're done working for the day and now have time to interact with him."

"But he's been doing it all day—nonstop. Well actually, he stopped for a few hours earlier, but still. I mean, what adult just fires off message after message after message when the person on the other end clearly doesn't want to speak to you at the moment?"

"Don't know," I said. "Seems a little immature."

"Exactly."

"Well, obvious resolution. Turn your phone off for the night. Anything work related will also come to me. I'll just let you know if it's something you need to know."

"Yeah." She hit a button on the side of her phone and dumped it into her pocket. Beth and I finished our dinner and settled up the bill. I left her in the lobby and headed up to my room. After a solid hour of television mixed with commercial breaks of researching where one could buy human-looking glass eyes, my cell phone rang. I clicked Talk and brought the phone to my ear.

"Babe," I said.

"Hey, you. How's Kentucky?" Karen asked.

"Meh. Nothing really got done on the investigation today. Aside from us getting in late, we stopped by a local precinct and just kind of made a plan of attack. The hotel here is nice, though. Beth and I just ate downstairs a bit ago."

"So what are you doing now?" she asked.

"I'm just kind of winding down in my room. Looking at a few things on my phone. I'll probably stay up for another half hour or so and call it a night. I want to be up early and get started on checking out some locations where our girls were last seen and had been taken from."

"You didn't really give me too much about what this investigation was about, other than the vague references of beheadings."

"Trust me—that's all you want. But if you really want the gory details, I guess I can give them to you."

"I think I'll pass."

"You sure? You'll probably catch it on the news within a few days, anyway. These guys here think they can kind of keep this all under wraps, which I'm pretty certain won't happen."

"Yeah, I'll still pass for now," she said.

"Probably for the best," I said. "What are you doing?"

"Surfing the Internet, looking at furniture that could go

with a new house—some things for kids' rooms."

"Probably would require a new house first?" I said. "And a kid."

"I've been meaning to bring that up," Karen said. "I think we should schedule something to look at that Leaf Lane place again. We're going to need to find a place soon."

"We'll talk when I get back—look at a few places, schedule some stuff."

"You said you liked that place, right?"

"I liked it. Can't say I'm all that jazzed about the price," I said.

"Everything around here is expensive, Hank."

"I'm aware. You sure you don't want to think about re-signing where we're at?"

"I think it's time we get a home," she said.

"Well, find some potentials, and when I get back, we'll start looking. So why do we need new furniture?"

"I'm just browsing. On another note, when you get home, we're going to have to talk about how we want to proceed with the adoption plans. Mainly, what age child we'll be a good home for. I was thinking that we should talk to our case worker and see what she thinks."

"I think that's a good idea," I said. "I told Beth the news earlier today and mentioned that you and I will have to have a real discussion about it."

"What did she say?" Karen asked.

"She was happy for us. And wanted me to tell you congratulations and all that. She seems to think we'll make good parents."

"Aw, that's nice of her. Tell her thank you. She needs to ditch that ex-husband and find a real guy to have a family with."

"Did you want me to tell her that part as well?" I asked.

"No. Not that part."

"Okay," I said. "I think she's about done with him, anyway. The quarreling seems to have escalated to the point where she might actually rip off the Band-Aid and be done."

"Good. Good for her. I mean, I've only met the guy the handful of times that we've been out, but he just seems like an ass. She's too nice to be with someone like that."

"Loving someone tends to affect judgment. Just be happy that you love me because I'm pretty much as good as it gets."

"Yeah, same," Karen said.

I chuckled.

"All right, baby. I just wanted to say hi and goodnight. I'll call you in the morning on my way to work. If I don't catch you, just call me when you get a chance."

"Sounds good," I said.

"Love you."

"Yup, love you, too. Have a good night."

I clicked off and tossed my phone onto the nightstand. My glass-eye research, which I wasn't coming up with much on, could resume in the morning. I reached for the remote control to actually find something to watch and heard my phone buzz from a call. I reached over and scooped it up, figuring Karen was calling back because she forgot to tell me something. The phone's screen said it was Beth.

I clicked Talk. "What's up?"

"Hank, come downstairs. I'm in the bar."

Beth clicked off before I could ask why. I stared at the screen of my phone, debating whether to call her back and ask her what she wanted. Her tone of voice struck me as odd. I scooped up my room key from the desk near the window, slipped on my shoes, and headed down the hall to the elevator.

CHAPTER NINE

As I walked down the hall toward the hotel bar, voices there were shouting at each other. I stepped through the bar's doorway and entered the dimly lit room filled with empty booths and tall vacant tables and chairs. I didn't see Beth anywhere, just two guys standing chest to chest near the bar.

When I glanced toward the far-right corner of the room, one of the guys shouted, "What's your problem?" pulling my eyes immediately back to the left.

I focused on the men and the lone female bartender behind the bar, who was threatening to call for security. One of the men had his back toward me while the other faced me but was blocked from my view by the other guy's back. In an instant, the guy with his back toward me pushed the other man and threw a punch, which landed.

A woman yelled, "Stop!"

The guy who got hit threw a single punch in retaliation, which sent the other guy to the floor. As the pair separated, I saw Beth seated at the bar behind where the men stood—she was the one that had yelled. I hustled over.

"What the hell is going on over here?" I asked in a loud voice.

Beth stood from the barstool. "Hank, it's fine."

"Fine?" I asked. "You called me, and I come down to whatever this is." I stopped before the group and pointed at the man who'd delivered the punch that sent the other down. "I'm FBI. You, stay."

The guy, who looked to be around thirty-five, a few inches under six foot, and husky, held his palms up toward me submissively. My attention turned to the man pushing himself off of the floor, whom I immediately recognized.

"This isn't any of your business, Hank," he said, rising to his feet.

"Aside from the fact that it looks like you probably just got what you deserved, what the hell are you doing here?"

"Hank, just leave it alone. Scott was just leaving. Weren't you, Scott?" Beth asked.

Scott stood before me, his lip bloodied. He wiped at it with his thumb and looked at the blood. Scott pointed at the man who'd floored him. "You're lucky I don't kick the shit out of you."

"Come and try," the guy said. "You don't treat women like that."

Scott tried to take a step toward the guy but ran into my outstretched hand. I looked him in the face. "Weren't you just leaving?" I asked. "Like, getting on a plane leaving?"

Scott looked past me at Beth. "You and I are going to talk, bitch."

I resisted the urge to put him back on the ground, knowing that Beth would rather I didn't.

"Yeah, that's about enough of that." I spun Scott by the

shoulders, balled the back of his shirt in my fist, hearing the fabric rip somewhere, and escorted him from the bar area. He tried pulling from my grasp once or twice but couldn't break my hold. I walked him to the hotel's exit and out front.

"Get the hell off of me," Scott said.

I let him go with a firm shove.

"The bitch goes out of town, and I catch her at a hotel bar talking to some guy." Scott paced the sidewalk and started back toward the doors to go inside.

I stepped in his way. "You should probably cool it with the whole *bitch* thing, and that's going to be your final warning with that."

"What are you going to do about it? I'll call her whatever I want."

Scott tried getting past me again, but I gave him another shove toward the sidewalk. "Just leave, Scott. Think about what you're doing here."

"Nah, I'm not going anywhere. Screw that guy. I want to press charges. He assaulted me."

"Dipshit. I stood there and watched you push the guy and throw a punch at him first. This is before he put your dumb ass to the ground. But, yeah, go ahead and call the local police and tell them."

Scott said nothing—just resumed pacing.

"Okay. Listen close because if you don't, we're going to have more of a problem than you just embarrassing yourself. Now, I don't care why you're here or what you think Beth was just doing. You're going to take your ass back home—on a plane, leaving town, back home."

"Who the hell are you to tell me what to do? That's my wife. This isn't any of your business."

"Okay. One, she's your ex-wife. Two, you're affecting my partner's ability to conduct a federal investigation. That means you're affecting my abilities because I have to worry about my partner's state of mind. I'll make this simple for you. If I see you again while I'm in this city, you'll be locked up for interfering in a federal investigation. Understand that? As in handcuffs, charges, sitting in a cell."

"You can't do that," Scott said.

"I can, and I'm actually kind of hoping that you test me out on this one. See, here's the thing…" I paused and shrugged. "I just don't care for you that much, so I'm completely fine with seeing you in cuffs and having someone put you in a cell."

"Yeah, okay, nice threat. Beth would never let you do it," he said.

"I'll just take it out of her hands, then. We can get you a cell right away, actually. I'll go back inside and talk that guy into filing a case. We'll get the local PD down here. Hell, I'd even go as far as saying I witnessed the whole thing to the officers. An FBI agent makes a hell of a witness. What do you think? You can walk yourself up the street and leave, or you can spend the night in lockup."

Scott stepped directly before me—his forehead equal with my nose. I assumed he was trying to exert some kind of dominance or something. His body language looked as though he'd done that before—a high-school sort of tough-guy move that he'd probably pulled out in the past.

I didn't budge. He puffed out his chest, which made contact with my suit jacket. I stared down at him staring up at me with anger in his eyes.

"You may want to reconsider your actions right now," I said.

"Oh, you think so?" he asked.

"I do."

"What are you going to do about it? You want to go a few rounds with me?"

"What?"

"I asked if you want to dance, Hank. You think you can take me?"

I furrowed my brows. "I'm actually just trying to figure out if you're serious right now. If you want to swing on me, do it. I'm guessing you won't like the outcome."

He jerked his chin at me as though he was trying to get me to flinch. I didn't move or bat an eye.

"What was that?" I asked. "Was that the part where I was supposed to get scared or something?"

He didn't respond.

"Look, I don't have all night. Are you going to just stand there like an idiot? Or throw a punch and then take a nap on the sidewalk?"

He let out a puff of air, mumbled, "That's what I thought," turned, and headed down the block. I watched him as he made the corner and walked out of view.

"What a jackass." I turned and walked through the hotel's doors to find Beth and ask what exactly had occurred.

She was inside, still seated at the bar and talking to the

bartender. The guy whom I'd told to stay had gone. I took a seat next to Beth.

The bartender stared at me. "Everything all right?"

"Fine," I said. "Can I just get a gin and tonic?"

"Sure." The bartender fixed my drink, set it before me, and walked to the far end of the bar, to give Beth and me a bit of privacy.

"Sorry." Beth held her head in her hands and stared down at the bar. "And thank you."

"No sweat," I said.

"Is he gone?" she asked.

"He is. Are you going to tell me what the hell that just was?" I lifted my glass and took a sip.

Beth took in a deep breath. "Well, apparently Scott had put one of those find-my-phone apps on my cell phone without my knowledge. He flew here to continue arguing with me, I imagine, because I wouldn't take his calls or respond to his messages."

That struck me as evidence that he had serious problems, but I didn't respond, waiting for Beth to get to the altercation.

"Anyway. I'm sitting here, having a drink and chitchatting with the bartender and the guy that you saw—just small talk, harmless. The guy said he owned a couple of small car dealerships and was in town for some kind of auto-industry conference or something. I don't know. Anyway, he said he'd lived in Chicago for a bit, so we were talking about that. The bartender said she'd just taken a trip to D.C. the prior year, so we were talking about that—like I said, just shooting the breeze.

"Then I hear a voice shouting my name—I recognize the voice immediately as Scott's. I spin on my barstool and see Scott staring down at his phone and then looking around. That's when I called you. So he ends up seeing me at the bar and storms over, asking me what the hell I think I'm doing. Him standing in front of me, and the look on his face, I just knew it was going to end up getting bad. I ask him how the hell he knew where I was, and he tells me he put something on my phone. Well, then he reaches out and grabs my arm to pull me toward him. I yank back, and the guy that was at the bar stands up and asks if there's a problem. Scott gets up in his face, telling him to mind his business. The guy—his name was James, I think—tells Scott to leave me alone, and then the two started going back and forth. I tried to defuse the situation, but Scott just wouldn't let it go. The bartender asks if she should call security, Scott accuses me of being a slut, the James guy is just trying to get Scott to leave, and then, well, I think you pretty much saw the rest."

"Just a run-of-the-mill Monday night," I said.

Beth smirked and shook her head. "What an asshole. What did you say to him outside?"

"I told him to leave. A couple different ways."

"Did he try to start something with you?" Beth asked.

"I think he was trying to." I lifted my glass, took another drink, and swallowed. "He was flapping his gums and got in my face a little bit. Puffed his little chest out at me. I think he kind of got the point that I wasn't screwing around with him and finally left. But he did it in a tough-guy kind of way, so he has that going for him."

"I'm sorry, Hank. I should maybe call Ball in the morning and see if he can send Scott or Bill out."

"Do you think that you need to do that?" I asked.

"I don't know."

CHAPTER TEN

William sat behind the wheel of his second vehicle, an old unmarked patrol car he'd picked up from a California police auction just a month or two prior. He stared through the windshield, across the street, at a restaurant parking lot. He'd been watching the side lot for the past few hours. He took the binoculars from his eyes and glanced at the time on the dash—a couple minutes past midnight. The restaurant had closed at eleven, and the only remaining people were staff. William imagined the remaining employees were cleaning up, possibly having a drink and talking about their nights, tips, problem guests, and the other happenings from the shift.

William had been a little more careful with each new capture. With the first couple victims he'd acquired, he was extremely reckless—merely stopping them as he saw them. Even Katelyn Willard had been a bit too dangerous for his liking. He'd seen her in a fast-food chain completely by chance and simply followed her back to her apartment. The parking lot was dark, and no one had been around where she parked.

William had since decided to stick with how he'd picked up the fourth woman, April Backer. Her method of capture, what he was currently in the process of doing, was a bit more planned out and provided a lot less risk. He brought the binoculars back to his eyes and looked across the street at the parking lot.

"About time," he said.

He watched as a couple of people funneled from the back door and stood around for a minute or two, smoking and talking, before heading to their respective cars. William kept eyes on a smaller female. The couple lights in the restaurant parking lot lit her up—yet, even through the binoculars, she was too far away for him to determine anything other than the fact she was a woman. She hopped into an older economy car parked near the end of the lot and backed up.

"Well, let's see what we get," William said. He started his car and waited.

Once she pulled from the restaurant's parking lot and made a left out onto the main street before it, William clicked on his headlights and pulled out from the lot he was parked in. He turned onto the main road and headed in the direction she'd gone. The streets, due to the late hour, were mostly empty. He caught her car in the roadway about three quarters of a block up.

William increased his speed a bit to keep her within a half a block but got no closer. He followed behind her the better part of four or five miles down the forty-mile-an-hour street until he caught her brake lights and her blinker showing a right turn. William took in the road as he made the turn after her, realizing he'd still need to wait for a lower-traffic street.

The woman drove straight ahead for another mile and made a left into a residential area—William followed. She made a right at the next street inside the neighborhood. William looked at the houses on the block—most of the lights inside were out. While the location wasn't ideal, the time to act had come.

William quickly rounded the corner and flipped the switch at the bottom of the dash for the red-and-blue lights in the grille of his car. The woman pulled to the side of the road. He killed the grille lights and then stepped from his car, leaving it running. He watched the nearby homes, looking for lights turning on, people watching, or anything of the sort—he saw nothing. William approached her driver's-side window and removed a small flashlight from his pocket. He flicked it on and pointed it in at her. Her window lowered.

"Detective Matt Paulson," William said. "Can you turn off your headlights and the vehicle?"

She did.

"Do you have your driver's license, registration, and proof of insurance?" William asked.

He kept the light on her, taking her in as she dug into the glove compartment of her vehicle. The woman appeared in her late twenties—she'd do. She removed some paperwork from the glove compartment and her ID from a small handbag and then held it out the window at him.

"Did I do something wrong?" she asked.

William took the items in his hand but didn't leave the

window of her vehicle. "Ma'am, is there something wrong with your vehicle?"

"No. Not that I know of. Why?"

"You didn't use your directional two turns back."

"Oh, um, I don't know. If I didn't, I apologize. I actually try to be a good driver," she said.

William took the light from her face, and aimed it down at her ID. Her name was Courtney Mouser. The weight listed was one eighteen. The street on the license was not the one they were on, and William was not familiar with it. With a quick bit of mental math, he put her age at thirty-one, a bit older than he would have liked. He wondered if there would be an elasticity problem in her facial skin. He pointed the light back on her for a quick check—wrinkle free.

William tucked the ID and paperwork into the inner pocket of his suit jacket. "Been drinking tonight, miss?"

"No—I mean, I had one drink after work. That's it. I'm not intoxicated," she said.

William paused. "Prescription drugs?" he asked.

"What?"

"Have you taken any prescription drugs this evening?" he asked.

"Absolutely not."

"Is there any prescription drugs on your person or in the vehicle that I should be aware of?" William asked.

"No, I don't do any of that."

William paused again, saying nothing as second after second passed. He kept the flashlight pointed directly into her eyes.

"Can you step out of the vehicle for me, miss?"

The woman pulled her head back at the request. "For?"

"Please step out of the vehicle, ma'am."

She let out a puff of air and opened her door.

"I'm going to ask you to take a seat in my vehicle there," William said.

"What did I do?" she asked.

"Your eyes are glazed over, and I have reason to believe that you're under the influence."

"I'm not under the influence of anything," she said.

William ignored her comment and walked her to the rear door of his car. "Place your hands behind your back for me."

"What?" she asked.

"Place your arms behind your back, ma'am. Don't resist."

"Am I under arrest?" she asked.

"You're being detained while I search your vehicle for contraband."

"There's nothing in there," she said.

"Ma'am, this is the last time I'm going to ask," William said.

"This is ridiculous," she said but obeyed his command.

William pulled a set of cuffs from his pocket and linked her up. He opened the rear door of his vehicle—behind the tinted glass, a metal grate was welded to the interior of the window frame.

"Watch your head," William said as he placed her in the back. "I'll be back with you in a moment, miss." William closed the door and took two steps forward. He looked left and right, spotting no one. He walked to her car, pulling a pair of rubber gloves from his back pocket. William put the gloves on, clicked on her ignition, and rolled up her driver's side window. He took her phone, purse, and keys from the vehicle, locked it, and walked back to his car. In William's mind, leaving each woman's vehicle in a bit of a different state would keep the authorities off his trail. He opened the driver's door, took a seat behind the wheel, setting her belongings on the passenger seat, and shifted into drive.

"What are you doing?" she asked from behind the metal grate separating the rear passenger area from the front.

William didn't respond as he pulled away from the curb.

"What's going on? Where are you going?" she asked. "What the hell is this?"

William didn't respond.

"Hey!" she shouted. "What the hell is going on here?"

"Ma'am, you're under arrest. I'm taking you back to the station."

"This isn't right. I didn't do anything," she said.

William didn't respond. He stopped at a stop sign, pulled the battery from her phone, and then made a right, leaving the neighborhood.

"No," she said. "Show me your badge!"

William chuckled and then spoke over his shoulder. "I must have forgot it at home. We'll see if I can dig it up when we get there."

"What?"

William lowered his window and tossed her cell phone out.

A long silence came from the rear of his car. William

waited for the situation to dawn on her—it had happened the same way with each woman he'd grabbed—the moment of realization that they were at his mercy.

A bloodcurdling scream broke the dead air inside of the car. The metal divider behind his head rattled and banged from the woman kicking it. William smiled, turned up the radio, and made the half-hour drive back to his house with her slamming her feet into anything she could—he'd stopped briefly to throw her purse into a trash bin at a gas station. William made a left turn into his gravel driveway and clicked a button on his visor to lift the overhead door on the detached shed. He pulled inside, lowered the door, and stepped out. After he closed the car door at his back, he could still hear the woman screaming and kicking in the back of the car.

"It's no use." William walked to the bench at the back of the garage, grabbed his catch pole, and returned to the car to open her door.

Her feet kicked at him as if she was pedaling a bicycle. She screamed and yelled and ripped back and forth. William knew from Kelly Paige's abduction—and getting kicked in the face—that the women were literally fighting for their lives when they were released from the vehicle. He'd since purchased the catch pole and devised a far more suitable way to subdue them and take them inside.

William stood at the rear quarter panel of his car with the catch pole and waited for one of her kicks. The second he saw a foot, he went to loop it but missed. He stood a few feet back from the open doorway, looking in at her, in an effort to get her to kick again. She did, and William's catch-pole loop found its mark around her foot. William yanked the tensioner on his end of the pole, securing the loop tightly around her ankle. He took a few steps back as he pulled. The woman slid across the backseat of the vehicle and landed squarely on her back and cuffed hands on the garage's concrete floor. The woman moaned in pain, moving slowly.

William dropped the pole, kicked her onto her side, and sprawled down, taking her back. He placed his left arm around her neck, grabbed his right bicep with his left hand, and placed his right hand behind her head. William rolled his shoulders back and pushed down with his right hand on the back of her head, tightening his grip—the move, a rear naked choke hold, was applied to perfection, and she went limp in seconds. William held the choke for another moment before letting go, quickly scooping her up, and carrying her from the garage. He walked to the back door of his home, twisted the knob with the hand holding her legs, and pushed the door open with the toe of his shoe.

The woman mumbled something as she began to regain consciousness. William hurried toward the basement in order to restrain her before she fully came to.

CHAPTER ELEVEN

I woke a couple minutes past six and got ready for my day. I showered, plotted out my individual stops for the morning, and picked up a cup of coffee from the lobby. I was still unaware of what Beth planned to do. The topic of her calling Ball and removing herself from the investigation was still up in the air. The idea, when she and I had left the bar the prior night, was that she'd sleep on it, decide in the morning, and let me know—that was after an hour-plus talk with her asking me what I thought she should do about the ex-husband situation. I didn't have much for her other than I didn't care for his behavior. I'd just finished up phone calls with Karen and Agent Duffield and was getting ready to head out when I heard a knock at the door and figured it was Beth. I walked over and pulled the door open.

Beth stood in the doorway, dressed for work, with the bag that she normally held investigation files in draped over her shoulder. I didn't spot a suitcase.

"Sticking around?" I asked.

"I am. Can I come in for a minute?" she asked.

I stepped to the side of the door, waved her in, and then

passed her, heading for my cup of coffee on the desk by the window. "I was just getting set to leave. Are you still planning on meeting with the friends and family, then?"

"I am. I guess I just needed to ask you a question."

"Shoot." I turned back to face her. She hadn't moved more than a foot or two from the door into the room.

"Are you planning on mentioning this to Ball?" Beth asked.

"What? Scott showing up here and being an idiot?"

"That—and everything else. Like, I'm one hundred percent not asking you not to. I understand if you do because of the nature of our occupation and all that. It's just… If you were going to, I'd like to be able to tell him myself, prior to him hearing it secondhand."

"I wasn't planning to," I said.

"But I don't want you to feel like you're keeping something a secret from your boss, you know?"

I held up my hand. "It's just not that big of a deal, Beth. So he showed up here unexpected, acted like an ass, and that's it. I kind of see it more as a personal matter. It's not really my or Ball's or anyone else's business. It could have just as easily happened anywhere, where I wouldn't have been there to see it. I mean, would you mention it to Ball if I wasn't there?"

"Well, no."

"Right. So something that was personal happened off the clock. Big deal. Shit happens."

"You don't feel weird about not mentioning it to Ball?" she asked.

"If you keep making such a big deal about it, eventually I'll feel weird about it."

She didn't respond to my attempt at humor.

"Look. Forget about it, already. Can you do your job over the next few days?" I asked.

"Of course."

"He's gone, I assume?"

"He is," she said. "I made sure."

I wasn't going to ask her how exactly she'd made sure, but I took her word for it. "Then we're good, partner."

"All right," she said. "Thanks for having my back last night. I appreciate it."

"Sure, no problem."

Beth took a seat on the foot of the bed. "What's your first stop today?"

"The business center downstairs. I need to print some photos of these women that I grabbed from the DLs. After that, I'm going to make a quick stop out at this Katelyn Willard's apartment complex. Then move on to the scenes where the women we know to be deceased were taken from. Then, I have a pile of things that I want to get into. I want to stop in at the paper that received the box. We need to speak with the guys from missing persons that created the reports. I still want to find out some details about the vehicle found on the side of the road with a flat tire. The list goes on and on."

"I know—we have a full plate," Beth said. "We'll just have to go down the list and start getting things checked off. You're going to the missing girl's place first, though?"

"I got the address from Duffield this morning. It's actually on my way to my first stop, so I figure I'll make a little pit stop at the area and just have a look around. The girl was pretty clearly abducted, I'm thinking, and while we don't know if it's connected to our investigation, I kind of think that a half hour of my time spent there is worth it. If it ends up being connected, at least I'll have viewed the freshest scene."

"Sure," Beth said. "Did you want to just give me a ring sometime throughout the day and let me know if you get anything new?"

"Yeah, I will."

"Okay," Beth said.

I grabbed my things and started for the door. Beth rose from the edge of the bed and followed me out. She rode the elevator down with me and left me at the lobby. I headed for the business center, got my photos printed, and left the hotel. The drive to the site of Katelyn's abduction took me a solid twenty-five minutes. On the way, I called the office of the Oldham County Sheriff, to see if they had any updates on their investigation into the girl's disappearance. Chief Deputy King said they'd had nothing new and the ex-boyfriend's alibi had checked out. He offered to meet me at the apartment complex, to which I agreed.

The robotic female voice on my GPS told me the address was ahead on my right. I slowed and made a right into the complex's main entrance. Each of the countless buildings rose two stories. I had the unit number Katelyn resided in, but with no point of reference and not seeing any signs that listed which units were where, I was driving blind. I figured I'd do a lap around the facility, looking for the chief deputy, prior to stopping in at the rental office to get the location.

I slowed at the first crossroads of the complex, looking up and down the crossing street. I spotted neither anything that looked like it could be law-enforcement issued, nor any vehicles not in the assigned parking stalls. I continued on, slowing at the next crossroads and then the next. The road in front of me terminated up ahead, allowing me to park in a visitor section or make a left or right turn. I slowed, checked both directions, and made a Y-turn to head back the way I'd come. As I drove back toward the front of the facility, a dark sedan driving my way stopped in the roadway, and the driver's-side window lowered. I recognized the car as a standard undercover issued Dodge Charger, and King sat inside.

"Saw someone driving slow and you make the turn down there. I thought that might be you," he said.

"I figured I'd make a pass through and look for you prior to stopping in the rental office and finding out just exactly where her unit was. They don't make it too easy to find what address is what back here."

"Sure don't," he said. "It's actually at the back, where you'd made the turn, and off to the left."

"Okay, I'll get spun around and follow you back."

He nodded and raised his window.

I turned around at the next crossroad and followed him back to the end of the road. King parked in one of the visitor section spots and stepped from his car. I pulled in beside him and did the same. After meeting him at the trunk of his car, we started toward where he'd said the girl's car had been parked.

"Did you get anything else from the car?" I asked.

"Nope," King said. "No prints other than what we confirmed to be hers. I guess she had a prior for shoplifting right around the time that she turned eighteen, so we found her in the system. The set of prints on the phone were hers as well. We either had someone wearing gloves, or they didn't actually make contact with her things. The car was parked back there." He pointed toward the far corner of the lot, next to a small square building. "The little building there is some kind of a service shack for water or something."

We walked toward the area. I noticed the parking lot wrap around the end of the apartment building and continue back toward the front of the complex.

"Does this lot turn back into a street and go back toward the entrance?" I asked.

"It does," he said. "There's the main road that we drove in on, and one on each far end of the facility that gets you in and out."

I nodded.

"So here is where her car was," he said, coming to a stop, "next to the shack here." He motioned toward the empty parking spot adjacent to the small building.

I walked around the vacant parking area and surveyed the ground looking for any little scrap of anything—I saw nothing. "What kind of vehicle?" I asked.

"Newer Hyundai. Mid sized," he said. "The roommate

said she usually parked way down here to avoid picking up door dings."

"Sure." I stopped searching the ground and looked up a light pole that sat behind the shed. I pointed to a camera mounted at its top. "That's the camera that doesn't work?"

"Correct."

I looked in the other direction, past where we'd parked, to the mirroring apartment unit on the far end. I spotted another pole at the back corner of the parking lot and what looked like a camera at its top. "What about that one?" I asked.

"We saw that as well. Also inop."

"Okay." I looked toward the apartment building nearest us. The ground floor held four banks of paired maroon entrance doors and four sets of sliding glass patio doors. Above the ground-level patio doors were small second-story patios set into the building. Groups of windows filled the remaining areas of the two-tone brown building. I assumed one of each of the paired doors belonged to a lower level and the other door to the upper. "What unit was hers?" I asked.

"It's on the other side of the building, facing the other way. Second-story unit. I think it's the first one in on the far side here," King said.

"So the roommate wouldn't have been able to see the vehicle from their apartment."

"Nope."

"So what she was saying about not noticing her car out here could hold up," I said.

"We kind of tossed around the idea that the roommate

was involved, back at the office. I mean, someone goes missing, generally you look at the closest person—especially with her vehicle being here and left in the way that it was. We just don't have anything to suggest that she was involved, yet we don't have anything to suggest that she wasn't, either. Her alibi of being home alone all day leaves a little to be desired, I guess."

"You checked over the apartment?" I asked.

"My guys said nothing seemed off."

"Did you run a forensics unit through?"

"We didn't, but it might be something that we have to do if we don't get something that points us in another direction," King said.

"Do you know if she's home?"

"The roommate?"

"Yeah," I said.

"I don't know. She just lives on the other side of the building, though. Did you want to pop in there and see?"

"I do," I said.

CHAPTER TWELVE

We rounded the building to the first set of doors on the far side. The doors themselves had small black numbers designating the address tacked to them.

"This is hers here." King reached out and knocked.

A dog immediately began barking inside. From the high pitched yelping, I figured the dog to be some kind of small breed.

A moment later, I heard the sounds of footsteps coming down stairs. The door pulled open.

"Ms. Bromley," King said.

"Oh, hi. Just Jessi is fine. Did you guys find anything out?" she asked.

"Unfortunately, not yet," he said. "We were just stopping out here for a look around."

"Sure. Did you guys want to come in?" she asked.

"Please," he said.

"Both of you are fine with dogs? There's one upstairs. It's a Yorkie, about this big." She held her hands up in about a ten-inch circle.

King looked at me.

"I'm a dog person. It's fine," I said.

She motioned us inside.

As we entered and walked up the stairs to the second-level unit, I thought about the fact that if the roommate was involved, she probably wouldn't have invited us up. I stepped from the top stair into an area of the apartment between the living room and kitchen off to my left. I looked toward the far side of the living room and spotted a small gray-and-brown long-haired dog perched on a couch cushion and staring back at King and me. The dog let out a good ten seconds of high-pitched barks, left the couch, and ran toward us.

"He's just showing off," she said. "Barney, you be quiet before Paul next door starts bitching."

The dog continued barking, and a moment later, we heard thumping on the back wall of the living room. The roommate grumbled, scooped up the little dog from the carpet, and held him under her arm. She walked to the far side of the room and banged her fist against the wall behind the television.

As she walked back, she said, "Sorry. The neighbor, Paul Something, isn't the biggest fan of my dog or me, I think. Any chance he can make that known, he does." She stood before the chief deputy and me. "What did you guys want to have a look at? Anything I can do to help, just let me know."

The second she finished her sentence, we heard more banging from the adjoining apartment.

"God!" she said. "He is just the worst. Like a week or two ago, I think he was trying to set up some kind of sting operation to bust me not cleaning up after my dog outside. I mean, my dog goes to the bathroom in one spot outside, and I'm a responsible owner. I pick up after him every time. It's just annoying. And then about a month ago, he called in the car of one of my friends, who was staying for the weekend, as being abandoned and got it towed. Anyways… Again, I'm sorry. What did you guys want to look at?"

King and I dismissed her neighbor issues, asked her if we could just have a look around, and proceeded to go through the apartment. I kept my eyes searching for signs of blood. After years of working in homicide, I'd learned the most commonly overlooked locations—the bottoms of door and wall trim, ceiling corners, kitchen-cabinet edges, under the lips of the kitchen counters. After looking high and low, I didn't see anything that raised any red flags. King let the roommate know that he would keep her updated and would be in touch. We left her and walked back out to the front of her apartment building.

"Probably not worth the trip, huh?" King asked.

I shrugged. "It was on my way. Figured it couldn't hurt to stop and have a look for myself. Do you know if anyone talked to the wall-banging neighbor?"

"I'd have to check the case file to see who we received statements from and what apartments they resided in. It's in my car. It would probably just take a second to check."

"Let's just go give his door a knock and ask. Obviously, he's home," I said.

"Sure."

We rounded the building toward the back side, where the

missing girl's car had been parked, and looked for the front door of the neighbor's apartment.

"If they shared walls, I'm guessing it would be just like her apartment was on the other side. So, the first bank of doors in." I pointed at the door.

We approached, and King pressed the doorbell. A moment later, a man wearing a blue sweater and khaki pants answered the door. The bottoms of his pants were tightly rolled—a style that had come and gone from fashion in the late eighties and early nineties. I put him in his late fifties by the amount of gray on the sides of his round, balding head. He adjusted his oversized glasses on his nose and stared at us.

"Agent Hank Rawlings, FBI." I showed him my credentials. "This is Chief Deputy King from the Oldham County Sheriff's Office."

"Okay," he said.

"Your name, sir?" I asked.

"Paul Samson."

I took my notepad from my inner pocket and wrote down his name. "Were you the one just banging on the wall?" I asked.

He pulled his head back. "Is that a federal crime? Wanting a little peace and quiet from someone's yapping mutt?"

We dismissed his remark.

"Sir, did you speak with anyone from my department regarding the missing woman in your complex?" King asked.

"Missing woman? No. I just returned home late last night."

"And you were where?" King asked.

"Visiting my father, who is ill, in Michigan."

"The date you left?"

"I was gone for over a week. Why?"

"Anything to prove that?" I asked.

The man grumbled and waved us into his apartment. "I'll show you my damn itinerary. Come up." When he turned to head up the stairs, a braided ponytail swung on the back of his balding head.

We followed the man into the apartment and upstairs. My nose filled with an odd smell I couldn't quite put my finger on. We stopped between the living room and the kitchen of his unit, which was a mirror image of the roommate's we'd just come from. I noticed his wood-cabinet-encased television, which looked like it was from the sixties or seventies. I glanced to the corner of the living room to see two suitcases with the tops open but fully packed—though the clothes appeared to have been worn. The outsides of the suitcases were covered in duct tape.

The man continued on to his small dining-room area and rummaged through some papers on the table. We followed him. I glanced around the rest of the items set on the table, including a clear resealable plastic bag with toiletries inside—his toothbrush had brown bristles, which was unsettling. My eyes went to the rest of the items—some airplane peanuts, a phone charger, a plastic hotel-room key card, and a set of headphones.

The man pulled a paper from the pile and held it out toward us. "Here, here's my itinerary." He dug back into the papers and pulled another. "Hotel information. I have my boarding passes in my carry-on over there."

We glanced at the man's papers briefly, including the boarding passes, and handed everything back to him. He either had a damn-well-thought-out alibi or was truthful. I had his name and could easily call to confirm if he'd made his flights and had in fact checked into his hotel.

"Just confirming," I said. "You haven't been here in the last week? Saw anything suspicious out back here?"

"No, I haven't," he said.

"Okay, thank you for your time, sir." I motioned at King, and we started toward the stairs that would take us back down to the front door.

"Out back?" the guy asked.

I turned back toward the man. "Correct."

"Wait a minute," he said. "What are you looking for? You think something may have happened back here?" He pointed toward his patio doors, referencing the back lot of the complex.

"We do," King said.

"I have a camera that's been running. I don't know how much it picked up over the last week, but we can take a look."

"You have a camera facing the back lot?" I asked.

"I set it up a month or so ago. People weren't picking up after their pets, and after stepping in dog mess a few times, I went to the management and filed a complaint. I told them to see who it was on the camera in the lot, and they told me they were having some difficulties with them. The cheap bastards just didn't want to replace them, probably. Well, I went out and bought a camera to see who the person was not cleaning up after their dogs. I figured I'd show whoever I got on tape to the management. And if that didn't work, at least I could confront the person."

I stood there thinking the guy shouldn't live in an apartment complex that allowed pets if he wasn't prepared for the occasional foot in poop. His wall banging and the extent to which he'd gone to bust a neighbor showed me that the guy probably shouldn't live around anyone. However, he might have had camera footage that would help us, so I played nice. "That's totally understandable. We have some irresponsible pet owners in my facility as well. It can be frustrating."

"Right?" he asked.

"Yeah, so that camera footage?"

"Sure—one second." The man walked to the patio doors, slid them open, walked out, and returned with a small handheld camera. "The light is still on. I guess their claim of a ten-day battery is fairly accurate."

Neither King nor I responded.

"This thing is motion activated and can pick up video at night fairly well. Hold on—I just need to get the memory card out and plug it into my computer."

"Sure," I said.

The man fiddled with the camera, slid out a small SD card, and powered on his laptop. He plugged the memory card in and brought up some app that must have been for the video camera. "Here we go. Any idea what you're looking for?"

The screen on his laptop flickered and played a clip of a car parking at night. I took a look at the screen, noting that the recording was black and white and not entirely clear. I chalked it up to being due to some form of night-vision feature the camera was using. My eyes went to the left side of the screen and the empty stall, where we'd been told Katelyn Willard normally parked. I knew that, while we wouldn't be able to get a look at anyone's face clearly enough for any kind of positive ID, we'd be able to get a pretty decent view of what happened, provided the camera had done its job and recorded when Katelyn Willard pulled up the night she went missing.

"Can you go by date?" King asked.

"This thing just kind of gives me a total run-time bar down at the bottom of the screen. I can drag to one spot or another to go forward or back. There are time-and-date stamps, so I don't think it will be too hard to find."

"We're looking for this past Saturday night, starting around nine at night," King said.

"Okay, I should be able to get that up. Did you gentlemen care for a cup of herbal tea? Maybe some Kool-Aid or a glass of milk with a little honey?"

The offer struck me as odd, which went along with just about everything else about the guy.

"No thank you," I said.

King quickly declined as well.

CHAPTER THIRTEEN

William sat on the top of his washing machine. His swaying feet made a metallic thumping sound as his heels contacted the metal door on the front of the washer.

"How's your breakfast?" he asked.

The woman, shoveling a handful of eggs into her mouth with her dirty hand, took a break from her chewing. "Go to hell."

"So the eggs are to your liking, then? Better than the dog food you've been eating?"

"Someone will find me. You'll burn for this."

"Doubt it," William said. "I almost have everything dialed in. It won't be long now."

"Yeah, you've said that before."

"Do you know what's interesting, Erin? You haven't once asked about what I've been doing with the women in the other room. I've heard you yell out to them and try to talk to them in the middle of the night. They can't respond to you, which I'm sure you've realized by now, but I know you can hear me with them through the wall. You can hear them plead for their lives. You can hear me kill them. You can hear the saw."

She didn't respond.

"What does that say about you that you have no questions or worry for others?" William asked.

She jammed another handful of eggs in her mouth and spoke over her chewing. "You're trying to play mind games with me, trying to scare me. I'm not that stupid. There's no other women over there."

"Then what is the noise? Where do the screams come from?"

"I don't care," Erin said. "A television, a recording, who knows? Maybe it's you sitting over there doing an interpretation of a woman. You put a hood over my head every time you take me from this room. You won't let me see what's going on over there. If there was blood and guts and dead people, I'm sure you'd want me to see that. Something to strike the fear of death into me. All I get is the little bit I can hear. You have sound deadening all over the walls in here. Barely audible voices that I can't make out and a scream or two every now and then is all I get. The fact is that you're a coward, William. You don't have the testicular fortitude to actually kill me, someone you've said multiple times that you want to kill. Why would you have the balls to kill someone else? You're going to keep me locked up and threaten me until someone finds me. Then you'll go to jail, and I'll go back to work. Forget the sports-anchor position—I'll be a celebrity after doing the circuit of talk shows before I end up getting a national anchor seat. If you actually had any intentions of killing me, you would have done it."

"Nice theory," William said. "We'll see. I think you'll

end up being impressed by my testicular fortitude in this matter."

She tossed the empty pie tin through the metal bars of the large metal crate she was locked in. The tin clanked off the floor, sending some remnants of scrambled eggs bouncing on the cement near the clothes dryer.

"That wasn't very considerate of you. Now I'll have to clean that up," William said.

She spat at him through the thick metal bars.

William chuckled, scooted himself off the washer, and grabbed the pie tin from the floor. "I guess we're going to go back to the dog food then, seeing as how you're being a little bitch."

Erin grabbed the bars of her enclosure and shook the door, which bounced and rattled the padlock keeping it closed. "Let me out of here!"

William caught the time on his watch. "I will around noon. Gotta take the dog for her walk outside so she can do her business. I'd enjoy the outdoors this time if I were you. Probably won't be too many more trips out in your future."

Erin screamed and wailed. William paid her no mind and left the laundry room. He closed the soundproofed door at his back and stared at the woman across the room, named Courtney, whom he'd picked up the night prior. She, like those before her, was restrained to the wall—her arms outstretched and shackled, her feet the same. William walked across the clean plastic-covered floor, around the table in the center of the room, and stood before her. The woman had been awake since the night before. William had woken a few times throughout the night and heard her crying, sniveling, and whining into the ball gag in her mouth.

William took her by her chin and turned her head to face him. Courtney didn't resist.

He stared at her face and turned her head from one side to the other. "You're older than I would have liked, but for my little test, I think you'll do just fine. I suppose I'm about ready to get this show on the road. What about you?" William reached behind her head, undid the straps securing the gag, and let it fall to her feet. He waited for her screams to come, but they didn't.

"Please," she said. Her voice was low, barely above that of a whisper.

"Please what?" William asked.

"Let me help you."

"What?" William cocked his head. "Help me? Help me with what?"

"Anything," Courtney said.

"Help me kill you? You know that's what's coming, right? I'm going to kill you." He stared at her, but her facial expression didn't change. "Do you want me to kill you?" William asked.

"No." She lifted her head and looked directly into his eyes. "I just think that there's maybe something we can do to avoid all of this. Maybe we can work something out?" A hint of a smile crossed her face.

"I'm not sure what that just was, but there's no avoiding it."

William turned and walked toward the knife lying on the

table. He took it in his hand and returned to her. He tapped the blade against the palm of his hand. "I'm going to stick this knife into your heart. Care to hear what I'm going to do after?"

"I think you'd like me better alive," Courtney said.

"Whatever," William said. "I don't much care for you either way. You're a head and a set of hands that I need to practice with. Nothing more. Nothing less."

He closed in on her and put his left hand against her upper chest, looking for the mark for his knife. She didn't pull away or make a sound but instead leaned into his hand.

William backed off. "No." He shook his head. "What's wrong with you? Are you some kind of nutcase or something?"

"Free me. Let me show you." She flashed him the same smile she'd shown a moment earlier.

William took another step back. He ran his hand along the back of his neck while keeping his gaze on the woman. "You were all full of piss and vinegar last night—screaming, kicking, fighting, all normal reactions. Now, whatever this is, isn't normal. Hmm. I have a hunch you're trying to play little games with me. I guess it's a good thing I didn't get a chance to clean up. Give me one second. I'll be back."

"Where are you going? Stay here with me."

"Nah, I think you need to see something." William turned, set the knife back on the table, and left the room.

He entered the basement den and looked down at the rotting mount of Kelly Page propped against the side of the end table—the only mount he hadn't smashed to pieces in his fit of anger and frustration. He took it in his hands, lifted it from the floor, and turned it to face him. The skin looked as if it had deteriorated even more since being removed from the wall. The pungent smell coming off her had only intensified—that was of no consequence as it would do fine for what he needed. He walked back across the basement, keeping the mount behind his back, and reentered the room where Courtney was shackled to the wall.

"I'm going to have you look at something for me, and then we'll see if you change your tune a bit," William said. He stood before her, the mount hanging from his right hand behind his back.

"What's that?" she asked.

William pulled the mounted head from behind his back and held it up before her face. "This is your fate."

William looked around the side of the mount to get her reaction. Courtney had a look of confusion on her face.

"Here. Get a good look. Smell her." He pressed the rotted flesh of Kelly Page's face against Courtney's cheek.

Courtney's body jerked, and he took a few quick steps back as she vomited. She gagged again and fought to get the word *help* to come from her mouth.

"Are you understanding this now?" William asked. "Is your fate clear to you?"

Spittle flew from Courtney's mouth. "Help!" she screamed once and again.

"I thought you wanted to help me—you know, work something out," William said over the woman's earsplitting shrieks.

He smiled, tossed the mounted head to the ground, and

walked to the knife on the table.

"Please, no!" she cried. "Help!"

"There we go. That's a little more like it." William walked to her, found his spot on her chest as she jerked and wailed, and plunged the knife in.

She went silent.

CHAPTER FOURTEEN

We'd waited for him to pull up the footage for the better part of ten minutes. He dragged the mouse one way and then back the other. I had a pretty good guess that I could have found the time in question about nine minutes earlier. While we'd been waiting, we'd identified the smell in the apartment as Limburger cheese—which he offered us, but we declined. He'd also informed us while we stood and watched him that we should refer to him as Big Paul as that's what his friends called him. However, the thought of that man having many friends struck me as a bit far-fetched. I figured I'd just stick with Mr. Samson if I did need to address him by name.

"Here. It's playing at eight fifty-eight on Saturday. Like I said, it's motion activated," Mr. Samson said.

"Right," I said.

We watched the laptop monitor as a car pulled in and parked in the back lot. Then a man exited the vehicle and walked back toward the apartment complex, disappearing from the screen. A moment later, the monitor went black. It flicked back on within seconds. I caught the time-stamp in the corner—9:33 p.m.

"That's her," King said.

The nose of her car approaching from the side of the building nearest her parking spot must have triggered the camera. We watched as she slowly pulled forward toward the parking spot. Then what looked like flashing lights lit the screen, illuminating the water shed and neighboring cars. Katelyn pulled into her parking spot. Headlights lit the back of her car as well as the strobing lights, which alternated between lighting the left and then the right side of her trunk. The lights continued for another few seconds before disappearing.

"What the hell was that?" I asked. "Was she getting pulled over or something?" I looked at King standing at my shoulder, and his eyes were fixed on the laptop's screen.

I looked back and watched. Katelyn never left her vehicle. A moment later, the figure of a man walked to her driver's door and lit up a flashlight. While the recording didn't give us a clear view, the guy looked to be in a suit as opposed to a police uniform. We looked on as the man stood at her window for roughly thirty seconds. An arm came from the driver's window and held a couple of items out toward the man. His light pointed at whatever he was handed. A moment later, the man took a step back. Katelyn's driver's door opened, and she stepped out. The man escorted her off screen. When the two walked off camera, the footage went black, only coming back on with a time-stamp roughly three hours later, when another vehicle pulled in and parked. We continued to watch the footage until it showed daybreak, just a few minutes in recorded footage later—no one approached the vehicle again.

"Did you want me to rewind it?" Mr. Samson asked.

"Not yet." I looked at King. "What time did the roommate say she'd noticed the car?"

He appeared to be in thought. "It's in my case file, but if memory serves, she said around nine yesterday morning."

"All right." I looked at Mr. Samson. "Mind if I try to pull up that time?"

"I'd prefer to be in charge of my own equipment," he said.

I shrugged and let out a breath.

He went back and forth on the timing bar at the bottom of the video screen for roughly a minute.

"Try a quarter inch to the right. You're still about eight hours behind where we need to be," I said.

"I'll have it for you in a second," he said yet didn't obey my instruction. I was beginning to think he was just trying to keep King and me there as long as he could. Another three minutes later, he'd found the time and date we'd requested—right around where I'd asked him to move the scroll bar.

"Here we are," he said.

The three of us watched the monitor as a woman, in daylight, walked around the corner of the building into the back lot and stopped in her tracks. From the build and style of hair, I figured it to be Jessi Bromley, the roommate. She approached the parked Hyundai belonging to Katelyn Willard slowly, rounded the driver's side of the vehicle, and looked inside. She removed her phone from her pocket and made a phone call as she paced the lot back and forth behind the vehicle. Then she appeared to hang up and make another call.

"Pretty much exactly as she described seeing the car and making the calls," I said.

"Agreed. I imagine, later in the recording, we'll see the police respond, look around, the vehicle being removed, et cetera. Let's rewind it back to where we think the abduction took place," King said.

Mr. Samson rewound the recording, and we watched the footage of her pulling in, parking, and walking back to the other car off screen with the man three more times.

"Do you know how accurate the time is on that camera?" I asked.

"Well, whatever timing method the camera uses has to be quartz, which even cheap quartz timing devices are normally pretty accurate—within a couple seconds per month, normally. When I set the time on the monitoring equipment, I synchronized it with my atomic watch here." Mr. Samson held out the watch on his wrist and turned it back and forth." This timepiece receives a signal every night and is accurate to one second per one hundred thousand years."

A simple *it's accurate* would have sufficed.

"We'll need that memory card," I said. "Someone from the bureau will need to go through it and try to clean it up to see if we can get a better look at our suspect."

"As long as I get reimbursed for it, sure," Mr. Samson said. "These go for about twenty bucks."

"It's evidence in an investigation of a missing woman," I said.

"And they still go for about twenty bucks," he said.

Mr. Samson held out his hand, expecting me to give him a twenty, I assumed.

I gave the guy my best not-screwing-around-or-giving-you-twenty-dollars face. "Are you sure?"

He grumbled and pulled the card from his computer. "Fine." He held it out toward me.

I took it and placed it in my inner suit pocket. "Appreciate it. Thanks for your time, sir." I motioned to King that we were leaving.

We walked down the steps of the apartment to the front door.

The apartment owner followed, and when I pulled the door handle to leave, he said, "Have them write my name as Big Paul if they include me in the news or paper or anything, so all my friends know it was me."

"Absolutely," I said.

I don't believe Mr. Samson caught my sarcasm, for he thanked me and asked if I needed the spelling. I told him that I didn't, and King and I left the apartment and walked to our cars. I looked back once to see Mr. Samson wave and give me a thumbs up.

"Odd duck," I said.

"That's putting it gently." King put his back to his trunk and dug into his pocket. He pulled out a pack of cigarettes, tapped one out, stuck it in his mouth and lit it.

"Okay, what do we make of the footage?" I asked.

King took a long drag from his smoke and exhaled. "I'm at a loss," he said.

"Well, this is your jurisdiction. Think it was someone from your department?"

"No. On the second watching of the footage, I caught it. The procedure was wrong. The way the lights lit up was wrong."

"What do you mean?"

"Our lights spin in our marked cars—LEDs inside the roof-mounted light bars with a rotating reflector."

"The guy wasn't in an official uniform. What about detectives?"

"We have two unmarked cars. This is one." He slapped the trunk lid he was leaning against. "The other mostly sits in our lot back at the station. Either way, neither goes home with anyone on the weekends, and again, the lights are different. We have strips in the top of the windshield and back glass. The strobe is five or six on red then over to blue. What was on the screen was back and forth. Here, look." He walked to his driver's door, opened it, and turned on the lights.

I walked to the front of his car and took a quick look, verifying the pattern as different from the video.

"No one has lights on any of their personal vehicles?" I asked.

He shook his head.

"So we have someone either from another jurisdiction, another branch, or someone simply posing as a cop who picked this girl up," I said.

He walked back to the trunk of his car, and I followed.

"Could have been anything equipped with lights," King said. "A fire chief's truck, tow truck, EMT vehicle, security vehicle. Security vehicle could make sense. We should check to see if this complex contracts a company for that." He finished his smoke in a few more drags, put it out against the bottom of his shoe, and held the butt in his hand.

I was quiet for a moment, in thought. King threw a bunch of alternative ideas against the wall and quickly made his case that it wasn't any of the vehicles from his office. I glanced down at his hand still holding the cigarette butt. I slid my sleeve up and looked at the time on my watch.

"I have to get moving here," I said. "We'll check on a security company for this place, and as soon as we get the video processed, I'll make sure your office gets a copy."

"Sure," he said.

"We'll be in touch, and thanks for shooting out here to meet me." I walked to the door of my rental car.

King left the trunk of his vehicle and walked to the driver's door. "No problem," he said.

I hopped into my car and backed out of my parking spot. I briefly stopped into the front office of the apartment complex and confirmed they did not have any kind of security vehicles or a company that provided the service for them.

I drove roughly a mile from Katelyn Willard's apartment complex, turned into a parking lot, pulled out my cell phone, and dialed Beth. She picked up within a couple of rings.

"Hey," she said.

"Not in the middle of something are you?" I asked.

"No. I'm driving to meet the parents of Kelly Page. I should be there in about five minutes. What's up?"

"Well, we have video of what I'm guessing is the abduction of Katelyn Willard from her apartment complex."

"Video? Really?"

"Yeah. It's fairly grainy, but you can see what goes down. Her neighbor had a motion camera on his patio. I think it was a cop who took her."

"What?" Beth asked. "A cop?"

"Looked like it, as much as the chief deputy was trying to sway me away from the idea by presenting a bunch of alternative theories."

"Chief deputy?"

"The chief deputy from the Oldham County Sheriff's office met me out there. We had a look around and met with a neighbor together. Neighbor had the video footage."

"How did it go down?" Beth asked.

I filled her in on the neighbor and gave her what we'd seen on the video.

"But you don't think it could have been anything other than a police officer?"

"Or someone posing as one," I said. "To me, the thing that sticks out is the way the guy approached the vehicle. He came up with a flashlight, must have had some words through her window, probably asked her to exit the vehicle, and she left with him. Nobody is going to do that unless they think they're dealing with law enforcement. Plus, she left her car open with her purse, phone, keys, and all of that in there. To me, that sounds like 'step out of the car and come back here.'"

"Yeah, you're probably right on that. So what's the plan there?"

“Not sure. I’ll turn the video in at the office, make sure the local sheriff’s department gets a copy, and I guess that’s it on it unless we can positively link the abduction with our guy.”

“Okay. You’re headed back to the field office after you make your stops?” Beth asked.

“I’m actually going to run back right now, drop off this memory card with the video, and then head back out to the scenes. But, yeah, I’ll be back there when I’m through for the day.”

“All right. I’m just pulling up to my first stop. I’ll meet you back there this afternoon.”

“Sounds good.” I clicked off, pulled up the navigation on my phone, and had it direct me back to the Louisville field office.

CHAPTER FIFTEEN

After my trip back to the field office that morning, I completed my rounds of viewing scenes or, more accurately, areas of town where the women had been last seen. By noon, I'd found the area where April Backer's vehicle with the flat tire had been discovered. I walked the stretch of roadway, which was fairly rural, and saw nothing that could be described as evidence. I made notes in my notepad to find out where the vehicle currently was, to see if anyone had found the source of the flat tire, and to get a report from whoever had inspected the vehicle.

From there, my trip took me back into the city. By one thirty, I'd walked the route around the University of Louisville that Jennifer Pasco, the woman who was last seen leaving a house party and walking back to her place, would have taken. I spoke with a handful of college kids that lived in the home where the party had taken place—it seemed the party was a bit of a free-for-all and none of them knew the girl personally.

From there, I headed back into the downtown area and visited the two locations where Kelly Paige and Trisha Floyd had been abducted somewhere between the bars they were at and their vehicles. I retraced the steps needed to get from point A to B at both locations and had talks with the bar staff as well as local business owners in the area. I discovered nothing new.

At a quarter to four, I found myself sitting in a trendy downtown diner over a dressed-up steak-and-cheese sandwich, which was delicious. I jammed the last bit of the sandwich in my mouth and took a drink from my soda. The waitress passed, and I requested my bill. I wiped my hands on a napkin and scooped my phone from the small white-tableclothed table. The light on the top corner of my cell was flashing that I had an e-mail. I clicked the prompts to pull up the message. The e-mail was from Ball, asking me to check in when I got the chance. I took another drink of my soda and dialed him.

"Ball," he answered.

"Hey, it's Hank. I just saw your message."

"I just wanted to see if anything was shaking. I hadn't talked to you or Beth today. I tried her a bit earlier, but she didn't answer."

"She's meeting with friends and family. I've just been out looking over the locations where these women were last seen."

"Anything at the spots?"

"Zip. I don't even know if you could really describe them as scenes. 'Missing from somewhere between here and here' doesn't give you much to look at."

"Did you stop in at the paper that received the package yet?"

"No. I was kind of thinking that maybe we should put together some kind of a press conference prior to doing that. An FBI agent walks into the paper and starts asking questions about the box that they had delivered, that contained what it did, and they could start spreading headlines. It doesn't take too many brain cells for them to realize it got kicked up the ranks and there is legitimacy to it."

"True, but both should probably be done, either way. Sooner rather than later," Ball said.

"Agreed," I said. "I'll call Agent Duffield in a second here and take his temperature on it. I'm just finishing up a late lunch right now."

"What about the house the package was shipped from?"

"Duffield said that the family should be back tomorrow, so I think I'll try to meet with them as soon as they're back in the area."

"Sure. Anything else? What about that latest abduction you told me about last night? Any news?"

"There is there, actually." I told Ball about the video footage and the fact that it looked as though a cop was responsible. He didn't seem to know what to make of that and left me with the instructions to leave it to the locals until we knew if it was connected one way or another.

"Okay," Ball said. "When you talk to Beth later, have her give me a ring if she hasn't already."

"Will do." I clicked off from the call and brought up the navigation on my phone. I entered the name of the newspaper and searched. The *Louisville Press-Gazette* showed as having eight different locations around the city—the closest being a few blocks, the farthest five miles or so. I realized I would need to look at the investigation file—which was in my car, parked at the meter around the block—to see which exact location was the one that had received the package. I dialed Agent Duffield.

He picked up within a couple of rings. "Agent Matt Duffield."

"It's Agent Rawlings. Hey, what are we thinking about a press conference on this?"

He let out a long breath. "It has to be done, huh?"

"Yes."

"Okay. I guess I could put something together for tomorrow morning," he said. Then he went silent for a bit before clearing his throat. "Yeah, it's going to need to be done. We should have something out there before another package shows up. If we don't, this could be all over the news and on the front page of every paper, and we'll look bad for being behind it. We can't assume another media outlet will handle it the same as the first newspaper."

"I agree, and speaking of the paper, would you rather I wait until tomorrow to meet with anyone from the paper that the package was shipped to? Whoever I talk to could put two and two together and craft a story prior to us getting a press conference put together."

"Well, it's probably too late for anything to be put together for print tonight yet," he said. "And they'd look pretty stupid with a speculation piece on the shelves in the morning when we give a press conference. You make the call."

"Okay. What newspaper location actually received the package? I searched the place and came back with a bunch of locations."

"One second—I'm grabbing a coffee from the lunchroom. Let me get back to my desk and get it for you."

"Sure," I said. "If it's close, I'll stop in and get it crossed off the list."

"Right. Anything else go on out at the scenes?"

"Nothing. What are you guys working on back there?"

"Well, it looks like I'll be putting together something for the press conference in the morning in a minute here. The tech guys are going over the video you dropped off. Aside from them trying to work a little magic on that footage to clean it up, I figured we'd try to get back into all the other footage we previously collected."

"Previous footage?" I asked.

The waitress passed and left a black padded-leather folder at the edge of my table. I gave her a smile and a nod.

"Just the stuff we came up blank with on the first go-around," Duffield said. "We had some traffic-cam recordings and the video from the bars these girls were last seen at. We're going to try to see if we can get anything that looks like an on- or off-duty patrol car outside or a police officer inside the establishments. That's kind of a shot in the dark there, seeing that we don't know if it's the same guy. Aside from that, I put a couple people on seeing if anyone local has sold any wooden plates for mounts or where the hell you could buy green glass eyes."

"I dabbled in looking into the glass-eyeball thing," I said.

"Not an easy thing to acquire, apparently."

"We're finding that out. Hell, I don't know. Just trying to keep my guys busy—maybe it will lead somewhere. Okay. I'm back at my desk. The package was shipped to their main office downtown on West Broadway. Need the address?"

I took the phone from my ear and looked at the map of locations, which I still had up. "No, I have it on the map here. I'm only a couple blocks away from it."

"All right," Duffield said. "So you're going to stop in there, then?"

"May as well."

"Maybe let them know that we're going to have a press conference in the morning. Ask them nicely to keep a lid on it until then. If you get the feeling that they won't, maybe ask them not so nicely."

"Got it," I said.

"Anything else?"

"That's all I need right now. I'm going to head over to the paper and then shoot back out to the field office. Was there a name of anyone associated with the paper that I should look for?"

"The report lists an Andrew Shalagin. It doesn't say what his position is there, though."

I wrote the name in my notepad. "Okay. I'll figure it out. How late are you sticking around the office?"

"I'll be here until six thirty or seven," Duffield said.

I took a look at the time. "I'll be back there before then. We'll talk in a bit."

"Sure," Duffield said.

I clicked off, paid my tab, and left the diner. In my rental car, I clicked the button on my phone to take me to the paper. The drive, as I was told by the navigation's robotic voice, took me just a bit over two minutes. I found the building, noticed a parking lot at its side, pulled in, and found a spot. I took my bag with the investigation file from the backseat and walked toward the main entrance.

As I rounded the corner from the parking lot, I looked up at the old six-or-seven-story tan stone building. I figured it had been built in the nineteen thirties or so, from the outside architecture. The windows were green glass, and near the front entrance, the corner of the building curved as opposed to being square. Toward the top of the building, six stories up from the main entrance, was a large clock inlaid in the stone. To the right of the clock were the words Louisville Press-Gazette in greenish copper lettering. I took my notepad from my pocket, memorized the name of the man I was looking for, and walked through brass doors set back into a copper alcove that featured an artwork relief. My feet clacked across the marble floors as I found my way to the front counter. I stuffed my notepad back into my pocket and removed my credentials.

An older white-haired woman wearing too much perfume, a flowered blouse, and a beaded necklace stared back at me. "How can I help you?" she asked.

"Hello. My name is Agent Hank Rawlings with the FBI." I flashed her my credentials and stuffed them back into my pocket. "I'm looking to speak with an Andrew Shalagin."

"Sure, is Mr. Shalagin expecting you?"

The fact that she referred to him as mister told me he was some kind of higher-up at the paper.

"No. I was in the area," I said.

"Okay. Um, let me give his office a ring and see if he's in."

"Thank you," I said.

The woman lifted her phone and punched a few numbers into the keypad. I gave her my back while she made the call and could hear her speaking in a low tone behind me. The receptionist informed whoever was on the line that an FBI agent was looking to speak with Mr. Shalagin, adding that I hadn't given a reason for my visit. The phone clicked back onto its base a second later.

"Sir," she said.

I turned back to face her.

"Mr. Shalagin is actually in a meeting at the moment. Did you want to wait or maybe schedule something?"

"I'm kind of tight for time. Is there maybe a manager or someone from your mail room that I could speak with?"

"Mail room?" she asked.

"Correct," I said.

She looked confused. "Let me make a call quick."

"Appreciate it."

I watched as she picked up the phone, said a few words, and hung up.

"You can take the elevator there. Just hit the B button, and it will take you down. Off the elevator, just walk forward to the first office on your left. You'll be looking for Ethan Bracknall."

"Thank you." I headed for the brass elevator with an analog display of what floor the car was currently on—four in that case.

I hit the button to take me down, waited, and allowed the people on the elevator to get out before I stepped on. The ride down was short but filled with the standard elevator music for my listening pleasure. The doors opened, exposing the lower level of the building, which wasn't what I was expecting. What I expected to see was newspaper machinery, people buzzing about, a mail room filled with people, and papers everywhere—what I actually saw was gray carpet, white walls, a hallway with a couple of offices, and some cubicles with people farther inside the room.

I walked to the first office on my left. The white door with the glass window was closed. In black lettering, it read Ethan Bracknall on the door's glass. I rapped on the door with my knuckles, and the man seated at the desk waved me in.

CHAPTER SIXTEEN

"Walk, dog," William said. He yanked at the chain attached to the shackles on Erin's wrists.

Erin mumbled something at him through the ball gag in her mouth. While his nearest neighbor was almost a quarter mile away, he still preferred Erin to not be screaming the entire time he had her outdoors.

William had taken her for a lap around his wooded backyard—mostly pulling her along as the shackles around her ankles only allowed her to take steps of a couple inches at a time.

William looked up at the sky, which was a shade of gray, and then at the backside of his home and the sliding glass doors leading directly into the basement. "Let's go," he said with another yank. He felt dead weight at the end of the chain. William turned back toward Erin to see her lying on the ground. "I said let's go. Your outdoor time is through. Get a good look, take a couple of deep breaths, and breathe the air in. Listen to the birds and wind. Feel the grass against your body. This could be the last time you're ever outdoors."

Erin stared downward, not facing William. From the

movement of her body, she appeared to be crying.

William walked to her and crouched down. "But you talk so tough. Am I seeing little chinks in your armor? This is what you get. I warned you."

She lifted her head and stared him in the face. Her eyes were pink and wet with tears. Through the ball gag, she mumbled what sounded like "I'm sorry."

William smirked. "Nice try. Way too late for that. Now get up and shuffle your ass back toward the house, or I'm going to drag you by the chains. I have things to do."

Erin made no attempt to get to her feet.

"Suit yourself," William said.

He looped the chain around his right forearm and took it in both hands. He took a few steps backward toward his house while pulling at the chain attached to her wrists. Erin flopped flat onto her belly, arms outstretched together. William pulled again, dragging her a few feet across his lawn. She still didn't attempt to get to her feet. He grumbled and put one foot behind the other, dragging her across a scrappy quarter acre of old grass, twigs, and patches of dirt. He stopped at the concrete slab at the rear patio doors. William kept hold of the chain and took a seat on one of the old railroad ties that bordered the concrete patio, sucking in lungfuls of air. Erin moaned and writhed in the grass.

"I told your ass to walk," William said. He let out a huge puff of air and pulled another in. "Now, get up. You won't like it if I have to pull you up the concrete and back into the house."

She mumbled and moaned for a bit before putting a

skinned knee underneath her and pushing herself up to her feet.

William looked at Erin—naked with scrapes and dirt covering her front side.

"You could have avoided that if you weren't so stupid." He rose to his feet and tugged at the chain. "Come on, back in your crate."

William slid open the patio door and walked her back inside. He stopped her at the lounge chair in the main room of the basement and placed a hood over her head. William led her through the rest of the basement, back into the laundry room. He put her in front of himself, gave her a shove, and then stuck a foot into the back of her knee, dropping her to the ground.

He pulled the hood from her head. "Crawl your ass back inside. You know the drill."

She crawled into the cage, and William locked the door. Erin placed her shackled wrists against the metal bars, and William undid the chain and removed it from her enclosure.

"Turn. Back against the bars," he said.

She obeyed, and William removed the gag from her mouth.

He pulled it through the bars and tossed it to the ground. "Did you enjoy your walk?" William asked.

"Screw you."

"No thanks," William said. "I thought you just told me you were sorry. Now you're back to being tough?"

"I can't wait until someone comes busting in. The thought of you rotting in jail makes me all warm and fuzzy."

"You really think that there's a chance you'll make it out of this, don't you?"

"I know I will."

"Well, I'd get to praying or whatever you have to do. I'm thinking tomorrow will be your last day."

"You keep saying that. Tomorrow will be your last day. Soon this will be over. Enjoy your meal—it will be your last. This is the last time you'll be outside," she mimicked sentence after sentence. "You're so full of shit. That's fine, though. The longer you do this, the better my chances get."

"I have a sneaking suspicion that you'll soon think differently," he said.

"Whatever, William."

"Okay. I have some things to go and take care of. You be a good bitch and sit in your cage." William took a step toward the door.

"I hope you get violated in prison."

William shook his head. "Wow, comments like that make me totally want to rethink my plans. You know, because you're such a good person and totally undeserving of what's in your future." He scratched at his beard stubble. "Erin, do you remember what I said to you right before I left the station in California?"

"Probably some asshole remark. I don't know."

"Think about it. Your response was quote, *I'd like to see that.* And then you called me pathetic."

She was quiet for a moment.

"Remember?" he asked. "Remember what I told you I was going to do?"

"Yeah, you said, *I'm going to mount your bitch head over my fireplace.*"

"There you go. I'll let you stew on that for a bit. Really think about it for a while. Think about everything I've said to you and everything you've heard. I'm going to show you something a little bit later that I think you'll appreciate. Enjoy your cage."

William walked from the room and closed the door at his back. A smile crept across his face.

CHAPTER SEVENTEEN

I closed the door of the office at my back, and its glass window rattled. "Ethan Bracknall?" I asked.

He stood from his chair and walked around his desk. "You found me." He held out a hand for a handshake, which I took. The man looked like he was pushing fifty with a gray buzz-cut, a blue button-up shirt, and jeans.

"Hank Rawlings, FBI," I said.

"Sure, what can I do to help?" He motioned for me to have a seat and then returned to his.

I sat down and put my bag beside my chair. I looked past him at the wall behind his desk and noticed multiple photos of him hunting. He took a drink from his coffee mug, which had an American flag printed on the side.

"I wanted to talk a bit about the package that came in last week."

"The film and letter?" he asked.

"Correct," I said.

"What did you want to know?"

"Just the process from when it arrived, who handled it, and how the decision was made to contact the authorities."

"Sure. Well, our mail here at the paper gets delivered in a push cart from the postman. He wheels it in through the back"—he jerked his head to reference someplace behind him—"and then our mail guys sort through it all by floor and take it upstairs to distribute it. Anything that's unaddressed goes into a separate bin and gets looked through after all the staff deliveries are made."

"Is getting unaddressed mail and packages commonplace?" I asked.

"Well, we get any number of letters a day that come in unaddressed. The packages would be a little rarer. The contents can be anything from fan mail for the column writers to potential news stories. At least once every few years, we'll get something that comes that's real news sent from an anonymous source. Basically, we just sift through the unaddressed stuff when we have the time and there's nothing else pressing. Sometimes, it sits for a few days."

"Was that the case in this instance?" I asked.

"Nah, pretty sure that one was same day."

"Okay, and the person who found the package? Who was that?"

"Temp worker named Zack Morton," he said. "Little wiry kid that started here a few months back. He found it, sorting through the mail, and brought it directly to me."

I took my notepad from my pocket. While I didn't know if Zack Morton's name was in my file or not, I wrote it down.

"Is this Zack here?" I asked.

"He is."

"Okay, I'll need to talk to him after you and I are through."

"Sure," he said.

"So after this Zack brought it to you, what did you do with it?" I asked.

"I looked it over and called upstairs. They made the decision to call the authorities—about it, really."

"How does Mr. Shalagin fit in?"

"He's one of the big shots upstairs. That's who I called when this package hit my desk. Pretty much anything that comes through here, we have to pass up to him. If it's newsworthy, he passes it along to whoever he'd like to take charge of the piece. It gets real chummy upstairs. Basically, you have to be an ass kisser to get any kind of good story. So after I call up to him—or his office, I should say—he came down here to my office. Mr. Shalagin had a look at the package for himself, and that was about it. The police came within about an hour and took the box, which they seemed to believe was a hoax, and that was the last I heard of it. Was it not a hoax?" he asked.

"We're investigating it," I said. "Just trying to get as much information as we can."

"So the local PD turned it over to the FBI?" he asked. The guy seemed to be putting two and two together as I pretty much figured he would.

"They informed us, yes. We're a little more accustomed to dealing with matters like this."

"So it was real? Son of a bitch. What was on the film? I mean, if you can tell me."

"Look, I won't try to b.s. you," I said. "Basically, it was

legitimate, and we're going to leave it at that for now. The Bureau will be releasing the information to the public tomorrow morning in a press conference. We'll make sure your paper gets the time of the conference and all of that. It would be appreciated if this didn't leak out prior."

"Hell, you don't have to worry about it coming from me. I'm in my own little world down here. I do my job until six o'clock every day, punch out, and try to forget about this place until the next. What the paper creates and reports on isn't really my concern. Shit, I don't even read it."

"Okay, well, again to reemphasize, this needs to be quiet until tomorrow morning when we can get the facts out to everyone."

"Yeah, say no more," he said.

"Appreciate that. Can we get this Zack in here? I just want to get a quick run-through from him, and then I'll be on my—" I cut my sentence short when the sound of the door opening behind me caught my ear. I turned to look and saw a midforties man dressed in a black suit and a red tie. His hair was styled and jet black, his face clean-shaven.

"I'm Andrew Shalagin. Were you the agent from the FBI that was upstairs requesting me?" he asked.

The man glanced past me and gave a nod to Ethan Bracknall, seated at his desk.

"I am," I pushed myself from my chair and shook the man's hand. "Agent Hank Rawlings. I'm just trying to get some firsthand information on the package that arrived last week."

"And?" he asked.

"And what?" I asked.

"Are you receiving your information?"

"Yes. We basically already have an account of what took place. I'm just crossing t's and dotting i's. I like to get firsthand accounts of everything on investigations I'm on."

"How did this get put through to the FBI?" He closed the door, walked into the office, and took a guest chair at my side.

"The local department turned the matter over to us," I said.

"So the letter was real? This person killed four women and plans to kill more. Did you find more victims?"

"Okay. I'm going to go over this again quickly because I just did it with Mr. Bracknall here prior to you walking in. Yes, the letter is legitimate. The FBI is putting on a press conference tomorrow morning. During this—"

"What time?" Shalagin interrupted.

I looked at him. "To be determined. I'll make sure you get the time."

He said nothing.

"Okay. During this press conference, we'll reveal what we know and what steps we're taking and lay the facts out from the investigation so far. The FBI would appreciate if we can keep this quiet until the time when we present everything."

Shalagin, again, said nothing.

"As in, no articles about this hitting the papers prior to tomorrow morning."

He still didn't respond.

"Are you getting any of this?" I asked.

"No mentioning of this until tomorrow," Shalagin said. "It's just news, you know, serial killer on the streets and all of that. Maybe just a headline of a possible serial killer and the announcement of your press conference in the morning?"

"Maybe not," I said.

He looked at me with a blank face. "You're asking the press to not report the news."

"No, I'm asking you to not go against the wishes of the FBI. This is an open federal investigation. Literally, lives could be at stake with this."

"Whose lives?" he asked. "Who is this guy after?"

I cracked my neck from side to side and looked him dead in the eyes. "Listen. We, as in the FBI, don't want this out in the open until tomorrow, when you'll all be more than welcome to report and also have facts to go along with your headlines. So if I see it in the paper prior to tomorrow morning, that would have to mean that you went against my request. See, something like that could affect my investigation, not to mention possibly putting lives in jeopardy. Do you understand that part? Your headlines will have to wait until the morning."

"Um, yeah, I get it. Don't say anything."

"And we're clear on that and the fact that I won't be pleased if someone talking about it affects my ability to do my job? You know, at the Federal Bureau of Investigation?"

"Crystal," he said. "You have my word, but we'll need something for tomorrow."

"What's that?"

"A couple-minute exclusive. Just one of my journalists and whoever is in charge of the investigation."

"If I don't see anything in the papers by morning, that's a deal," I said.

Shalagin did a little fist pump, which rubbed me the wrong way.

"You realize that this person is killing young women, right?" I asked. "Living, breathing young women with families and futures ahead of them? Does that sound like it should be a reason for you to get excited? To be celebrating with your little fist pump there?"

He said nothing.

"Do you have children?" I asked.

He fumbled for words. "I, uh, I have two teenage daughters."

"Why don't you think about that for a while?" I turned my attention back to Bracknall, who'd been sitting quietly. "Can we get this Zack in here for a couple questions? I'm going to need to get back to the office."

"Sure. One second," Bracknall said.

I stayed seated as Bracknall left the office in search of his temp. Shalagin peppered me with questions regarding the investigation as I waited—I debated just getting up and leaving after the fifth or sixth. To every question Shalagin asked, I delivered the same canned response: "You'll get everything you need regarding the investigation tomorrow." My parroting of the same line over and over didn't seem to dissuade him from trying to rephrase the questions and asking again.

CHAPTER EIGHTEEN

Duffield called me just as I was leaving the front doors of the newspaper. I clicked Talk as I walked toward my car.

"Rawlings," I said.

"Hey, Hank. I was just going to leave you a message. Figured I'd get your voice mail."

"I'm leaving the paper now. Headed back. What's up?"

"Anything there we didn't know?" he asked.

"Nah, just got their account of how they received the package. About it." I unlocked the doors on my rental car, tossed my bag in the back, and got behind the wheel.

"Okay. And they were fine with keeping a lid on it?" Duffield asked.

"I had to ask nicely once, not so much the second time, but I think I left seeing eye to eye with them."

"Sure. Well, I was calling to let you know that we're going to have a meeting in a little bit here. If you can make it back in time, great. If not, no worries. It's just going to be to gather everyone and get them up to speed. Beth is back here, so she could probably just fill you in if you miss it."

I fired up the engine and pulled from the lot. "I'll be back in about twenty minutes. When are you starting?"

"Half hour or so. So that should be perfect. I'll get everyone gathered and see you in a bit."

"Sounds good." I hung up and pulled up the navigation on my phone to have it direct me through downtown back to the field office. Twenty or so minutes of classic rock on the radio later, I parked my rental car in the Bureau's parking lot, ventured through the building, and walked into serial crimes. I found everyone gathered in one of the larger conference rooms, entered, and took a seat between Beth and Duffield, who was sitting at the head of the table.

"Okay," Duffield said. "Looks like we're all here. Let's get rolling." He clasped his hands in front of himself on the table. "Basically, I wanted everyone in to go over where they are and what they're currently working on. Everyone on the same page would be good, and everyone knowing what everyone else is working on is also good. We're going to have a press conference tomorrow morning at nine. It's going to be short and sweet—pretty much a This Is What We Have, and This Is What We're Doing."

I glanced up and down the long conference table. Duffield held down the end, and four agents were seated across from me. Next to Beth at my side, were a couple guys from the tech department whom I'd been introduced to when I dropped off the memory card with the abduction video earlier that morning. Sitting in a chair in the corner was a thin, forty-something-year-old man with dark hair, wearing a lab coat. One foot was crossed over and resting on his other knee. I'd been introduced to the man, named Frank

Witting, when we viewed the package upon our arrival to the bureau office—he was the forensics department lead.

Duffield looked toward the agents sitting at the table across from Beth and me. "Houston, where are we at with the wooden mounts?"

The agent seated farthest left at the table—in his thirties, with a square face and short blond hair—spoke up. "You could buy them from five or six places within about a fifty-mile radius—mostly the taxidermists we'd already looked into. None reported selling any." He brushed a finger across his equally blond mustache. "Basically, I got responses that they would sell them if someone called, but no one had called. I expanded by a bit to a couple of other places but received more of the same responses. From there, I started looking online. You can buy them virtually anywhere. The shape that these are—I guess it's kind of a shield shape—is pretty damn common. I just don't think we're going to have much luck there, unfortunately."

"Okay," Duffield said. "Do you think that's it on that?"

"I do," he said. "There's just too many online places they can be purchased from, no real brand to look into. I even found places overseas they could be purchased from for resale. It's endless."

"Right." Duffield turned his attention to the agent seated next to Agent Houston. "Braine, how are we on finding where those glass eyes came from?"

"Well, we have a number of places where they could have come from, but seeing as how we have a quantity, if I can find a place that sold multiples, we should have our spot. I was going to start straight with the distributors and work my way down. By morning, I should have all the subpoenas going to get their sales reports, specifically for green human-like glass or acrylic eyes sold in the last year. There's around five or six places that are on my top level. From there, I'm just going to try to follow them down—call each place and see if they've sold multiple sets and to who. I'm kind of bookmarking my entire day tomorrow to hammer on it."

"Good," Duffield said. "Houston, if you're done with the wooden mounts, give Braine a hand with the eyes."

"Sure," he said.

I had a thought brewing, so I spoke. "What makes you so certain that we're dealing with any kind of quantity on these eyes?" I asked.

The agent named Braine showed me a confused look. "Four women, four sets of green eyes, maybe more if he's continuing."

"Who is to say he doesn't just have one set," I asked, "switching them from one mount to the next? We don't have a photo of all the mounted heads together to see if they all have eyes."

The agent was silent for a moment. "I guess I didn't think of that," he said.

"I think starting with the distributors is fine to follow them down to where they went," I said. "That part is smart. It will give us retailers that we won't be able to find with a simple search. I'd have to say we need to find all of these that were sold though, even if it's just individual sets."

"Houston, you take the small and mid-level places that

sell the eyes. Call each," Duffield said. "Any sets sold, we need to know. Braine, continue with what you had planned out with the larger suppliers. I want to either know where the hell those eyes came from and who they were sold to, or get it crossed off the list entirely as a dead end."

They both agreed.

Duffield turned his attention to the other two agents, who had yet to speak. "Collette, Tolman, what do you have working?"

"Well," the one on the right said, "I touched base with the missing persons departments that were dealing with the girls we have IDs for. What you see in the files is what we have—nothing that we don't already know there. So after that, I started working with the missing persons departments across Kentucky and neighboring states. I wanted to see if this may have extended beyond the Louisville area. Basically, what I'm looking for is a number of women, all fitting the same age criteria taken from a single geographical location in a short period of time."

"And?" Duffield asked.

"We haven't found anything that would suggest it."

"Collette?" Duffield asked, turning his attention to the other agent.

The last agent, yet to talk, piped up. "I've had my plate full. Since we got the investigation, I've been trying to work with other agencies and expanding our reach as much as possible, looking for bodies of women found that were missing heads and hands. Kind of drawing a blank, though. There have been a few, but they're scattered across the country, and we haven't found any unknowns. Basically, the women's bodies that have been found like that, we know who they are and who was responsible. Seems dumping a body minus a head that can lead to an ID through dental records or hands, which can do the same via fingerprints, isn't entirely uncommon."

"All right. You two keep doing what you're doing." Duffield looked toward the tech guys. "Anything new on our video?"

The tech lead, named Aaron Koechner, flipped through a couple pieces of paper in front of him. He wore a gray polo shirt and khakis. I put him somewhere in his later forties. "We went through everything that we had previously gathered again and tried to see if we could connect anything with the footage that Agent Rawlings picked up this morning from the abduction of the Willard woman. My guys and I had pretty much all day with it. There's just nothing there. On a little bit better note, we did clean up the footage of the abduction a bit and sent it over to the Oldham County Sheriff's Office. We did a few points of reference on the footage and estimated our guy's height and weight. It's looking like he's around five ten or eleven and roughly one hundred eighty pounds. We blew the footage up a bit, and it looks like she hands him a slip of paper as well as a driver's license."

"Two things a cop would ask for at the window," I said. "DL and registration." I pulled out my notepad, flipped to a clean page, and jotted down the estimated height and weight.

"Anything else?" Duffield asked him.

"Nothing concrete, but just from my personal observation, I'd say the body movements of this man look like someone in his fifties."

"The reasoning there?" Beth asked.

"Just the stride length," Koechner said. "It's a couple inches shorter than it should be for a person of the height. Stride length decreases with age."

I wrote down *fifties* with a question mark in my notepad.

Duffield looked at Beth. "Agent Harper, anything we didn't know from the friends and families?"

Beth rubbed her eyes. "I made stops with everyone we had on file, except one, which I'm scheduled to be over at in about an hour. Pretty tough day with nothing to show for it," she said.

"Grieving families can be rough," Duffield said. "Never a part of the job I'm too eager for."

"The meetings are worse when the families have been told that their loved ones are dead, we don't have a body, and they can't see the photographic evidence that we have. It makes for some hard interviews—just a full day of tears and questions I had no answers for. Not a single thing new that we didn't already know."

"Okay, Rawlings?" Duffield asked.

I gave the room an overview of my day, which aside from finding the video that morning, had been fruitless. However, something on my list did demand an answer, and as I thought back to what I'd watched on the video, it created additional questions.

"Anyone know where April Backer's vehicle currently is?"

I asked. "The one that was found with the flat?"

"City impound probably," Agent Collette said.

"The bureau never processed it?" I asked.

"Hold on," the agent named Tolman said. He paged through a stack of papers in front of him, pulled a few sheets, and read them over. "She went missing eight days ago. Locals went through the vehicle, found nothing. No prints that weren't hers. This is all on the missing person's report and file. It doesn't say where the vehicle currently is."

"I've looked it over, but you have it right in front of you there, does it mention if the window was down, personal items remaining inside, keys in the vehicle, anything like that?" I asked.

Agent Tolman shook his head. "No."

"All right. I'm going to make some calls on that as soon as we're done here. I want to see that vehicle and talk to whoever found it."

"You're thinking that it could be under circumstances similar to how Katelyn Willard's was found," Duffield said.

"Well, it's a thought," I said. "We need to know one way or another."

"Agreed," Duffield said.

"If you need us to go through it, just let me know, and I'll get a team out," Witting, the forensics lead said—those were the only words he spoke during the meeting.

I nodded.

Duffield finished compiling his notes and went around the room with questions he needed clarification on—then he wrapped the meeting and instructed everyone to be in by eight the next morning for the conference at nine.

CHAPTER NINETEEN

William had snapped the final photos of his completed mount of Courtney Mouser with both his cell phone and his film camera. He scooted his chair closer to the table the mount was sitting on.

"So much better," he said. "I think this may just work out."

He'd prepped the head in the same fashion as the others, prior to testing out his new technique. Her skin had been removed from the skull and gently fleshed—he'd sealed the back with spray lacquer. The woman's eyes and brain had been removed from her skull prior to him boiling it and removing the bits of flesh that remained. Her hair had been set aside, trimmed and dyed. William had sculpted the modeling clay to the skull and replaced the facial skin. After that, as he'd been doing with the hands, he dunked the head in a pot of melted flesh-tone wax. When the wax dried, he smoothed it to a perfect shape, cut the wax away from the glass eyes, applied false eyelashes, airbrushed features, and replaced the hair. The completed result was far superior to the previous attempts.

William was almost ready to place the mount on the wall, but he had something else in mind first. He scooted his chair back, took the mount from the table, and walked downstairs to the basement. He stood before the laundry room door, and an uncontainable smile broke across his face. William set the mount outside the door and entered. He looked to the right, at Erin in her cage—both of her hands were through the metal bars and holding the lock that secured the door. William stared at her wrists and saw the handcuffs were removed. His eyes went to her ankles, where her shackles were also gone. Erin's head quickly snapped up, and her eyes met his. She yanked her hands from the lock and immediately retreated to the back of the cage and away from the door.

"Well, well, well. It looks like you've been busy down here," he said.

She didn't respond.

"Pick up the cuffs and place them back around your ankles. Do the same with the ones that should be around your wrists."

"No."

"Either do it, or I'll leave you to starve to death in that little cage, covered in your own mess. Don't think for a second that I won't. I'll brick off this damn room and leave you in here to rot."

He stared through the metal bars at her and crossed his arms over his chest while he waited. A solid minute of silence passed before she began moving and obeying his orders. She clicked the cuffs back around her ankles and then resecured her wrists.

"What did you get a hold of to get you out of the cuffs?" he asked. "Toss it onto the floor. Outside the cage."

"I don't have anything," she said.

"Right." William approached, crouched, and looked around the lock area where her hands had been when he walked into the room. He spotted a small piece of metal hanging from the keyhole of the lock. He couldn't identify the piece or where it might have come from. "Where did you find this?" He pulled the piece of metal from the lock and held up the small, thin scrap, not much bigger than a toothpick, in front of his eyes.

Erin said nothing.

"Looks like I walked in just in time." William walked to the washbasin beside the washer and dropped the piece of metal into the drain. Then, he returned to Erin and knelt in front of the door. He inspected the lock and gave the door a yank. "It looks like your lock-picking skills still need some work."

"I only needed another few minutes," she said with a bit of a smile. "I will get out of here."

"Good luck with that." William ran his knuckles across the door of the cage, making a thump with each bar they hit. "So are you ready for the big reveal?"

"What the hell are you talking about?"

"It goes along with what I told you that I wanted you to think about earlier."

She said nothing.

"This has all been leading up to this." William smiled, baring his teeth at her. "Here it comes." He rose from in front of the cage, walked to the laundry-room door, and scooped up the mount from just outside. He walked it back to Erin and held it next to the bars as he crouched back down. "Ta-da! What do you think?"

Her eyes were locked on the mounted woman's head.

"You see how the hands are arranged? That's going to be where you hold the microphone. See, I've been practicing building these. This one here is my latest. I think her name was Courtney or some shit. I dunked her head in wax after I peeled her face off, scooped out her brain, and got her all ready. I think the wax will do the trick so she doesn't start decomposing like the others."

Erin's eyes remained fixed on the mount. She still didn't make a sound.

"Well? Come on. Don't leave me hanging." William chuckled to himself. "Don't leave me hanging. That kind of fits with the whole mount thing."

William watched her. She appeared to be leaning in to get a better look at his creation.

"Get up and close. She won't bite." He put the mount just an inch from the metal bars. "Arr rarr rarr!" William shouted, making his best dog impression as he yanked the head back and forth.

Erin slinked back to the far end of her crate. "That's not real."

"It most certainly is," William said. "Well, do you see the resemblance? She looks just like you. Same hair, same eyes, same high cheekbones and trashy-looking fake eyelashes. I imagine your mount will be pretty spot-on. I've had plenty of practice."

"You're not scaring me with your little game here," Erin said. "And your whole threat and what you just described don't really work together."

"What do you mean?"

"A wax head above a fireplace?"

"Oh, yeah, the fireplace here doesn't work, so we'll be fine," he said. "Aside from that, that was more of me just saying it. Hell, I didn't even have a fireplace at the time. Just kind of a coincidence that I do now. That is where you're going to go, though. So I guess it all kind of works out."

"Whatever. More little games," she said.

William stood, took a few steps back, and stared at her in her enclosure. His nose twitched. Annoyance overtook him because she still didn't believe her fate. William turned and left the room without saying a word. He walked to the den, hung the mount on the wall by the cable hanger on the back, and took a moment to straighten it. He returned to the laundry room and picked up the chain he'd been using to walk Erin. William fished the cage key from his pocket, knelt, and unlocked the door. He jammed his foot in front of it so it wouldn't open all the way.

"Hands through the gap," he said.

The woman didn't obey.

"Put your damn hands through, or I'll get the pole."

Erin sat in the back corner of her cage, not moving.

"Do I need to count like you're a child?"

She crawled on her knees to the door and placed her hands through the gap. William attached the chain and let the door open. Erin crawled out on her hands and knees.

"Stand," William said.

"Where are we going?"

"Not far. Come on." William walked toward the door and tugged at the chain.

Erin, her ankles shackled, shuffled after him. William led her from the laundry room and paused a few steps into the larger room with the table in the center. He looked back at Erin, who'd stopped just outside the doorway of the laundry room.

"This is what you wouldn't let me see? A room covered in plastic?"

"Well, it's usually covered in blood. Sometimes there's a headless body on the table when you come through. I wanted the whole thing to be a surprise."

She said nothing but rolled her eyes.

"This one or one of the far ones?" William asked.

"What?"

"Freezers," William said.

"What are you talking about?"

He said nothing and tugged at the chain, leading her to the chest freezer across the room. He stopped before it and pulled back the plastic hanging over it. "Lift the lid and have a look inside."

She didn't move.

"You're so difficult." He wrapped the chain around his left forearm in case she tried to get away and reached out his right hand. His fingers moved under the lip of the chest freezer's lid and lifted it up. The cold air escaping the freezer hung before them. "Well, have a look." William stared at Erin, waiting for her reaction.

She looked inside. William watched the horror cover her face as she stared down at the headless, handless, frozen female corpses.

CHAPTER TWENTY

I sat at an empty desk in the serial-crimes unit and waited on hold for a deputy by the name of Eric Vernon. After a couple phone calls to the Shelby County Sheriff's Office, I'd learned April Backer's car had been released to her family, and the deputy I was waiting on hold for was the first to respond to the vehicle. A minute or two later, a man came on the line.

"Deputy Vernon," he said.

"Agent Hank Rawlings. I've been informed that you were the first to respond to the abandoned vehicle belonging to an April Backer. I had a couple of questions regarding the vehicle."

"I tagged it," he said. "I didn't hear about anything else regarding her being reported missing until days later, and the car had already been towed."

"You tagged it, meaning a tow-away warning?" I asked.

"Correct," he said.

"Okay. Well, the questions I have are regarding the vehicle itself if you have a second."

"Sure," he said.

"Were her personal items inside? Purse, phone?"

"I did a quick look through with my flashlight. I didn't see a purse or phone or anything, though. Yet someone could have taken them from the vehicle. It was open."

"Was the driver's window down?" I asked.

"Actually, yes, it was," he said.

Got him. That was the first real clue linking things together. We more than likely had our guy on video. Another thought came just as quickly—we also had another possible victim.

"What about the keys? Were they in the ignition?" I asked.

"I guess I didn't really look. The tow company might know. I'm pretty sure they have to do a check-in or walk around or whatever you want to call it with the vehicles they bring into their lot."

"Do you know the name of the company that towed it?" I asked.

"The place we use is called Shelby Tow and Haul. Their lot is just down the road from the station here."

I pulled out my notepad and a pen and wrote down the name of the tow company. "Phone number there?" I tapped the tip of the pen on the page.

"I don't know it off hand," he said.

"Do they tow twenty-four hours a day?" I asked.

"They do."

"Okay. I'll just look the place up. I appreciate the help."

I clicked off from the call and searched the tow-truck company on my phone. A listing came up that included business hours for their office, which had closed a good hour and a half prior. I tried their twenty-four-hour tow line to see if I'd have any luck. The phone rang in my ear.

"Shelby Tow," a man answered. "This is Herb."

"Hi, maybe you can help me out. My name is Agent Hank Rawlings with the FBI. I actually had a question on a vehicle that you guys picked up."

"What's the question?"

"Well, I need to know if the keys were in it when it was towed."

"What kind of car, and how long ago was it picked up?" he asked.

"One second." I dug through the file to find the information from the missing-person report. "The vehicle was a 2003 Honda. One week and one day ago."

"So that was last Monday, then?"

"Correct."

"That would have been Clint who picked it up," he said. "I have Mondays off. You'd probably want to speak with him."

"Last name?" I asked.

"Ruben."

I jotted the driver's name down. "And do you have a number for this Clint?"

"Well, I'd probably want to check with him before handing out his phone number. I'd appreciate it if he did the same for me."

"Can you do that for me?" I asked. "I'm knee-deep in an investigation and need to get this checked off my list. It's kind of time sensitive."

"I guess I can give him a ring."

"Appreciate it," I said. "Let me give you my direct number to call me back."

He took my number down, and I clicked off. I scooted my chair back and walked to Duffield's office. He stood at his door, clicking off the lights inside.

"Duffield," I said. "Our guy on the video might actually be our guy."

"Did you find something out with the car?" he asked.

"I just got off the phone with the deputy who put a tow-away warning on April Backer's car. He said the window was down when he came up on it, just like Katelyn Willard's."

"Were her personal effects still inside?"

"He said he didn't see anything, but someone seeing a car with the window down out on the side of the road in the country could have stopped and helped themselves."

"Not out of the question," he said.

"I tried the company that towed it. I'm waiting on a call back to see if the keys were still in it when they showed to take it away."

"It would help," Duffield said. "Just the window down, while probably not a normal occurrence for a vehicle left on the side of the road, could still be a coincidence. If we start adding a couple of things to that, keys in the ignition and the like, we could pretty safely link it up with Katelyn Willard's abduction."

"Shit. I just thought of a couple of other things that could help."

"What's that?"

"In the video, the guy never hands back whatever the paper was that Katelyn Willard handed him," I said. "Odds are it was her vehicle registration, but we need to be certain. I need to check to see if it is missing from her vehicle. Then, I need to see if the registration from April Backer's car is in the vehicle or not."

"Both missing would be another connection," Duffield said. "I was just about to head home, but if you need a hand, I could probably stick around."

"No, that's fine," I said. "Beth already left. I'm just going to take care of these couple things and call it a wrap for the night anyway."

"All right. If you come up with something, give me a ring."

"I will," I said. "Have a good night."

Duffield nodded and disappeared down the hall. I walked back to the empty desk and had a seat. I took out my cell phone, found the number for the Oldham County Sheriff's Office, and dialed. After a recording came on instructing me to dial 9-1-1 if I had an emergency, I pressed zero and was connected to the front desk.

"Oldham County Sheriff," a man said in a gruff voice.

"Agent Hank Rawlings, FBI. Is Chief Deputy King in?"

"I think he's gone for the evening," he said. "Did you want me to put you through to his desk to leave a message?"

"Actually, I don't think I necessarily need the chief deputy. I'm looking to see where the vehicle belonging to Katelyn Willard is. She's a woman who was reported missing yesterday."

"Let me see if there is anyone around that can help you out with that. Can you hold for me for just a minute?"

"Sure," I said.

I heard a click and then some light jazz music. A second later, a beep sounded in my ear, signaling that I had another call. I took the phone from my ear and glanced at the screen. The call was coming from a number I didn't recognize. I clicked over.

"Hank Rawlings," I said.

"This is Clint Ruben with Shelby Tow and Haul. I just got a call from Herb Spiner, saying you had a couple of questions about a vehicle."

"Yes, I do actually. Can you hold on one second for me?"

"No problem," he said.

I clicked over to the call on the other line, heard jazz music, and clicked back.

"Still there?" I asked.

"Yup."

"Okay, basically I needed to know if the keys were in the vehicle when you arrived to tow it."

"In the vehicle, no. But I found them when I was hooking the car up—kicked them, actually. The owner must have dropped them when they were trying to deal with the flat, I guess."

"Were there any personal items in the car? Phone or purse?"

"I didn't see either," he said.

"Okay."

"What's going on with this vehicle, anyway?" he asked.

"I mean, that the FBI is calling and questioning about it."

"It's an open investigation, so I can't really discuss it."

"Figured as much."

"I appreciate the call back," I said.

"Yup."

"Take care." I clicked back to the other call. The music was still playing, so I sat and waited another three or four minutes until the gruff-sounding dispatcher came back on the line.

"Agent?" the man asked.

"I'm here."

"All right. I asked around the station here a bit and didn't get anyone who really had any info on this vehicle, so I called the chief deputy at home. He wanted me to give you his number so you could just call him."

"That will work," I said.

The dispatcher rattled off the number, which I wrote down. I thanked him, hung up, and then dialed the number for King. He picked up within a single ring.

"King," he said.

"Hank Rawlings."

"Is something going on?"

"I just wanted to confirm something with the vehicle of Katelyn Willard," I said.

"What's that?"

"That there is no registration in the vehicle. Basically, I want to see one way or another if that's what she handed our guy in the video."

"Well, the car is in our garages. They're within our

complex. How time sensitive is this?"

"I'd like to know by tomorrow morning," I said.

"What time in the morning would you need to know by? I go in pretty early, six thirty or seven in the morning. I'd like to be there, but I'm about an hour away. Can it wait until morning, or do we need to do this tonight?"

"I guess it could wait until morning. I'm going to need to be back at our field office at around eight. So if I was going to meet you, it would have to be right around seven so I can get in, out, and back here."

"Seven would work," King said.

"And you said the vehicle is there at your station?"

"Our garages are attached at the far end. You can just meet me in the main building, and we'll walk over. Same place you guys came in when we met with the family and roommate."

"Okay." I ended the call and leaned back in the office chair that I sat in. "One more call," I said.

I looked through the investigation file to find the contact information for April Backer's family.

CHAPTER TWENTY-ONE

I finished my phone call with Ball back in Manassas and walked into the hotel. Beth was seated at the bar, where her text message a couple of minutes prior had said she'd be. As I walked up, she was tapping away at her phone's screen. I pulled up a stool next to her, and Beth put her phone into her purse, which was hanging from the back of the bar stool.

"Drinking away your sorrows?" I asked.

Beth looked over her shoulder at me and gave me a quick smile. "Just a rough day. Dealing with the families was hard. This is ginger ale, though."

"So who was your last visit with, and how did it go?"

"Trisha Floyd's father, and not so hot. It's hard watching a big, fifty-some-year-old man break down in tears with nothing you can say to him that's going to help." She let out a long breath. "He didn't know anything that could help us, either. He'd last talked to his daughter the day prior to when we believe she was abducted. After the guy was done with the tears, he started requesting the photos the FBI said they had that proved his daughter was deceased."

"What did you tell him?" I asked.

"That I didn't have the photos to show him. Then he asked me what the photos were of, to which I just told him that I hadn't seen them. I didn't know what else to say, and the guy didn't seem like he was going to stop. I thanked him and left. The whole situation just wasn't good. These families need some kind of closure, not just the FBI saying these women are dead. I mean, I don't know."

"Do you think we should show them photos of their daughters decapitated?"

"No," Beth said. "What about you? Did you get anything with your phone calls?"

"A bit," I said. "April Backer's vehicle was also found with the driver's window down. The keys were on scene but not in the ignition."

"Window down, just like our missing Katelyn Willard," Beth said. "People don't leave their vehicles with the windows open. It's a connection."

"I still want to link up a few more things, but the chances are getting a little better. In the video, the guy takes a piece of paper from Katelyn. I'm thinking it was the registration. I'm meeting with Chief Deputy King from the Oldham County Sheriff's Office tomorrow morning at seven to get a quick look at her car in the impound lot. I want to see if there's a registration in it or not. I also called April Backer's mother to see if I can have someone check her vehicle, which is back in possession of the family, to see if there is a registration in it. Still waiting on a call back from her, though."

"You probably won't see that call until late tonight or the

morning would be my guess," Beth said. "When I went out to meet with her earlier today—Nancy is her mother's name—she said she was a second-shift worker."

"Good to know," I said.

"Have you checked in with Ball?" Beth asked.

"I just got off the phone with him a few minutes ago. I brought him up to speed with where everything is at."

"All right. Well, it looks like we have some wheels in motion. I'll tag along with you in the morning."

I nodded in agreement. The bartender walked over to see if I needed anything.

"Same as hers," I said.

Beth let him know she was fine for the moment.

"So, this new information could help out with the press conference," Beth said. "Does Duffield know?"

"I talked with him a bit, but I'll give him the rest in the morning after we look into Katelyn's car and hear back from April's mother. Having a possible suspect is a hell of a lot better than telling the press that we pretty much have nothing other than 'Someone is killing people.' I doubted the 'No bodies, no evidence, no suspects, no leads' was going to go over well."

"Yeah, probably not," Beth said. "Though I'm not sure the 'We think it might be a police officer or someone posing as one' will go over too well either."

"Not something we have any control of. It is what it is."

The bartender set my drink before me. I took a sip. Beth's phone chirped in her purse next to her. She ignored the sound. A second later, her phone chirped again. Beth shook her head, yanked her phone from her purse, and held down the button to power it off.

"He just doesn't get it," she said.

"Scott, I'm assuming."

"He's acting like him showing up here and making an ass out of himself was supposed to be endearing—supposed to show me how much he cared. Now, he's trying to make me feel bad for making him leave town when he came all that way to try to talk to me. He got on a plane and traveled states away just to see my face and try to resolve an argument—his words, not mine."

"You do realize that there's something wrong with him upstairs, right?" I tapped the side of my head. "I mean, seriously. Ex-husband, current boyfriend, or whatever aside, his actions aren't that of a normal person."

"I just… I don't know what to do, Hank. He just won't stop. If I turn on my phone, I get endless texts, instant messages, or e-mails from him. It's never-ending."

"Get a different phone number," I said. "Or phone, that isn't bugged."

"I deleted that immediately," Beth said.

"Doesn't take away the fact that he put it on there without your knowledge."

She didn't respond.

A couple minutes of silence stretched on. I sipped at my drink—she did the same.

At about the five-minute mark, Beth broke the dead air. "So what is our tomorrow looking like?"

I ran through it with her. "Katelyn's car, talk with April

Backer's family, press conference, meeting with the mailbox family, and catching our guy."

"Good plan. The mailing from that specific mailbox still seems like too much of a coincidence. He had to know that the family was out of town."

"Did we ever get occupations for everyone in the household?" I asked.

"I don't think so."

"We should do that tomorrow," I said.

"Are you thinking it could be a coworker or something?"

"Well, if we think he knew that these people were out of town, that leaves postal workers or someone else connected—friends, family, coworkers, neighbors."

"Hmm," Beth said.

"Hmm what?"

She took a sip of her ginger ale. "Do you think we should do a little door knocking around the area when we finish with the family?"

"They've done it already. But I guess expanding the radius a bit couldn't hurt. There isn't much penciled in for our day after we're through meeting with Mr. and Mrs. Mailbox."

"Mr. and Mrs. Mailbox," Beth said with a smirk. "I like that."

I shrugged. "Thanks?"

"Did you eat anything?" Beth asked.

"Not since… Hell, I don't even remember. No."

"Did you want to grab something from the restaurant here or find some place to go or what?"

"The restaurant here is fine," I said. "I'm kind of wiped, and it looks like we'll be getting an early start tomorrow."

"Sure."

Beth and I finished our drinks, got a bite to eat at the restaurant, and called it a night. I was up in my room by a couple minutes after nine thirty and stretched out on the hotel-room bed. I was a solid twenty minutes into channel surfing when my phone rang. I figured it was Karen and reached over for my phone on the nightstand, but the caller ID on the screen was a number I didn't recognize. I clicked Talk.

"Hank Rawlings," I said.

"Hello, this is Nancy Doyle, April Backer's mother." The woman's voice was quiet and strained.

I sat up in bed. "Hi. It's Ms. Doyle, you said?"

"Yes."

I found the remote for the television and clicked the mute button. "Okay. This is Agent Hank Rawlings with the FBI. I actually had a question regarding your daughter's vehicle that I was wondering if you could help me out with."

"Did you find something new?" she asked.

"Possibly, but we're trying to match a couple of things up to know for certain."

"Oh," she said. "Whatever I can do to help find who did this."

"Do you know if the registration for your daughter's vehicle was in the car?"

"I guess I don't know why it wouldn't be. April is..." A long pause came from her end of the phone. When she spoke, her tone of voice was lower than it had been a moment prior. "She was mindful of those kinds of things."

"Is there a way that you could check to see if it is there?" I asked.

"I'm at work right now. I'd have to go home and check. Let me go tell my supervisor that I'm leaving early. It will take me a few minutes to get out of here and about twenty minutes to get back to my house."

"You don't have to leave work to go and check—just as soon as you can," I said. "We would just like to know by morning."

"It's fine, and if I can do something to help find who did this to my daughter, I'm not going to wait around to do it. They'll understand here."

"Okay, could you just call me back after you check?" I asked.

"I will."

I gave her my cell-phone number and hung up.

CHAPTER TWENTY-TWO

William's hands were gloved. He pulled the roll of film from his camera and walked downstairs to the laundry room.

As he opened the door, he heard scratching and shuffling. His eyes shot to Erin, who was backing away from the door of the cage. She cowered in the back corner.

"Come here and put your finger through the bars," William said.

Erin said nothing and didn't obey.

"Do it!" William shouted.

She tucked her fingers to the palms of her restrained hands and clutched her legs, making herself small.

"Get your ass over here and do what I say. If you don't do it. I'll get a saw and take both of your hands this second. You saw the bodies. It's something that's in my plans either way."

Erin scooted to the cage's door and stuck a dirty index fingertip through the metal bars.

William walked to her, crouched, and pressed her fingertip to the edge of the roll of film.

"Thank you," he said. "I'll bring you your food in a little bit."

He turned and left the room, closing the door at his back.

William walked back upstairs, into the kitchen, and placed the roll of film into a box on the kitchen table. His letter had been crafted and already sat inside. William sealed the box and searched the kitchen for his car keys. He wanted to get the package in the mailbox of the family he'd seen leaving with suitcases while he was driving to the dump the week prior. He planned to deal with feeding and walking Erin when he returned.

CHAPTER TWENTY-THREE

The sound of my cell-phone alarm woke me from a dead sleep. I cracked my eyelids and glanced over at my phone, lit and buzzing across the surface of the hotel-room nightstand. I stared at it in disdain for a moment before reaching over, silencing it, and kicking my feet off the side of the bed. I clicked on the lamp and rubbed my eyes. The time was five fifteen in the morning. Beth and I were going to have to leave in an hour to get over to the impound lot to meet the chief deputy at seven.

I went through the process of shaving, showering, and dressing for the day. A couple minutes before six, I heard a rap at the room's front door. When I walked over and pulled it open, Beth was standing in the hall, dressed and ready to leave. She held out a tall cardboard cup of coffee toward me, which I took and thanked her for.

"Morning," she said.

"It damn well is." I waved her into my room.

"Are you almost ready? I can give you a bit if you're not."

I took a drink of my coffee. "I just need to grab my bag, and I'll be set."

"Hear from April Backer's mother?" Beth asked.

"I did. No registration or proof of insurance in the vehicle. She left work last night and went and checked. She said that April had two envelopes in her glove compartment. One read insurance, which was empty, and one read registration, which was also empty."

"Furthers the 'Police officer requesting the information' theory," Beth said.

"Correct. I also asked her about the flat tire, but she didn't really have much to offer there. Basically said that it was repaired at a service station when they got the car back. I got the name of the station but didn't get any further information as far as what caused the flat."

"I'd bet that tire is long gone now. And that vehicle and tire were never processed, right?" Beth asked.

"Unfortunately not. Nobody knew what they were dealing with prior to the family getting the car back and the tire changed."

"So that is probably dead in the water. What is Duffield going to do with the new information on our suspect, or I should say that we may have the suspect on video?" Beth asked.

"I need to call him and see. I tried last night, but I didn't get an answer on his phone. I'd assume that he'd call me first thing this morning." I glanced at my watch. "I'd have to think he heard my message and would be up by now. Let me call him quick." I set my coffee down on the cabinet holding the television.

Beth took a seat at the foot of the bed. I pulled my phone

and dialed Duffield. He picked up a moment later.

"Rawlings, I was just about to call you," he said.

"You got my message?" I asked.

"I did right when I woke up this morning. I've been circling the wagons and trying to get the tech guys into the office to get me some stills from the video footage."

"So you're putting this guy out there as our potential suspect?" I asked.

"I kind of think we have to. We don't have much else to work with. I'm thinking if we can get this guy that we have on video in—well, worst-case scenario, we can get to the bottom of what happened to Katelyn Willard. Best-case scenario, he is in fact our guy, and we can put this whole thing to bed."

I couldn't argue with his reasoning though I knew that putting out the fact that the suspect could be a police officer, or could be posing as one, might ruffle some feathers with the local departments. Another thought came a split second later—the public could then fear being stopped, which could possibly put officer's lives at risk.

"Have you given any thought to how we're going to approach the possible law-enforcement aspect of this?" I asked.

"It's a sticky situation," he said. "I'm still kicking that part around. I'll make my decision prior to the press conference."

"Okay. Beth and I are headed to the impound lot to view Katelyn Willard's vehicle, and then we'll be in. I'm guessing we'll be there shortly after eight."

"Sounds good. We'll see you in a little bit."

"Yup." I clicked off.

"He's going to give the description of the guy to the public?" Beth asked.

"That's what he says. Said he was calling in some tech guys to get stills from the video we got."

"What did he say about the possible law-enforcement thing?" Beth asked.

"That he was still tossing around how he wanted to handle that part."

"He should probably figure that out."

"Agreed," I said. "All right, let's get a move on." I grabbed my bag and scooped up my coffee, and we headed out.

We drove the roughly twenty-five minutes to the Oldham County Sheriff's Department. The time driving was spent spitballing the case and trying to think of the best way for Duffield to approach the possible law-enforcement angle—at the end of our conversation, we had no good course of action on the topic that we'd be able to share with him. Beth found us parking on the street next to the old red-brick building with the white trim and white balcony. We stepped out of the car and walked toward the front doors. I held the door for Beth, and we entered. In the lobby, the chief deputy, dressed in uniform, waited for us.

He glanced down at his watch. "Seven on the nuts," he said.

"King," I said with a handshake.

He shook Beth's hand also and waved for us to follow him as he turned toward the secured door. "You can get to our garages from inside here. Follow me, and we'll go over."

Neither Beth nor I responded but followed him into the building when the door buzzed us in. King guided us through the room with the bullpen and offices. He made a right down a short hall and through a door that led to a longer hallway with offices off to its sides on the right and left. From the look of it, I imagined it to be the patrol division. He pushed open a door at the end of the hall that led to the garage. I spotted parked cruisers to my left and right. A back area off to the left appeared to be where the patrol vehicles received service. He headed in that direction.

"Her car is back here," King said.

We followed him around the nose of a couple of cruisers. I took a glance at the light bars on the roofs, confirming the rotating reflectors inside. I spotted the Hyundai sedan belonging to Katelyn Willard parked near the back wall, near the hoist for vehicle service.

"Did you take a look before we got here?" I asked.

"Nope," he said. "I actually just walked in a second or two before you guys. So you wanted to check to see if there was registration in the vehicle?"

"That's correct," I said.

He stopped at the front of the car and waved me toward it. "Have at it," he said.

"You've already processed it?" I asked. "I don't need to glove up or anything?"

"No. The car is actually going to go back to the family in a day or two. We're done with it here."

I pulled open the passenger-side door and had a seat with my feet hanging out of the vehicle. The passenger-side floor was covered in trash—mostly receipts with more garbage sprinkled in.

"What is it with women and garbage in their cars?" I mumbled to myself.

Beth walked around the front toward the driver's side, looking over the car. I popped the glove box, which was wedged top to bottom with papers, what looked like the car's owner's manual, napkins, more receipts, and air fresheners. Something hit my knee, and I glanced down—sitting on top of the foot-well trash was a ball of what looked like hair ties that must have fallen out. Beth opened the driver's door and crouched in the doorway.

"Looks like the inside of my car between cleanings," she said.

"I believe it to be a woman thing. Karen's truck is usually jam-packed full of garbage as well. Here." I pulled a two-inch stack of paper and whatever came with it from the glove box and set it on the driver's seat. "Look for a registration in there."

Beth looked through everything I'd placed before her. I took an equal-sized stack and started flipping through it—some fast-food order tickets, a warning for speeding, a grocery list, a receipt and the results from an eye exam, and some miscellaneous garbage.

"See anything?" Beth asked.

I held up a receipt. "Pedicure receipt. Seems like something really important to keep. Aside from more crap like this, no." I shook my head and continued through the stack. "If there was a registration in here, how the hell would she even find it?"

"I'm guessing the same way we are going through it," Beth said.

"Nah, on the video, she handed the guy at the window whatever the paper was and her ID pretty quickly."

"Finding anything?" King asked.

I glanced up through the car's windshield at him standing at the front bumper and watching Beth and me. "Not yet," I said.

Beth and I continued through the contents of the glove box, never finding anything that looked like it belonged to the vehicle itself and not finding a registration. Beth stacked all her papers and handed them back to me. I stuffed everything back in the glove box and closed the lid.

"See anything on the floor there?" I asked.

Beth leaned in and looked around the carpet. She reached below the driver's seat and came back with a blue cardboard envelope. She smiled and held it up. The front of the envelope had the words *car docs* written on it in black marker.

"Probably what we're looking for," I said.

Beth opened the flap and pulled out the documents within. "Maybe she left it on the seat, and it landed on the floor when it was towed or something." She turned the papers in her hand and went through them one by one. "Looks like the paperwork from when she purchased the vehicle, some oil-change and service receipts. And..." Beth flipped the final paper. "No registration." She held out the papers toward me.

I took them in hand, paged through them, and

confirmed the absence of registration. "Okay, so it's not in the car. I guess that's about all we need to know."

Beth stood from her crouched position. I put the papers back in the folder and left it on the passenger seat as I got out and closed the door.

"And no prints here that weren't hers?" Beth pointed to the driver's door as she closed it, possibly referencing powder remaining on the door, which I couldn't see.

"None," King said. "And from the video we looked at, it doesn't seem like the person at the window actually came into contact with the car." King went silent for a moment. "Am I ever going to find out what exactly the hell is going on here with the FBI and this missing girl? I mean, I'm doing my part and all to assist—just kind of like to know what I'm assisting with."

Beth said nothing and looked at me to field the question.

"We're going to have a press conference at nine this morning to tell the public what we know."

"And that is?" he asked.

"The area has an apparent serial killer on their hands. The case was transferred to the bureau from the Louisville PD to investigate."

He stood before us with a blank expression on his face.

CHAPTER TWENTY-FOUR

Duffield had decided to reveal to the public that our possible suspect could have been posing as a police officer but had left out the possibility that he might actually have been a police officer. He'd brought in the chief of police from Louisville Metro PD to speak for a moment. The police chief stated that he'd informed all his officers to dress in uniform and only make stops if they were in official vehicles. He went on to say that he was working with other departments to ensure the same thing. He also stated that, if people had the feeling that they were being approached by someone who wasn't official law enforcement, they should tell the officer they'd like to call 9-1-1 or their local department in order to verify the officer.

As I listened to the words the police chief was saying, I mentally shot holes in each part laid out. His plan was filled with flaws, flaws that would affect the ability of the officers to do their jobs, as well as potentially putting them in unneeded danger.

The police chief stated a few more steps they planned to take, one of which was to be on the lookout for any civilians driving retired patrol or detective cars, which I thought was a good idea. He finished his speech and turned the podium back to Duffield, who answered a few questions and wrapped up.

We'd concluded the press release a few minutes before ten o'clock, and I spent twenty minutes with a journalist from the *Louisville Press-Gazette* as per my agreement with Andrew Shalagin from the paper.

I found Beth in Duffield's office, gave the door a tap, and walked in.

"It was his idea," Duffield said.

"Whose idea?" I asked, taking a seat next to Beth.

"The chief of police, with the whole 'Dressed in uniform and verifying officers' thing."

"Oh, yeah, that's all pretty much worth crap," I said.

"I tried telling him that before we started. You know, the fact that he's limiting the ability of his own guys out on patrol."

"I was punching holes in it as he was rambling on," I said. "The official uniform and vehicle part was pointless. Our guy could go and buy a Halloween police costume, and the vehicle he was driving is already believable enough to get people to pull over. When you factor in the cover of nightfall…" My words trailed off.

"I think he just wanted to show his face and say he was doing something," Duffield said, "even if what he planned on doing was useless." Duffield ran his hand over the top of his short black-and-gray hair and leaned back in his chair.

"So why again are we leaning just toward the 'Posing as

an officer' as opposed to 'May actually be one'?" Beth asked.

"I agreed with the chief deputy that we weren't going to put that as a possibility out there. Until we know for certain that it's a police officer, and not someone posing as one, that's the route I agreed to take. Which, after watching the recording countless times, I think is the right one. There were just too many things wrong with it. Hank, you said that you were PD at one point, right?" he asked.

"I was. Homicide detective and then sergeant," I said.

"Patrol?" he asked.

"Years and years ago."

"Okay, but you have to remember the procedures—safe ways to conduct a traffic stop."

"Being?" Beth asked.

"Watching your ass," Duffield said. "Every traffic stop an officer makes is one of two things—risk or high risk. Basically, risk because you never know who you're walking up on, or high risk when you know—a driver with felony priors, evading, warrant, et cetera. The point is, if you've ever made a stop, those essentials of being cautious are kind of ingrained into you. You're not going to make a stop in a dark parking lot and walk directly up to the driver's window and stand there—no spotlight, no being mindful and approaching cautiously from behind the vehicle, or anything—just casually walking up to the window and standing square in front of it."

I thought about watching the footage. Duffield did have a point.

"I bet our guy probably already knew who was in the car," I said. "He has a type of female he is after, from what we can see with the victims. Driving around randomly stopping cars would be a bit too risky and time-consuming, I would think. But I agree with your thinking on the walk-up."

"Well, if he was watching or following Katelyn Willard, where did he first come upon her?" Beth asked. "As far as we know, prior to her going missing, she went from her work to her mother's place and then home, where she was taken. I mean, unless the guy had maybe followed her from her work—but then he would have been sitting in front of her mother's house for however long she was there—hours. I guess we don't know."

"She drove home at nine o'clock, I think her mother said." I pulled out my notepad and flipped through the pages until I found the one from our meeting with the mother, sister, and roommate. I confirmed the time in my notes.

"Something about a television show just starting and the DVR switching to the program," Duffield said. "So that time is probably pretty accurate."

"I have to think, due to the time, that our guy was familiar with her and her vehicle prior or knew where she lived. I doubt, with the cover of night, that he picked her out driving."

"Unless she made a stop on her way home," Beth said.

"Maybe," I said, a number of thoughts rolling through my head. "I know I saw the time-stamp on the video of when she pulled into her apartment, but I don't remember it off hand. I'd like to get that exact time and see how long it actually takes to drive from her mother's to her apartment. If the times don't add up, we can assume she made a stop. It gives us some places to check."

"We'll probably want to ask her mother and see if she knows the route she would have taken as well—on the chance that there are multiple ways," Beth said.

"Good idea," I said.

"Did you want me to get someone on that?" Duffield asked.

"Beth and I will dig into it. After this meeting with the family the package was mailed from, the rest of our day doesn't have much on it." I glanced down at my watch. "And speaking of this family, what time are we supposed to go over there?" I asked.

"When I spoke with the man..." Duffield pushed around a couple of papers on his desk and brought his fingertip down onto a name, "Chris Emmerson, he said they were getting in early Wednesday morning and he'd be willing to meet with us then. We don't really have a set time. Let me try giving him a call and see if they're back in the area."

"Sure," I said. "If he can't meet with us until later today, maybe Beth and I can get on this right away."

Duffield nodded and scooped up his desk phone. He punched in the number written on the piece of paper underneath the man's name. A moment later, someone must have answered.

"Mr. Emmerson," Duffield said.

Beth and I sat quietly as Duffield completed his phone call, which didn't take much more than a minute or two.

Duffield then hung the phone back on its base. "He says he can meet with us now if we wanted to drive over."

"They're back pretty early. Must have taken a red-eye flight or something," I said.

"He said they got in at one this morning." Duffield rocked his head back and forth. "Which technically is early Wednesday morning, like he said. Did you guys want to shoot over there right away or get going on the other thing and schedule a meeting with them later?"

"Let's get the meeting with the family knocked out now and checked off the list," I said. "The address is in the file, correct?"

"It's in there," Duffield said.

I pushed my chair back and stood. "I'm guessing we're just going to come back here when we're through. We'll get going with the calls we need to make on the Katelyn Willard thing and then go start with that."

"Door knocking too," Beth said.

"Damn, that's right."

"What's that?" Duffield asked.

"We wanted to do a little door knocking around these people's house that the package was shipped from, as well," I said.

"We've done it once," Duffield said. "As soon as we found where it was shipped from."

"Another round couldn't hurt," I said. "We'll expand the original radius a bit. What was the last name? Emmerson?"

"Yeah, Chris Emmerson is the man. Didn't get the rest of the family's name. Why don't I tag along with you guys? Another set of eyeballs and another pair of feet walking around and knocking on doors will probably help."

"Absolutely," I said.

Duffield rolled his chair back from his desk and stood.

"I'm just going to grab a coffee from the break room, and we can take off."

"A coffee actually sounds like a pretty good idea," I said.

We followed Duffield from his office, made a quick stop for a couple coffees, and walked to the cars.

CHAPTER TWENTY-FIVE

William walked through the laundry-room door and turned toward Erin in her cage. His catch pole scraped along the ground as he approached. "It's moving day and, well, your last day."

She said nothing but cowered in the back of her enclosure.

William crouched before the door.

Erin tried to inch back farther, holding her knees in her arms.

William stared in at her—watching her as she sniffed and trembled—her eyes were pink and wet. He saw a tear run down her cheek. "I'd have to say it looks like you actually believe me now." He set the catch pole beside him on the floor, took the cage door in both hands, and shook it.

Her feet slid back across the metal tray at the bottom of her enclosure as she gripped her knees more tightly to her chest.

"Aww, is my little captive scared?" he asked. William cocked his head to one side and smiled. "If not now, you will be soon. I have a surprise for you as well."

She again didn't respond.

"Well, say something," he said.

Erin didn't utter a single word.

"Silent treatment, hey?" he asked. "But you've always been so chatty. You know—spreading rumors about me around Channel Eight, water-cooler talks about how I was creepy. I'd imagine some pillow talk and lies with Mark, before you guys got married, to get me fired and let you skate into my job. You know how annoying it was watching you on the telecast every day?"

Erin let out a small cough. "William, I'm sorry. It's been years. I'm… I'm a different person now."

"Oh, okay. That's so good to hear. All I ever wanted was for you to say that you've changed from the shitty person you were." William took the key from his pocket and reached for the lock on the cage door. "Here, let me let you out of there and get those cuffs off of you. Since you've seen the error of your ways and changed, you're free to go." He stopped with the key in the lock cylinder and then pulled it back out. "Hmm. You know, on second thought, I think I'm actually just going to go ahead with my plan of killing you and mounting your head."

"Please," Erin said. "I'm—"

"No." William waved his finger at her. "You can talk when I'm through. I want you to know your fate. And not just the end result, which you've seen, but the process involved. It took a fair amount of trial and error. See, killing you is just the beginning. As soon as you're dead, I'm going to cut your head off with that Sawzall out there and toss your body in one of those freezers on top of the practice girls."

"William, no," she said. Tears welled in her eyes.

He smiled. "Tears and fear. Now we're getting somewhere. But I haven't even gotten to the good stuff yet. All right, so after I saw your head off, I'm going to drag your head upstairs by your hair, probably thumping it off each step as I walk up. Then, once upstairs, I'll cut and pull the skin from your face. After that, I'll remove your hair and scalp."

"William," Erin said, her voice cracking.

"Wait, wait, wait. Okay, so when I get all the skin from your face and scalp from your head, I'll scrape away the meat still attached to your skull. Now, your skull itself is another process. First, I'll dig your eyes out. Then, I'll go in from your eye socket with a coat hanger and kind of whip and pull at your brain until it's completely out." William made a motion with his hand and arm as if he was completing the process. "It's surprisingly difficult to get all of the brain out, but I've come up with a couple of tricks."

"God, stop!" she screamed.

"Shh. I'm not finished, Erin. Just hear me out. If you interrupt me again, you won't like it." William continued, "so, once I scoop pretty much all of your brains out, I'll get some water boiling in the kitchen and plop your skull into the pot. I'll leave it in there for a few hours. All the scraps of meat that are still attached will just kind of fall off after that."

"Help!" she screamed.

William jammed the end of the metal catch pole through the metal bars of the door and violently poked at her body.

Between her shouts of pain, she continued to scream for help.

"Shut your damn mouth." He jammed the pole into the side of her head, striking her in the temple twice.

She winced and went silent.

"Good. No more with your mouth and screaming and shit. No one is going to hear you, and honestly, it's just starting to piss me off." He let out a big breath. "Okay, where was I? Oh, skull in the pot. So once your skull is done with the boiling, I'll take it out and let it dry and cool. Then, I'll start with putting everything back together. I'll kind of mold your facial features with clay, drape your skin back on and attach it. After that, I'll put in your glass eyes and mount your skull to the board with this little rig that I've created. Then I'll dunk your head in wax, let you dry, and then put on your hair and makeup and get you just right with all the little details. And then you go up on the wall." William clapped his hands together, held them out, and turned them up and down like a card dealer at a casino table would. "And then that's it."

Erin took a couple of erratic breaths. "How… how many people have you killed?"

William looked up and scratched at his chin. "Six, getting ready for you. Well, actually seven. That's the surprise that I mentioned earlier." He stopped talking and stared at her, waiting for a comment. She didn't say anything.

"Oh, the suspense is killing me. I'm horrible with secrets. I'm actually really proud of myself that I kept it this long. Okay, here goes." William pointed both index fingers at her.

"Did you want to do a drumroll sound or something?"

She didn't respond but turned a bit in her cage.

"Hmm. When I envisioned telling you, there was always kind of a drumroll sound in my head before the big news. Are you sure you don't want to do it?"

Erin said nothing.

William slumped his shoulders. "Okay, fine. I—" He stopped his sentence short. "No, it just isn't right without the drumroll. I'll do it." William flicked his tongue against the roof of his mouth, making the sound he desired and finished it with his best impression of cymbals clanking together. "I killed Mark."

"What?" she asked between short, choppy, breaths.

"Yeah. Your hubby is dead. I blew the top half of his head off."

Her body jerked as she cried and sniveled and shook her head. A low, sustained moan came from her mouth. She rocked back and forth, clutching her elbows with her hands over her chest. Erin raised her head. Her bottom lip quivered. "Tell me that you didn't. William, tell me you didn't do anything to Mark."

"Yup. He's worm food. Good riddance. That's what you get for firing me so your trampy little girlfriend can take my job. And then he goes and marries you? What an idiot. You slept with half of the station. Real prize."

Erin began to cry more loudly.

William spoke over the top of her noise. "I made sure the trajectory was right and put a gun in his hand. Shot him under the chin and splattered his brains on the ceiling. I figured he might be able to cause problems for us, so it was better to just remove him from the equation. But I did it smart. He left a suicide note that said that he killed you and dumped you in the Pacific. Couldn't live with himself. It seemed like everyone bought it. I'd imagine that any signs that the suicide wasn't legit probably disappeared by the time they found him, which was like ten days if I remember right. It was on the news and all that. I caught a little coverage of it on the Channel Eight website. They had some memorial to-do for one of their own, meaning you, being a victim."

She continued to wail.

"So, you see, everyone thinks you're dead." William smiled wide. "There isn't a single person looking for you. Don't worry, though. Everyone will know that I'm the one who did this to you. You think you taking my job and getting your face in front of the cameras made you famous—not even close. You'll be national news soon, but it won't be anything like the coverage I get. You'll be a footnote in the bigger story while I get the limelight."

CHAPTER TWENTY-SIX

We slowed and pulled in behind Duffield, two wheels in the muddy grass in front of a single-story beige brick home at the end of a long, straight blacktopped driveway. Beth killed the motor on our rental car, and we stepped out. My feet squished in the wet grass as I walked around the nose of the car.

"Did it rain overnight or something?" I asked.

"I don't think so," Beth said.

I shrugged and stamped my wet feet on the road.

Duffield swung his driver's door closed and stretched his back. We met him at the front of his truck.

"Ready?" he asked.

"Yeah, let's see what they have to say," Beth said.

We made a right into the driveway and walked toward the home. I glanced left at the black mailbox and green newspaper box at the far edge of the driveway, near the street. We passed along the side of a black couple-year-old Ford pickup parked in front of the garage and made our way up the single step to the front door. A bay window sat to the front door's right. The television was on inside the house.

Duffield reached out for the doorbell, but the front door swung open before his finger pressed it in. A woman, looking in her late thirties with long dark hair, stood inside the doorway behind the still-closed white screen door.

"Ma'am, Agents Duffield, Harper, and Rawlings," Duffield said, pointing to each of us with our respective names.

"Hi, I'm Emily. Come on in," she said. She opened the screen door and held it as we entered the home. "We can probably go to the kitchen table, right through there, straight ahead." She pointed the way to the kitchen.

We walked toward where she pointed, through the living room area and past a hallway that shot off to our left.

Mrs. Emmerson stopped at the hall. "Chris!"

A man faintly yelled, "What?" as a response.

"They're here!" she called and walked into the kitchen behind us. Mrs. Emmerson motioned to the table, and our group had a seat. She put her back to the kitchen counter. "Chris will be out in just a second."

"Sure," Duffield said.

Mrs. Emmerson brushed at the front of her black blouse.

A man, looking equal in age to the woman, with dark-rimmed glasses, jeans, and a hooded sweatshirt, appeared from the hall and entered the kitchen. "Hello," he said. "Chris Emmerson."

"Mr. Emmerson," Duffield said. "I was who you spoke to earlier."

He approached Duffield and shook his hand. Beth and I went through a round of introductions and handshakes with the man next.

"So I guess we don't really know what is going on here or what you'd like to talk to us about. Basically, all we've been told is that someone mailed a package from our house while we were out of state. First the police call us, then the FBI, and now the FBI wants to meet with us. What's this all about?"

"We actually just wrapped up a press conference prior to us coming here," Duffield said. "While we can't get into the specifics of the actual investigation, we can basically tell you what we told the press."

"This sounds pretty serious," Mrs. Emmerson said.

"It is," Duffield said. "We believe we have a serial killer operating in the area. A package he mailed to a local newspaper came from your mailbox."

"Serial killer!" Mr. Emmerson said.

"Oh, God," Mrs. Emmerson said.

"Why us?" Mr. Emmerson asked. "Why did he pick our house?" He paused in thought. "How did he know that we weren't home?"

"Are we in danger?" Mrs. Emmerson asked. "What about our kids? They're with their grandmother now, but I don't want them coming back here if there is a serial killer lurking around our house."

Duffield held out his hand to slow down their onslaught of questions. "We're going to go through everything with you," he said.

"I sure as hell hope so," Mrs. Emmerson said.

"First, we'll need to know everyone that knew your family was leaving out of town," Duffield said.

"Well, people from work obviously knew. Family, friends…" Mr. Emmerson said.

"The Osweilers down the road knew, too," Mrs. Emmerson said.

I cleared my throat and spoke up. "Maybe you guys could start putting together a list. I assume this was a planned vacation?"

"It was," Mr. Emmerson said. "We took the kids to the Grand Canyon and some theme parks out west." Mr. Emmerson looked at his wife. "Honey, can you grab us a piece of paper and a pen?"

She nodded, went into one of the kitchen drawers across the room and rummaged through it. She walked back to her husband a moment later and set the paper and pen on the counter behind them. Mr. Emmerson gave us his back and started writing.

"Were there any other neighbors or locals that may have known about your absence?" Beth asked. "Passersby that may have seen you loading up for your trip?"

"Hell, I'm sure a couple of cars had to pass while I was packing up the truck, but I can't say that I remember any of them," Mr. Emmerson said, pausing from his writing and looking back at us over his shoulder.

"None of them looked like it could have been a police patrol vehicle or perhaps an unmarked one like a detective would drive?" Beth asked.

"I can't say I remember seeing anything like that," he said.

"Any neighbors that you know of own a vehicle like that?" I asked.

He shook his head and turned back toward the counter.

"We asked the Osweilers to kind of keep an eye on the place while we were gone," Mrs. Emmerson said. "Have you talked to them?"

I looked at Duffield.

"We've spoken with a couple of people in the neighborhood, but we'll be doing that again today," Duffield said. "What direction and how far away do the Osweilers live?"

"They're down the road a property to the south," she said. "Dark-blue two story with white shutters."

Mr. Emmerson turned back to face us and held the piece of paper out toward his wife. "That's about all that I can think of for me."

From what I could see of the paper, he'd written down about a dozen names.

She took the paper in hand and, like her husband, turned to use the countertop to write.

Mr. Emmerson crossed his arms over his chest, leaning against the counter. "So what the hell are we supposed to do here? Whoever mailed this package, or whatever, from our house had to know we weren't home."

"Which is why we wanted to talk to you and see if we could come up with a connection. I don't suppose that you know anyone who maybe seems off or work with anyone who could be a bit questionable? Past criminal history, mental-health issues, anything like that?" Beth asked.

Mr. Emmerson shrugged and lifted his hands. "I work at a bank—personal banker. Only a handful of people knew that I'd be out of town, and I honestly can't think of anyone that isn't pretty straight up that I work with. They kind of have to be."

"Do you know anyone that drives or owns a retired police vehicle?" I asked.

He slowly shook his head. "No. I can't say that anyone I know owns one of those. Babe, know anyone who has an old cop car?"

Mrs. Emmerson turned around, walked a few steps toward us, and held out the paper, which Beth took. "Old cop car, no. Is that what this guy has or something?"

"We believe so," I said.

Mrs. Emmerson pointed at the paper, which Beth was looking over. "That's everyone that we can think of, I guess," she said.

"Thank you," Beth said.

"What is this person doing?" Mr. Emmerson asked. "I mean, if my family is in any kind of danger here, we'll have to try to figure out somewhere to go."

"We could maybe go to my mother's," Mrs. Emmerson said.

Mr. Emmerson's face twitched. He apparently wasn't keen on that idea.

"We can't get into the finer details of it," I said. "Let's just leave it at taking lives of younger women. The age range seems to be in the earlier twenties."

"So we are or are not in danger, here?" Mr. Emmerson asked.

"We have no way of telling you that. Perhaps going to a

different location might be the prudent thing to do," Beth said.

He nodded, but the rest of his body language said he was reluctant to do so.

Beth was still staring at the piece of paper with the names. "Could you maybe tell us what each name is in relation?" She reached into her pocket and removed a pen. "I'll just say the name, and you can say co-worker or friend or family."

"Sure," Mrs. Emmerson said.

Beth ran through the list of names with the couple, writing down the association with the Emmersons next to each. We spent another ten or fifteen minutes with them prior to thanking them and heading for the door. They'd said that they planned on leaving the home and staying with the wife's mother, as she'd suggested. Duffield told them he'd call if we needed to follow up.

Mr. Emmerson held the door for us as we walked out. Beth and Duffield led, with me being the last to exit.

I stopped at the front step and turned back to Mr. Emmerson. "Our team has already looked over your mailbox, but do you mind if I have a quick look as we head out?"

"Sure, go ahead," he said. "I don't know what more you're going to see, other than an empty mailbox, but you have our permission, sure."

"Thank you," I said. "Take care."

I took a couple quick steps to catch up with Duffield and Beth, who were talking as they walked down the driveway. The topic of conversation seemed to be what they were going to do with the names on the list.

"I'll take a photo of it and send it back to the office," Duffield said. "I can get some of the guys on running the names for priors right away. After that, I'll get them on registered vehicles." He turned his head to look over his shoulder at me. "Do we want to interview these people personally or just try contacting them by phone?"

"Let's just see what we can get from the list and go from there," I said.

The three of us neared the end of the driveway. I jerked my chin at the mailbox. Homeowners says it's fine if we check it out. Figure I'll give it a quick look."

"Looks like a mailbox," Beth said.

"Never know. There could be something in the grass that went overlooked. Wrapper, cigarette butt, gum, who knows." I approached and looked down, noticing muddy tire tracks between the road surface and the mailbox itself—I figured they were from the homeowners checking the box when they arrived home or from someone delivering a newspaper. To me, the time of day seemed too early for the regular mail delivery. I stood directly before the box, my feet on the street to stay away from the mud. I surveyed the grass and surrounding areas.

"Anything catching your eye?" Beth asked.

"Nope." I looked into the newspaper box, which was empty, and reached out to flip down the door on the main box. It came down with a squeak of rusty hinges.

"Son of a bitch," I said.

"What?" Duffield asked.

I pointed inside the mailbox.

Beth and Duffield both closed in for a look inside.

"Same looking as the other," Beth said. "Plain brown cardboard box."

"Are we sure it didn't come from the homeowner? Maybe they forgot to put the flag up. Who is it addressed to?" Duffield asked.

I put my face close to try to read the address, which was typed on a white adhesive label. "Unless the Emmersons are sending something with no return label to the *Louisville Press-Gazette*, we're going to need a forensics team." I looked back over my shoulder to see Duffield already pulling his phone from his pocket.

CHAPTER TWENTY-SEVEN

Within the hour, the forensics team from the local office was on the scene. They photographed the area and removed the package from the mailbox. Beth, Duffield, and I gave them space. I stared over, watching one of the forensics guys pour plaster into the muddy tire tracks while another was dusting the mailbox for prints. The forensics lead, Frank Witting, stood at the trunk of his vehicle with the package. He slipped it into a clear evidence bag and pulled the backing off the adhesive end to seal it. The package wouldn't be opened until he had it back in his lab in a controlled environment.

"Are we ready to go?" Duffield called.

Witting turned his head toward us. "Ready when you are if you need to head back with it," he said. "I'm going to need some time with it at the lab."

"That's fine," Duffield said.

Witting nodded and placed the sealed bag with the package into a tote in his trunk. He closed the trunk lid. "My guys probably have another half hour or so, and they'll be headed back with what they got as well."

"Okay, give me a minute here. I have to call Collette and

Tolman and see where they are, and we'll head back," Duffield said.

Witting confirmed and went to the driver's door of his vehicle.

Duffield took a few steps away to make the call.

"So these guys are doing the door knocking now, and we're going back with the package?" Beth asked.

"That's the plan, I guess," I said. "Wait around to see what's inside the box and take it from there."

Duffield clicked off from his phone call and walked back to Beth and me. "The guys should be here any second," he said.

The sound of the home's screen door clacking shut caught my ear. I looked over to see the Emmerson couple dragging suitcases from the front door. They loaded them inside their truck, and the husband walked down the driveway toward us.

"We're leaving," Mr. Emmerson said. "You guys have my number if you need anything." He held out a scrap of paper and waved it around for someone to take it.

Duffield took it from him and glanced at it.

"That's a few more names that we thought of that knew we were gone," Mr. Emmerson said. "If we come up with any more, I'll call."

"Thanks," Duffield said. "We'll be in touch."

He gave us a quick nod, turned, and walked back to his truck. We stepped to the sides of his driveway so they could pull out. The truck slowed as they made a right turn at the mailbox, probably to look at what the forensics guys were doing.

"Do we know where we're at with the names that we already had?" I asked.

"I haven't heard anything," Duffield said. "Just a confirmation that Houston got the image of the list that I sent to him and was going to get someone on it. I'll send these latest ones over to him now." Duffield snapped a photo of the names on the list, clicked a few buttons on his phone, and tucked the piece of paper into his inner suit-jacket pocket. He looked up from his phone and jerked his chin toward the road.

A dark-gray sedan was pulling to the side of the road behind our rental car.

"That's them. Let's go," Duffield said.

We walked toward our cars.

Witting sat idling at the far side of the street with the window down. "We're good?" he asked.

"Two seconds," Duffield said.

Witting raised his window.

Beth, Duffield and I walked to Agents Collette and Tolman, who were exiting their vehicle.

"Just door knocking?" Collette asked as he slammed the driver's-side door. "How far out do you want us to go?"

"Let's stretch it out to about a two-mile radius from here," Duffield said. "I think we went a little short of that the last time."

"And the drop point?" Tolman pointed at the mailbox. "Do we need to sit on it for any reason?"

"Forensics guys should be here for a bit yet. After they're done, we're done here. The homeowners have already left."

"Okay," Tolman said.

"Anyone you make contact with, take in their height and weight to see if it hits our suspected marks," I said.

"On top of that, get the names of each person you talk to as well as other adults in the houses," Duffield said. "Run each person for priors and registered vehicles."

"Got it," Tolman said.

"Check in with me in an hour or so. Obviously, if you come up on anything, call me immediately."

After both agents confirmed, Beth, Duffield, and I got in our vehicles and followed Witting from the area back to the field office. We pulled into the Bureau's parking lot a couple minutes before two o'clock, grabbed our bags with the investigation files from the car and walked toward the entrance to the office. Our group entered the building, and we followed Witting straight to the forensics center on the second floor. Witting weaved around the stainless-steel tables and workstation to a lab at the back of the room, and we all entered.

Witting set the package down on the table in the middle of the room, gloved his hands, and looked at us with a confused expression. "Um, like I said, this is going to take me a bit, guys. I can't just pop this open without about twenty other things first. First, I'll need to log it in and take a couple of photos. After that, I'll need to check the box itself for prints and trace. Then, I'll need to remove the tape and do the same with prints and trace on that. I'd also like to try to match the tape up with the tape from the previous package. You're looking at a solid hour or more before I even approach the point of breaking the seal. Plus, I guess I'd kind of like the room to be clear when I begin. I'm not super big with people staring over my shoulder while I work."

"Just do what you can as fast as you can. We'll be right there." Duffield pointed through the lab's glass window at the nearest stainless-steel table in the main room.

"Sure," Witting said.

We left the lab and went to the table. Duffield went to one side so he could face the lab that Witting remained in. Beth scooted up a nearby stool, tossed her bag onto the table, and had a seat. I leaned against the table and rested my elbows on its surface.

"Sit and wait, I guess," Duffield said. "Hell, you guys probably could have just stayed out."

"If you need Collette and Tolman back, we can shoot back over there and take over the door knocking," I said.

"We need to know what's in that package," Duffield said. "Let's just stick to what we're doing. Collette and Tolman can handle it."

I nodded but said nothing. The thought of just standing around for an hour and wasting the time doing nothing as opposed to something nagged away at me—I had a good hunch Beth was feeling the same. Fifteen minutes passed of brief bursts of talk about the investigation between spans of silence. I looked down at my watch. The time was inching up on two thirty.

"Beth, do you want to maybe call Katelyn's mother and see if she knows the route she would normally take to get from her mother's house back to her apartment?" I asked.

"Good idea," she said. Beth slid her bag from the table, draped the strap over her shoulder and took her phone from her pocket. She walked into the hallway outside the forensics center.

I looked at Duffield. "I'm going to walk up to the tech department quick to get that time-stamp on when Katelyn returned to her apartment. I'll be back in a minute."

"Sure," he said.

I left the room and found Beth in the hall on the phone. She held up a finger toward me signaling me to wait, so I did.

Beth clicked off from the call a moment later. From the topic, I knew she'd gotten a hold of Katelyn's mother and received the route.

"Have it?" I asked to confirm.

"Yeah. Main roads, basically."

"Okay, I'm going to go and get the time-stamp for when she returned to the apartment from the tech department. I'll be back down in a second, and we'll check in with Witting again. If he's going to be much longer than another half hour, we should head out and start looking into this."

"Not a fan of standing around either?" Beth asked.

"No. And unless he pulls prints or something inside says who this guy is or leads us directly to him, we're wasting time here."

"I agree," Beth said. "If the contents of the package are similar to the last, it will give us some information but won't be a direct lead. We need to keep pounding the pavement."

"Right," I said. "Back in a second." I headed for the stairwell leading up.

CHAPTER TWENTY-EIGHT

Erin ripped back and forth at her restraints.

"It won't do you any good," William said. He plugged the reciprocating saw's cord into the wall and walked back to the table in the center of the room. William lifted the saw and gave the trigger a couple of pulls. The motor whirred, and the blade flapped back and forth. "I've been kicking around the idea of sawing your head off while you're still alive. What do you think?"

"Please," Erin said, staring at the floor.

"Please what? Please do that?" William asked.

"Just stop this, William. It was a job. How is losing a job a reason to do any of this?"

"A job? It was my entire life. Everything I ever worked for, the only thing I excelled at. My passion. My only point of existence. I think it's pretty safe to say that you took more than *a job* from me."

"I'll do whatever you want," she said.

He walked the saw to Erin and held it out as though serving it to her. "I want you to saw your own head off."

She said nothing.

William returned to the table, set the saw down, and lifted the ten-inch knife from the plastic-covered table's surface. He removed its sheath, which he tossed back down on the table, and then slapped the blade against the palm of his hand. "I'll wait until you're dead to saw your head off, I think. If you jerk around or yank your pretty little head in an unexpected way, there's a chance that I could hit your face with the saw, and we wouldn't want that. Plus, the blade is kind of dull from the other girls, so it probably won't be as clean and quick of a cut. I'll probably have to work at it a bit. You know, I was thinking about something else as well." William let the knife hang from his hand, walked back to Erin, and stood before her.

"Did you just know that you'd never be good enough to take the position from me, and is that why you did what you did? I mean, sure, you've got the looks, but I've seen you stumble and yammer on camera. Did you see a life of on-location high-school games in your future? Because until I was through, there was just no way that you were taking the anchor seat from me. Your catchphrases on big plays are awful. Your timing is worth shit. Your on-camera work, even up to the present, shows that your knowledge and preparation is lacking. In reality, you're just not that good. I think if it ever came down to a "Who is better for the position?" decision, there's just no way that you would have won."

She didn't respond.

"Do you think you could actually best me in front of the cameras in a head-to-head?" William chuckled. "Head-to-head. That's kind of funny, considering what your future holds."

She still said nothing.

"I seriously want to know what provoked your actions. I mean, I did my job every day for twenty-one years. I was a fixture at the station—respected by everyone there. And William Allen David with Channel Eight Sports," William said in his best interpretation of the studio narrator's deep voice.

"Then one day, I hear from one of the camera guys that you were saying something about me making inappropriate advances at you. I was blown away by the accusation—I mean, I'd never really said as much as two words to you and damn well never made an advance at you. All I knew was your name and that the station hired you to do bit spots. But then you just escalated things after that. Told people that I'd sit outside of the women's restroom and try to catch peeks inside. Had a drug problem. Every week or so, it was something new, all coming back that it came from you. When the rumbling finally reached the execs, they called me upstairs for a talking-to. They didn't seem to believe that I'd done nothing wrong and every last accusation was completely unfounded and fabricated. Well, then you start sleeping with Mark and who knows who else, and the next thing you know, I have a sexual harassment claim against me. The whole "Resign, and she won't take legal action" was a nice touch, though." William paused and stared at her.

"Do you have any idea how many places I applied at after that? It seems that being forced to resign due to sexual harassment doesn't go over too well on the old resume. So after two straight years of applying for positions, I finally get a callback—some piece-of-shit station here in Louisville. I pack up and move across country, buy this ratty-ass house out here in the sticks, and wouldn't you know it, not two days after I'm on the job, I get called into the station-manager's office. Seems all of their background checking finally came back. They spoke with Channel Eight, who told them the reason for my termination. Sorry, forced resignation. The station manager apologizes to me that the position was offered prior to getting the background results but informs me that he has to let me go. Hell, I never even got to step foot in front of the cameras before I was canned."

Erin turned her head and stared William square in the eyes. "I was just trying to climb the corporate ladder."

"You mean you wanted what I had, so you took it. And you didn't care about ruining my life to do it," William said.

She didn't respond.

"Tell me that you would have never been as good as I was," William said.

"I wouldn't have been as good," she said.

"I know. Soon, the rest of the world will know, too." William reared back with his hand holding the knife in an overhand grip. With every last bit of force he could muster, William slammed the knife into her chest.

A gasp came from Erin's mouth. William yanked the blade from her chest and hammered it into her again, hitting bone before he moved the blade and slipped it between her ribs into her heart. He let the knife hang from her chest and took a step back. Erin's body jerked back and forth—her eyes were fixed on the knife handle protruding from her chest.

"Look at me," William said.

She didn't.

He stepped toward her, grabbed her chin, and lifted her face. "I want to be the last thing you see."

William could feel the resistance of her neck muscles fighting his hand. He stared into her green eyes, which were opened wide in shock. He took in every last second of life that remained in her body. Her struggle against his hand lessened and then faded completely. Her eyelids hung. He took his hand from her face, and her chin dropped to her chest—she was dead. He stood in place for minutes, staring at her lifeless face, before he reached for the keys to her restraints in his pocket. After unlocking the shackles that bound her, he let her body fall to the ground. William cracked his neck from one side to the other, crouched beside her, and pulled the knife from her chest. The blade came out with a sound of wet suction. He watched blood pour from the wound and pool on the plastic-covered floor.

William wiped the bloody blade across the side of her face to clean it before standing, returning to the table, and replacing the knife in its sheath.

"Okay." William turned to face Erin. "Let's get that head off of you and get going."

He cleared the table of all the items on it before walking back to Erin's body and scooping her up into his arms. He lay her across the table's surface and positioned her so her shoulders aligned with the table's edge and her head and neck hung over the side.

William took the saw in hand and positioned the blade where her neck met her shoulders. He held down the trigger and began his cut. Blood spattered her chin and hair—more sprayed back toward him, peppering his face and clothing. The blood that spattered his lips and seeped through into his mouth tasted like warm salted metal. The saw's blade popped through her windpipe, and a moment later, blood poured to the floor from the sides of her neck as the blade passed through her carotid arteries.

Something caught his ear—a sound he couldn't distinguish over the noise of the saw. He took his finger from the trigger and listened but heard nothing. William resumed cutting and felt the blade make contact with her spine. The dull blade caused her entire head to shake violently back and forth. The noise caught his attention again. William took the saw from Erin's neck and placed it on her chest—he stood silently and waited. The doorbell chimed upstairs.

"Oh, that's perfect timing." William walked across the room, leaving bloody footprints behind him with each step and opened the door to the main room. He stared across toward the television and the patio door leading out back—the vertical blinds were drawn shut, blocking the view into the lower level. William walked to the stairs, trying to keep his noise to a minimum as he climbed the steps to the main level. With each footstep upward, the blood on the soles of his tennis shoes squeaked against the linoleum stairs.

William craned his neck around the stairway door and

looked through the back windows of the kitchen—he didn't spot anyone. The doorbell chimed again, followed by a couple loud knocks. He left the doorway and walked across the kitchen to where the dining room met the living room. William poked his head around the corner and looked toward the front door. The curtains on the bay window at the front of his house were drawn. The front door had no windows—whoever was outside wouldn't be able to see in from the front—however, the side of the house was a different situation. William stared over at the two windows facing the driveway—both pairs of blinds and curtains were open.

As he stared, movement in the left window caught his eye. Williams head snapped left, his eyes fixed on the window. Two men were walking toward his shed at the end of the driveway. Staying low, William made his way to the window for a better look. The two men wore suits and were trying to get a look through the shed's side windows. He knew they wouldn't be able to see his two vehicles inside—he had packed shelving units covering the only two windows.

Then both men turned away from the shed and started back down the driveway. William quickly ducked and sat with his back against the wall next to the window in silence. He could hear the two men talking as they passed and continued back toward the street. The nature of the conversation, he couldn't make out. A silent minute later, he heard a car's motor start. William again stayed low and moved as quickly as he could to the front window. At the bottom corner of the window, he moved the curtain and spread the blinds with his bloody fingers. William stared out. A dark-gray sedan that looked police issued pulled away from the front of his house and drove down the road.

William's mind raced with everything that still needed to be completed.

He rushed back through the house and took the stairs down to the basement three at a time. William fumbled through the couch cushions for the television remote and clicked on the television to the local news channels. He found commercials, commercials, and more commercials. William took a seat, not much caring that his bloody clothing would stain his couch. He waited, staring at the television screen, flipping back and forth between channels. One channel went to weather, and he flipped back to the others.

"Come on. There has to be something somewhere."

Minutes of channel surfing passed before a man and a woman anchor sat at a desk—the top corner of the screen read Serial Killer Lurking Louisville.

"There we go!"

William held down the volume button to turn it up. As he stared at the television, his feet pitter-pattered on the carpet. The top corner of the screen that had the headline switched to a photo of a silhouette of a man beside a car at night. William immediately recognized where and when the still was from—when he'd stopped and taken Katelyn Willard.

The two news anchors spoke to each other and gave an estimated height and weight, which was fairly accurate. They went on to say that the suspect might be posing as a police officer to acquire his victims—also accurate. They mentioned a retired patrol vehicle—somewhat accurate though the car sitting in the shed wouldn't be the first, second, or probably tenth guess for an undercover vehicle. The coverage cut away to a FBI press conference labeled Recorded Earlier at the top right. A man stood at a podium, giving details of what William had been doing, but he didn't include a word about the mounted heads.

"Come on." William rolled his eyes. "That's the hook. They have to know about the mounts. They're the sizzle to the whole thing."

The agent mentioned a package being mailed and the area from which it was sent. After another couple of minutes, the podium was turned over to the chief of police, who went on to state what measures were being taken at a local level.

"Hmm," William said.

He muted the television, pulled out his cell phone, scrolled through the contact list, and dialed Glen, a retired construction worker that lived a mile or two away from him. William had seen the man's name and number on a handyman sign stuck in the ground in his neighborhood and had hired him for a bit of work on his soffits when he moved in. The phone rang in his ear. A moment later, he heard the click of someone picking up.

"Hello," a man's voice said.

"Hey, Glen. It's William, down the road from you there. You did my soffits a couple of weeks back."

"Yeah. Hey, William. Ready to do that roof?"

"Not quite yet. Soon, though."

"Sure. Well, what can I do for you?"

"I was actually calling to see if you had anyone stop over at your house asking a bunch of questions in the last hour or so."

"The pair of feds. Second time in a couple of days that they've been in the neighborhood," Glen said.

"Really? First time they've been over here. What the hell is going on? They wouldn't really tell me anything."

"Well, from the looks of things, and what has been on the news this morning, I'd have to say it has something to do with this serial killer they're after."

"Serial killer?" William asked. He tried to place as much question in his words as possible. "They damn sure didn't mention that."

"It's been all over every channel this morning. You can probably find something about it if you flip on the news. Someone in the city killing young women, I guess."

"No shit? What are they doing out here?" William asked.

"They said something was mailed from our area and asked if Delores or I saw anything out of the ordinary around here lately. Basically, the same questions they asked the other day as well. This time, they mentioned the Emmersons' specifically, and I saw a pile of people over at their place earlier when I went out. It looked like a bunch of detectives or something. Maybe that's where whatever this was got mailed from."

"The Emmersons?" William asked. "I don't think I've met them yet."

"They're a few miles from you. Back on the main road heading east. Married couple with a pair of little ones. I've done some work for them in the past."

"Hmm," William said. "Yeah, this was the first time they've stopped over here."

"Maybe they're expanding their search a little. It seemed like they were just going door-to-door."

William heard the sound of a woman's voice telling Glen that they had to go.

"That's about all I know," Glen said. "Hey, the wife's on my ass. We need to go and get some plants for the yard this second, apparently. Let me know when you're ready to tackle that roof. Like I said when I was over there, better to get it done sooner rather than later."

"Will do," William said. "Probably a couple of weeks or so, and I'll be ready."

"Sounds good. Let me know."

"All right, take care," William said.

"You too." The neighbor clicked off.

William tossed his phone beside himself.

He leaned back into the couch cushions and thought out loud. "So they found out where it was mailed from. I wonder if they found the second package."

William wondered how close they actually were. He had no way of knowing. The one thing that he did know for sure is that he wouldn't be caught without finishing and sending off everything else. William pushed himself from the couch and went back to finish removing Erin's head.

CHAPTER TWENTY-NINE

I walked back into the forensics lab. Beth and Duffield stood with their backs toward me, watching through the glass as Witting worked inside. I stepped to Beth's shoulder.

"Time was nine thirty-three," I said.

Beth pointed into the lab.

Inside, Witting was opening the side of the box and carefully removing the contents. He set a roll of film on the table and then removed a single sheet of paper from the box.

"I thought we were waiting at least an hour?" I asked. "It's been half of that."

"I asked him to find a way to get it open sooner," Duffield said.

Witting walked to the glass of the lab. In his hand, he held the piece of paper by a corner with forceps. "Box is clean—no prints, no nothing. Here's your letter." He held it up so we could read it.

I pulled my phone from my pocket, focused on the page, and snapped a photo. Then I put my phone away and began to read. The letter was typed, like the previous one, though much shorter than the last. The letter began with a heading that read, "Step one complete". Then my eyes moved to the content of the letter itself. He stated that he'd killed two more, had found a suitable method for his mounts, and had finished practicing. He said he'd leave the bodies of the women he'd killed somewhere they'd be found in the near future. He signed it The Sportsman.

"That's it?" I asked.

"Appears so," Beth said.

"So two more? One of which we believe to be Katelyn Willard. Who's the other?"

My question didn't receive a response.

"We didn't have another call of a missing woman come through?" I asked.

Duffield shook his head. "Not a peep."

"And why the hell is this guy sending off packages with what he's doing and to who?" I asked. "What the hell is the point? All the packages are doing is giving us a way to find him. He's giving us the names, with which we investigate their disappearance. Sooner or later, it will lead us to him. I mean, if he never sent anything, this probably would have all gone unnoticed."

"Maybe he wants to be noticed," Beth said. "Maybe that's the point."

I looked up at Witting behind the glass. "What can we do with the film? How long will that take?"

"I'll have one of my guys get on it as soon as I'm done processing the film roll itself. We should have some images from it by five o'clock or so, I'd think. Maybe a bit sooner. If you guys are done reading the letter here, I'm going to start processing it."

"That's fine," Duffield said.

Witting took the letter back to the table, and Beth, Duffield and I backed away from the glass.

"More dead girls," Duffield said.

I glanced at my watch. "So we're back to waiting?"

"Appears so," Duffield said. "I'm going to head up to my office and make some calls. I haven't heard anything back from Collette and Tolman yet. I need to see how it's going out there."

"Okay," I said.

"One second." Duffield banged on the glass of the lab's door and entered, apparently to speak with Witting about something.

"Did you want to take the drive and see if these times line up?" I asked.

"It's either that or sit here, I guess," Beth said. "Hold on, let me check something." She tossed her bag on the nearest table and pulled out our files on the investigation.

I rounded the table and took a seat. "What are you looking for?"

She pulled out her phone and stared at it. "What do you know? Ten new messages from Scott." Beth poked her fingertip at the phone's screen, deleting the messages. "I want to look and see how long my navigation says it should take from point to point." She clicked away at her phone's buttons in between looking at papers in the investigation file, which I figured were the addresses of Katelyn Willard's apartment and her mother's place. "Nav says twenty-one minutes. What did you say the time-stamp from the video said, again?"

"Nine thirty-three."

"How accurate do you think the time on the video was?" Beth asked.

I thought back to the man's ramblings about synchronizing the time with his super watch. "Pretty safe to say it's accurate," I said.

"Well, if she left at fourteen after, we're pretty much dead on. If she left at nine o'clock, we have a discrepancy of thirteen minutes. There's kind of a lot of unknown variables there."

"So do you want to go and drive it or no?" I asked. "It looks like we'll have enough time before we get any kind of photos to look at."

"Sure. Maybe something will stick out at us," Beth said.

The lab door opened, and Duffield looked back into the doorway. He told Witting to call him upstairs the second he got anything.

Behind the lab's glass window, Witting nodded in agreement and returned to what he was working on.

"Are you guys going to stick around here?" Duffield asked.

"I think we're going to go and try to get this trip between Katelyn Willard's mother's place and her apartment checked off the list. It looks like we'll probably have enough time before we get any kind of word back on these photos."

"Sure," Duffield said. "I'll call you as soon as I hear something if you're not back."

"All right."

We left Duffield in the hallway outside the forensics

center, where he went toward the elevators—Beth and I opted for the stairs back to ground level. We hopped in our rental car and headed for Katelyn Willard's mother's house. I dialed Ball back in Manassas, and he picked up right away.

"Ball," he answered.

"It's Hank."

"Have an update? How did the press conference go?" he asked.

"The press conference went about as well as you'd imagine. I do have an update though it isn't really one of the good variety. We found another package this morning. The letter inside states that he's killed another two women and his—whatever you want to call it—*perfecting his method* is now complete."

Ball grumbled into the phone.

"Was there a roll of film?" he asked.

"There was. The local forensics unit is just getting going on it. The lead said they should have some images from the film before five o'clock. When we get them, I can make sure they're sent back to you."

"Okay. So that was it? Another letter and roll of film?"

"Correct. I snapped a photo of the letter. I'll send it over as soon as we're off the phone."

"Okay. That was the gist of the letter, though?"

"It was. There was something a bit different, though. The top had a header that read, 'Step one complete'."

"Step one complete?"

"Correct."

"What the hell is step two?" Ball asked.

"Good question."

"You guys haven't got any call ins since the press conference?"

"Not a word."

"What are you guys doing now? It sounds like you're on the road."

"We are," I said. "We wanted to see how long exactly it will take us to get from the mother of a missing person, who we believe to be one of this guy's victims, to her apartment. The thinking is that he was following her. We have a pretty good idea when she left and know exactly when she pulled up to her apartment, so if the times don't line up, there's a chance she made a stop. It will give us a place to look if she did."

"Did you look into her bank records?" Ball asked. "It probably would be easier."

"No purchases the evening she went missing on her debit or credit cards. But she had just gotten done with work a few hours prior and probably had a pocket full of tips. She was a waitress. A cash purchase isn't out of the question."

I felt a swat on my shoulder. I looked over at Beth and cupped the mic on my phone.

"We're pretty close here. The mother's house is about a block up," Beth said.

I nodded and brought the phone to my mouth. "Hey, we're about to start our little timed drive here. Let me check back in with you a little later."

"Sure," Ball said. "If you guys need anything from us back here, just give us a ring."

"We will. I'll talk to you in a bit." I clicked off from the phone call and quickly sent Ball the image I'd taken of the letter.

Beth turned around in the street and pulled to the curb.

"That's her house there." Beth pointed at a brown single story outside my window. "Are you ready?"

"Yeah." I clicked the button to start the timer on my phone. "Go." I tossed my phone onto the dash and crossed my arms over my chest.

Beth pulled from the curb. "So if we end up having a discrepancy of ten minutes or so, we kind of have to assume that she made a stop. If that's the thinking, what kind of stop takes about ten minutes?"

"Gas station," I said.

"It fits." Beth jerked her chin toward me. "Get out your notepad. Any place that we pass along the way that you could think of being a ten-minute stop, write down."

I nodded and pulled my notepad from my inner suit jacket. I pulled the pen from the binding and found a clean page. "What else?"

"Traffic."

"I doubt there was any at nine something at night."

"Unless there was an accident, but we could probably find a record of that fairly easily. Um"—Beth scratched at her chin—"I guess the usuals. Cigarettes if she was a smoker, which I guess we don't know. Beer or booze. Fuel. All of those could be at a gas station. Grocery store probably wouldn't allow for enough time, but she could have run through a drive-through or something."

"So gas stations and drive-throughs. That should only

give us about a thousand options," I said.

Beth clicked on her turn signal to make a right. I wrote down the name of a gas station on the corner, as well as a burger joint across the street.

CHAPTER THIRTY

We made the trip in about the exact amount of time that Beth's navigation had stated—a bit over twenty minutes. Beth called Katelyn's mother back, trying again to get as accurate a time as possible for her departure. Her mother stated that she left mere minutes after nine o'clock, not more than a couple. She also said that Katelyn had not sat out front but had immediately pulled from the driveway and driven off. Beth asked her if she mentioned picking up anything on her drive home, or knew of a place that she would regularly frequent between the two points—the mother answered no to both questions. With all things considered, our only assumption was that she had in fact stopped off for something, somewhere.

Beth and I sat in Katelyn's apartment-complex parking lot. I stared at my notebook and then flipped to the next page, which was also covered in names of gas stations and restaurants. I'd counted each plausible stop.

I turned to face Beth. "Sixty-three places."

"How do you want to handle it? We'd literally have to go into every place on the list and request to see video footage from a few minutes after nine until nine thirtyish." Beth appeared to be pondering something. "Figure five or six probably won't have video, which leaves us, well, let's just call it sixty. So sixty stops at about a minimum of twenty minutes each. My mental math says that will take us, split up, two full days."

I didn't question her math but took it as pretty close, more than likely. A thought perked in my head. "We may have a quicker way," I said. "At least to get part of this list checked off."

"How's that?"

"Well, just for the gas stations. And it's kind of two part. First, I can call back to the chief deputy to see if the vehicle is still there and ask him how it's looking on fuel. Completely full tank could point us to a gas station. A low-fuel light could maybe eliminate that as a stop. You'd have to think, if she's almost out of gas, that she would get that as well if that was where she stopped."

"Okay, let's say the car is topped off, which gas station?" Beth asked.

"That's part two. Everyone has a gas station that they like or chain that they prefer. I know around my place, there's only one or two that I go to. I pass probably three or four to get there."

"So how are we going to know that?"

"Her garbage-strewn car. There were receipts everywhere. If we have a number from a single gas station or chain of gas stations, maybe that can be where we start."

"It's an idea," Beth said. "What if she has a half of a tank?"

"Then we're shit out of luck and are going to have to do it the hard way." I pulled out my phone and dialed the Oldham County Sheriff's Office. I waited as the recording informing me to dial 9-1-1 if I had an emergency played in my ear. A moment later the phone rang, and a man picked up.

"Oldham County Sheriff's Office," he said.

"Is Chief Deputy King in?"

"Who's calling?"

"Agent Hank Rawlings, FBI."

"One moment," the man said.

Hold music played in my ear before the phone rang again repeatedly. King's voice mail picked up a moment later, stating he was out of the office for the rest of the day.

"Shit." I hung up and looked at Beth. "He's gone for the day." I scrolled through my call log to find his personal number. I found it and clicked the button to call.

"King," he answered.

"It's Agent Hank Rawlings."

"What can I do for you, Agent?"

"I tried you at the station but got your voicemail saying you were gone for the day."

"I left about a half hour ago to take care of a personal matter. What do you need?"

"We'd actually like to stop back out at your station and have another look at Katelyn Willard's vehicle."

"Something new you need to see?"

"We wanted to see how the car was doing on fuel. We think she may have stopped on her way home that night and also wanted to see if we could find anything inside her vehicle to correspond with that theory—maybe in some of the trash in there. It should just take us a couple of minutes."

"Do you need me there for this?" he asked.

"I don't believe so, as long as we can get access to the vehicle."

"Can you hold on for me for just a second?"

"Sure," I said.

I heard him thanking someone on his end of the call and saying the words "come on" to someone.

"When can you be over there?" he asked.

I cupped the mouthpiece on my phone. "How long do you think it will take us to get back to the sheriff's department?"

"Katelyn's mother's place is probably only about five minutes from there," Beth said. "I'd have to say twenty-five minutes, plus or minus a couple."

I took my palm from my phone and brought it back to my mouth. "Half hour or so," I said.

"I'll meet you there," King said and hung up.

I slid my phone back into my pocket. "Back to the Oldham County Sheriff's Office. The chief deputy is going to meet us."

Beth pointed at the clock on our rental car's dash. "We should probably have photos pretty soon. Are you sure you want to go now?"

I nodded. "Photos aren't going to get us any closer to finding this guy. Unless there's a photo of his DL mixed in, which I doubt. Start heading for the sheriff's office, and I'll make a call to Duffield to check in."

"Okay." Beth wove around Katelyn Willard's apartment building and took us from the main entrance back out onto the street.

I clicked through the call log on my cell and clicked Duffield's name to call him. He picked up after a couple of rings.

"Well, what was the verdict?" he asked.

"We're thinking she made a stop. We're actually going to head back out to her vehicle for another look."

"Is it at the sheriff's office still?"

"It is. The chief deputy is meeting us there in about a half hour. What about you there? Photos yet?"

"Not yet," Duffield said. "We have a bit of a development on the roll of film, though. Witting found a partial on it, which he got into the system right away. That was what the delay was with getting the images. Nothing through IAFIS on the print yet, though—still searching. One of Witting's guys is getting the film set now with the film scanner. We should have everything contained on the film shortly."

"Okay. Give me a ring when you get the photos or get a hit on that print."

"Yup."

I clicked off from the call.

"Print?" Beth asked.

"I guess Witting found a partial on the roll of film."

Beth furrowed her brows. "No prints or trace on anything—ever—and there's a partial on the film inside of the box?"

"Could have been overlooked," I said.

"I guess we'll find out. No hits on it yet, though?" she asked.

"No," I said.

We headed back in the same direction we'd come from. I glanced at every gas station and restaurant on our way. My eyes went back and forth, looking at my notes and out the windows. When we pulled up in front of the red brick Oldham's County Sheriff's Office, King was stepping from the sedan I'd seen him driving when I'd met him at Katelyn Willard's. He pointed at the parking spot at the curb directly in front of the building's entrance. A sign posted between the curb and sidewalk marked the spot for official vehicles only. Beth turned in the street and nosed the car into the spot. We stepped out and went to greet Chief Deputy King.

"Afternoon," he said.

"Thanks for meeting us, again." I shook his hand.

While Beth greeted him, I glanced over at his car to see a teenage boy sitting in the passenger seat. King nodded his head toward his vehicle.

"I had to go and pick Junior there up from school. Seems he got wind of some of the guys from the football team picking on his little brother and took it to some of them."

I thought back to my youth and my older brother. While he'd regularly poke, prod, and rough me up, he was always the first person to have my back, which I appreciated until I was old enough to handle myself. I figured that I should call my brother and shoot the breeze for a bit when the investigation was over—we hadn't spoken in a couple months.

"Standing up for his brother, I guess," I said. "Mine did the same for me, growing up."

"Yeah, I said the requisite things about fighting and put on my best disappointed face while we were dealing with the principal, but I think he knows that I'm not going to go too hard on him for sticking up for his little brother. Come on, let's go check out your car again. You said you wanted to check on fuel and for some receipts?" King started toward the garages attached to the end of the building.

Beth and I followed.

"So anything further since the press conference?" he asked.

"We found another package," I said. "Our team is still working on sorting through the contents."

King stopped at the garage door leading into the building. "So from what I gathered from the press conference, this guy mailed a package that showed photos of the deceased as well as their driver's licenses."

"Correct," I said.

"And now we have another?"

"Correct," I said.

"And we believe that Katelyn Willard was taken by the man that you guys are out looking for?" he asked. King was leading me down the path to his eventual question, which I figured to be whether he was going to have to notify Katelyn's mother that her daughter was deceased.

"We don't have the identities of the latest victims yet," I said. "The letter that came with the package stated that he'd killed two more."

"But there's a good chance that this girl is one of them?" he asked.

"We don't know for certain right now, but yes," I said. "She very well could be one of the victims."

King let out a hard breath and waved us into the garage without responding.

Beth and I approached the car with King following behind. I went to the passenger side and Beth to the driver's, as we'd done the last time. I pulled open the door and had a seat.

Beth opened the driver's door and crouched in the doorway. She took the keys hanging on a metal wire around the steering column and placed them in the ignition. She clicked the key forward to power up the dash.

I looked over to see the fuel gauge bounce from empty to full before settling on a click below three quarters of a tank.

"Well," Beth said. "Swing and a miss."

"On to the garbage," I said. "Let's see if any of this crap has our time and date that we need."

"Do you just want to hand me a pile of garbage, and we can start sorting it?" she asked.

"Sure." I scooped two handfuls of receipts and miscellaneous paper up onto the driver's seat.

"How do we start?" she asked.

"Just organize the receipts as to what they're from. Make a pile of gas stations. It looks like there is a good chunk of ATM receipts as well. Make a stack of those." I reached down and picked up receipts and scraps of paper. My fingertips got covered in an unknown brown gooey substance on about the fifth or sixth receipt that my hand touched.

"Gross," I said.

"Huh?" Beth glanced over at me from her pile of papers.

I held up my hand and spread my fingers. The slime on them made a bridge from one finger to the next.

"I don't even want to know what that is." Beth tossed me a napkin from her pile and continued sorting.

I wiped my hand and let the napkin drop to the floor of the car—which was fitting. I pushed on and used the top of the dash for organizing. Five minutes later, I had neat stacks of gas-station receipts, ATM receipts, fast-food receipts, and miscellaneous papers. Then I checked each paper on the dash for time and date, but none matched up with the night she'd been taken.

"Anything?" I asked.

"A couple to go, but no," Beth said.

I rummaged around through what garbage remained on the floor—some cellophane wrappers from packs of cigarettes, a couple of gum wrappers and packages, and two bags from fast-food restaurants. One of the bags appeared to be leaking something, which was probably where the mystery goo on my fingers had come from. I reached down for the unslimy bag and pulled it up onto my lap for a look inside.

"I'm through. Nothing," Beth said.

I stared into the white paper bag to see a couple of french fries at the bottom, along with a few napkins and a crumpled hamburger wrapper. I reached in to move the napkins and found a three-quarters-eaten hamburger with what looked like a receipt below it. The burger looked as though it could have been made that day. I shook the chunk of burger to the other side of the bag so I could get a look at the receipt. I stared in and read the date from the top corner of the bill—two months old. I took my hand from the bag and turned it to see where it was from—a famous burger chain. I set it back down on the floor and picked up the other bag with the questionable substance. I carefully uncrumpled the bag and pulled it open between my legs so I didn't get a lapful of whatever was leaking. I stared inside at a couple of open containers of sweet-and-sour sauce and an empty box that said Chicken Nuggets on the side.

Beth reached out and tugged at the edge of the bag, tearing something from its side.

"Receipt," she said, taking a quick look at it. Then she held it out at my eye level. "We have our spot. Let's go."

CHAPTER THIRTY-ONE

William had dug out Erin's eyes and brains prior to dropping her skull into a pot of boiling water. After the skull had boiled for his pre-selected amount of time, he scraped away the bits of meat that remained, let it cool, and began his process of getting it affixed to the mount. William had just finished molding the clay to the bone of Erin's skull.

"Getting there," William said as he leaned forward in his chair and stretched his back. He brushed the back of one hand against his bushy mustache, satisfying an itch.

William picked up a can of spray adhesive and sprayed down the clay-covered skull. He set the can back on the table. The adhesive would need a minute to tack, so William reached over, flipped open the lid on a large jar, and selected two green glass eyes. He took them in one hand and stared down at them.

William recalled how he'd come upon them and how the idea of what he would do to Erin had hatched. By chance, William had stumbled upon the dolls the eyes had come from. He was wandering around a local superstore, half drunk, the day after he was let go from his new position in

Louisville. While walking toward the liquor department in the store, he saw racks and racks of the dolls on clearance—each one in its own box standing three feet tall. The dolls all had human-sized heads attached to infant-sized bodies. The dolls' eyes all stared at him as he passed. Something about the color and the little flecks of brown mixed in with the green in the doll's eyes stopped William in his tracks. It took him a moment to think through his drunken haze and recognize the familiarity—the dolls' eyes were almost identical to Erin's. William panned left to right, looking at all of Erin's green eyes staring back at him. He remembered what his last words to Erin were, and the decision was made. He loaded a cart with dolls and made for the checkout line. The next day, he'd packed a bag and booked a plane ticket to California.

William held one of the glass eyes between his thumb and forefinger. He pressed it into the clay in her eye socket. He did the same with the next eye. Then he looked at the table to his right, leaned over, and picked up the skin from her face. After a quick spray of adhesive to the backside of the flesh, he was ready to bond it to the clay. William draped the skin over the skull and carefully arranged it just perfectly. He smoothed the creases and made sure the skin adhered properly around her eyes. From there, he ran his hands along the neck, making sure it bonded with the framework attached to the mount.

With the hands having already been set on the mount, he was nearing the point of submerging the whole mount in the melted wax, which according to William's internal clock, should have been about ready in the kitchen. He lifted the mount and walked from the room to check. William entered the kitchen and saw steam rising from the large pot on the burner—the wax inside neared the pot's rim. The coat hangers mounted to the bottom of his upper kitchen cabinets, where he would hang the mount to dry, awaited his wax-coated piece. William set the mount down on the kitchen table and walked to the stove. He scooped up a long aluminum spoon and plunged it into the wax. He carefully stirred and poked, searching to see that it had all melted. His eyes went to the timer on the stove, which showed fifty-some seconds remaining.

"I think we're just about ready."

William picked up Erin's mount from the table and walked her back to the pot—large enough to accommodate dunking the entire mount at once. He flipped the mount so her head was facing the floor, and he gripped the edge of the wooden baseplate. He crouched as he lowered the entire mount into the wax. William submerged her, allowing the mount's base to rest on the pot's rim. Then, he lifted her straight back up and hooked the coat hangers to the metal wall hangers attached to the wooden base. The head dangled there, wax dripping to the pan on the kitchen counter below. He'd allow her to dry and cool for a half hour.

William turned off the burner on the stove and moved the pot of wax to a cool burner. He walked from the kitchen back into the spare bedroom, where he planned to prepare his supplies for when the mount was ready. He took a seat at the table where he would apply her hair and makeup. His eyes went right to Erin's scalp and hair, draped over a mannequin head. He reached over and ran his fingertips through the blond hair, from which all the blood had been washed. William refocused his attention on the makeup before him.

"Blush, lipstick, eyeshadow, eyelin—" William cut his verbal checklist short. "Damn, out of eyeliner."

CHAPTER THIRTY-TWO

Beth and I drove toward the fast-food restaurant the bag had come from. The restaurant was a nationwide chain, large enough to all but ensure that they'd have video.

"Nothing back from Duffield yet?" Beth asked.

I pulled out my cell phone and took a look at the screen. "Nothing, but we need to call this in with him anyway." I pulled up the number for his desk and dialed. After eight or nine rings, I got his voice mail in his office. I scrolled my call log and dialed his cell phone, and within two rings, he picked up.

"Agent Duffield," he said.

"It's Hank. We may have something here."

"Okay. Hold on. Give me two seconds."

"Sure."

I heard muffled talking from Duffield's end of the phone—it sounded as if he was giving someone orders to "get everything."

He came back on, "Sorry. Complete whirlwind around here. I've been running back and forth, upstairs, downstairs, phone calls, the works."

"Something going on?" I asked.

"Yeah, but I don't know what the hell to make of it."

I caught Beth's gaze from the driver's seat. "Duffield, I'm going to put you on speaker so Beth can hear."

"All right."

I clicked the button on my phone and placed it in the cup holder between Beth and me. "Go ahead," I said.

"Well, we have copies of the photos that were on the film."

"And?" I asked.

"Same as before. Photos of their identifications, them alive, decapitated, and mounted," Duffield said.

I dug my index finger and thumb into my eyes. "The identities?"

"Katelyn Willard and another by the name of Courtney Mouser."

"Courtney Mouser, you said?"

"Correct."

I pulled my notepad from my suit pocket. "Spelling on this Courtney's last name?"

Duffield gave it to me.

"What do we know about the second victim?" Beth asked.

"A little older than the others—thirty-one. She was never reported missing, but we looked up registered vehicles and got a hit on her plate. Her car was found parked in a neighborhood about three miles from her residence. We're just getting going on getting everything we can now—finding the officer that found the vehicle, the tow company that picked it up, where it is now, everything. After that, we need to get contacts, employment, friends and family, and see what we can do about trying to piece together when and how she was taken."

"Have Katelyn Willard's mother and roommate been notified?" Beth asked.

"Calling the Oldham County Sheriff's Office is my next call," Duffield said. "Right now, I'm knee-deep in something else."

"What's that?" I asked.

"We got a hit on that partial print, which is the part that we can't really figure out what to make of."

"Who did it come back to?" Beth asked.

"A woman by the name of Erin Cooper-Connelly."

"Who the hell is that?" I asked.

"That is a missing woman from California who was presumed dead. She was reported missing about a month and a half ago."

"That is a bit before this all started," Beth said. "So what is she? A victim? Or accomplice?"

"Well, it gets stranger. So we get a hit from this woman on the print, and I call the number that I'm supposed to contact—a missing-persons department out there in California. It seems that this woman was a local television sports anchor. Well, her husband, also employed by the same television channel, committed suicide and left a note that he'd killed her and disposed of her body in the ocean—thus the reason for the suicide, he couldn't live with himself."

"Interesting," I said.

"Still not the most interesting part," Duffield said. "DL lists her as twenty-seven, five foot nine, one hundred seventeen pounds, with blond hair and green eyes."

"So she might be who these are modeled after," I said.

"Could be," Duffield said.

"So how the hell does this woman's print get on our film out here?" I asked.

"That's the million-dollar question."

"So if her husband killed her then himself, our guy has to be connected with them in some way or another. Especially if he's modeling these after her. Anything odd about the suicide?"

"I need to get in contact with whoever was in charge of the scene to find out," Duffield said. "So, yeah, you could say that I have my hands full at the moment, weeding through this. You said you guys got something?"

"We're driving right now. We know where she stopped," Beth said.

"Where?" Duffield asked.

"A fast-food chain between her mother's and her apartment. They should have video," I said.

"Call me as soon as you view it. If I have anything for you guys prior to that, I'll give you a ring."

"Sounds good," I said. "Anything from Tolman and Collette?"

"I just talked to Collette a second ago. They're still out knocking on doors. Nothing of any interest so far. He said that they had a couple of homes with no answer that they were going to check back in with. I guess that's about it out there."

"Okay. I'll call you as soon as we're done here, but we'll probably be heading back right after."

"All right. Talk to you guys soon." Duffield clicked off.

I lifted my phone from the cup holder, ended the call, and dropped my phone back into my pocket.

"What do you think is up with the mystery woman?" Beth asked.

"I don't know. Missing from California, possibility that these mounts were made to look like her, and then her print showing up here. There's obviously a connection somehow." I shrugged. "We'll see. Sounds like Duffield has wheels turning for getting everything we can on her. Where is this place?"

Beth pointed out the windshield. "Another mile or two. Navigation says it will be on our right."

"Do you have the receipt?" I asked.

"It's in my shoulder bag inside of the little evidence envelope the chief deputy gave us. The time on it says eleven minutes after nine o'clock."

"Okay."

Beth continued to drive. A couple of stoplights later, I saw the restaurant at the far end of the next intersection on the right. Beth passed through the green light and turned in. We parked in the lot and stepped from the car. As we approached the side entrance of the building, I glanced at the giant painted cement chicken mascot, complete with a championship belt around his waist, standing to the side of the order board for the drive-through. Above the outdoor menu, a camera was attached to the corner of the building behind it. I held the door for Beth, and she led the way toward the front counter. A couple of people stood off to the sides, waiting for their orders, I assumed. We waited as a mother and three small children in front of us placed their order—more customers entered and stepped into line behind Beth and me. I looked at the wall to my left, which contained plaques, awards, and some kind of rating from a restaurant agency, which said A+. The largest plaque had a photo of a man, a woman, and a couple teenagers—one boy, one girl. The words *This franchise proudly owned by The Jacobson Family, Inc.* were engraved on a brass plate below the photo. On the plaque above it, another photo, titled Employee of the Month, pictured the kid standing at the cash register.

The kid, who looked about sixteen or seventeen, wore a brown-and-white uniform and a plaid brown-and-orange paper busboy hat, just as he did in his employee-of-the-month photo. He flashed Beth and me a smile as the mother and children in front of us moved.

"Welcome to The Chicken Champ. Would you like to go a few rounds with one of our Ultimate Chicken Combos today?"

"No thanks," I said.

"Sure. What would you like to order?" he asked.

"Agents Harper and Rawlings, FBI. We actually need to speak with a manager," Beth said.

He tapped his name badge, which read Kyle Jacobson with the title Assistant Manager below it. "That would be me. How can I assist you today?"

"You're the manager on duty?" Beth asked.

"Yes, ma'am."

"We'd like to talk with you about the video security here," I said.

"Absolutely, sir," he said. "Can you give me one second?"

"Sure," I said.

The kid looked over his shoulder and requested someone named Kevin to take the counter. A moment later, a man, looking in his late twenties approached the front. The assistant manager waved Beth and me to one side and let his employee take over the register.

He walked from behind the counter and motioned toward the nearest table, where Beth and I took a seat.

The assistant manager slid out a chair, sat, and clasped his hands on the table. "Now, what can I help you with?"

"We'd like to view some security video if possible. We believe you may have captured something that led to a crime on your footage," I said.

"Oh, geez," he said. "When did this happen?"

"Last Saturday evening," Beth said.

He turned his head and looked up as though in thought. "I closed last Saturday. I can't say that I remember a thing out of the ordinary."

"This wouldn't be a crime happening on your property here," I said. "A victim came here and ate prior to a crime happening. We just want to see some footage of that. We believe she used your drive-through."

"I'd be more than happy to allow that, yet I'll need to make a call just to verify that it is all right. If you don't mind, it will only take me a second."

Beth gave the kid a nod.

He rose from his chair, slid it back under the table, and reached down to pick up a straw wrapper from the floor. He walked back toward the counter, tossing the wrapper in the trash on his way.

"The kid is pretty well spoken, an assistant manager, acts like he actually cares about the place. Yet he looks like he's fifteen," Beth said. "I wonder how that came to be."

"Parents own the franchise," I said. "He's going to go call one of them right now to ask what to do."

"How would you know that?"

"I was a detective. I detect."

Beth gave me a blank stare.

"I was looking at the signs on the wall while we were waiting," I said. "There's one that says the place is owned by the Jacobson family. The assistant manager kid's last name is Jacobson. If I had to guess, I'd say he's in the process of being groomed to take over when needed."

"Sharp eye," Beth said.

"Yup."

We sat and waited as minutes passed. I watched as customers walked past and took their seats with buckets of chicken. The woman who had been ahead of us in line with the three kids sat just a few booths away. The kids jammed chicken nuggets and tenders into their mouths. My stomach grumbled. I stared past Beth at the menu on the back wall behind the counter—a Smothered Philly Chicken Sandwich caught my eye.

"Did you want to maybe grab something to eat from here when we're leaving?" I asked.

"I don't do deep-fried greasy chicken," Beth said.

"Have them hold the grease," I said. "I'd say it's a pretty safe bet that they have some kind of chicken-and-rabbit food on the menu for you."

"Nah, you go ahead. I'm saving my appetite," Beth said. "I guess I have dinner plans later this evening."

"What?" I asked.

"Nothing really important. I'll fill you in later." Beth jerked her head to the right.

I looked over and saw the kid walking toward us from behind the counter.

He walked up to the edge of our booth but didn't take a seat. "We got the go-ahead. Did you two want to follow me back to the office?" he asked.

"Sure," I said.

CHAPTER THIRTY-THREE

Beth and I followed the kid down a short hallway leading to the restrooms and then through a door marked with an Employees Only sign at the end of the hall. He led us past the kitchen to a small office tucked into the back corner. He motioned to a pair of chairs on one side of the desk in the center of the office and took a seat in front of the computer facing the other. Beth and I took our seats.

"Do you know what time we're looking for on Saturday?" he asked.

"We have a receipt that says nine eleven," Beth said.

"Okay, that would be when her order was placed. And you said drive-through?"

"I guess we don't know for sure. She could have ordered it from inside to go," I said.

"We'll check both. Maybe I should start a couple minutes before?" he asked.

"Sure," I said.

The assistant manager clicked buttons on his computer's keyboard and wiggled his computer mouse back and forth, clicking on various things—from the position of his monitor, I couldn't see exactly what he was doing. A moment later, he turned the screen so it faced Beth and me. He slid his keyboard to the side and scooted his desk chair around the edge of his desk so he could man the controls while we watched.

"This is Saturday night here," he said.

On the monitor was a full screen of vehicles in a line at the side of the parking lot with the drive-through. I counted eight cars and trucks bumper-to-bumper, stretching from the sidewalk near the street to the corner of the building where the drive-through lane bent around the back side. Other vehicles sawed back and forth in the parking spots, trying to either park and go in or back out and leave. Random people walked the lot, coming and going. It looked like a mess.

"Lots of business on Saturday nights, huh?" I asked.

"Yeah, we give out free ice cream for those twelve and under Saturdays after five. It brings the families in. Usually, things slow down a bit around nine o'clock or so, but it looks like we were still going pretty strong. What kind of vehicle are you looking for?" he asked.

"Newer dark Hyundai Sonata," I said.

"Okay," he said. "I'm thinking we can probably pick that out."

I kept my eyes on the screen's time-stamp in the bottom corner. From the number of cars waiting in the drive-through, I figured Katelyn Willard would be in line at any moment. Another thought registered in my head—the amount of time it had taken her to leave her mother's, stop for food, and get home. We'd been watching for a couple minutes, and the line had only advanced a few car lengths. The time on her receipt was just four minutes later than the time on the monitor.

"Does this time on your video camera here match up with the same time as your receipts?" I asked.

He nodded. "It does."

"Let's get a view inside of the building," I said.

"Front counter?" he asked.

"Yes."

He clicked away at his computer, minimizing that screen and then bringing up an alternate view.

"You don't think there's enough time for her to get her order in, either?" Beth asked. "I was just thinking about that."

"The cars in the drive-through aren't moving fast enough." I pulled out my notepad and found the page where I'd written down what she'd been seen wearing when she left her mother's house.

"Here you go," he said. "Five minutes prior to the time that was on the ticket."

"Is this the only view inside the building?" I pointed at the screen, which showed the front counter and five or six people in line.

"We have one on the indoor dining area as well as the kitchen," he said.

"Okay. Let's fast forward this a couple of minutes to see if we get her at the counter," I said.

He did as I'd asked. I held out my notepad toward Beth

so she could get a look at what I'd written down that Katelyn was wearing—a pink hooded sweatshirt with the word *love* on it and a pair of blue jeans. A minute or two prior to the time on the receipt, the color pink entered the frame.

"Play it there," I said.

"That's her," Beth said. "The hood on the sweatshirt hangs down over the letters, but you can still see that it says love."

We watched as Katelyn approached the counter, placed her order with the young woman working, and stood off to the side, where she waited on her order to come up. She walked off screen for a couple seconds and came back with a handful of napkins. A moment later, she took a bag from another employee, who was placing the ordered food items on trays on the counter and calling ticket numbers. She left with the bag off the screen, toward the side opposite the drive-through.

"Do you have coverage of that side?" Beth asked.

"We do. Our payment and pick-up windows are on that side. One second." The assistant manager clicked away on his computer and brought up the footage. He fast-forwarded it a bit to catch up to the time.

"Hold on," I said.

He allowed the video to play.

"That's her pulling in there," I said.

We watched as she pulled into the lot, parked, and walked into the restaurant. A line of cars paid and picked up their orders nearest the building. I took note of where she'd parked. I didn't see anyone standing outside at that moment and didn't notice anyone inside any of the vehicles parked near her car.

"Okay, run it until she exits," I said.

"Sure." The kid continued with the fast-forwarding.

A few minutes of fast-forwarded footage later, we saw her return to her car with the bag. One vehicle belonging to a customer at the drive-through window pulled away but exited the lot before she did. The vehicles in the area where she'd parked remained, and no new ones had come into the picture. Katelyn backed from her parking spot and pulled to the exit of the lot.

"Doesn't really look like anything happened here," the kid said.

"Wait," I said. "We need to see the next couple of vehicles out."

We watched in silence. Katelyn made a right from the restaurant's lot out into the street. Not fifteen seconds later, a car pulled around the building and made a right into the roadway without as much as tapping the brakes.

"What kind of car was that?" Beth asked.

"Sedan, dark, but moving too fast," I said. "May have been a Chevy. Rewind that."

The kid rewound the footage and played it again—I still couldn't make out what kind of car it was or the tag number.

"Let's get the video from the other side just before the guy pulled around the building," I said.

"Sure. Hang on." The kid brought it up.

I glanced at the time-stamp, just under a minute before the footage of him pulling from the lot in a hurry.

"That looks like the car there," Beth said. "Can you make out that plate?" she asked.

I stared at the car on the screen parked toward the end of the lot farthest from the street. "No."

We continued to watch the footage. A few seconds later, a man came from the side entrance of the building, gave a wave to a car in the parking lot that allowed him to pass in front of it, and jogged to the car.

"There he is," I said.

The man got in his car, and the brake lights flashed before the whites of reverse clicked on. He backed from the parking spot with the rear of his vehicle coming square to the camera. By the shape of the two round taillights on each side, I put the car as an early two thousands Chevy Impala, which some departments used as law-enforcement vehicles—the car was possibly a match to what we were looking for.

"Pause it," I said.

He did, with the rear of the car and the plate centered in frame. The tag number was legible, 6MHL880—all strung together, no dashes. I pulled out my notepad and jotted down the plate number. I looked at the rear window, trying to spot any kind of light bar—I couldn't tell.

"Doesn't look like a Kentucky plate. Or Indiana," the kid said.

"It's California," I said.

"California lines up with the girl that our print came from," Beth said.

"Looks like a Chevy that could be used in law enforcement as well," I said.

"Do you want to call it in to Duffield?" Beth asked.

"One second. I want to see if we can find any kind of contact between these two inside the building." I turned my attention back to the assistant-manager kid. "Can we get some footage of the indoor dining area? I'd like to have a look at this guy inside the restaurant."

"Yeah," he said. "How far back do you want it to go?"

"I want to see everything you have from the second this guy pulls up until the point he leaves."

"Okay. Well, we know where he parked and when he left. It would probably be easiest to get a time if we just rewound this until he pulls in. That way, we can kind of follow him from camera to camera."

I nodded.

The kid rewound the footage at high speed until we saw the car pull out of the lot in reverse—some twenty minutes prior to the time he actually left, according to the time-stamp on the recording. He clicked Play. I looked for any kind of lights mounted to the front of the vehicle as we watched the car pull in—again, I couldn't make any out. The man parked, walked into the building, ordered from the counter, and took a seat to eat. I took in the man's height, build, and everything else I could from the video while he was walking around. The height and weight that we had estimated on our suspect seemed in line with the man on the video. I made a mental note of his appearance—dark short hair; thick mustache; scruffy, unkempt beard; and dressed in a suit, which was another similarity. He sat at his table, alternating between taking bites from a leg of chicken and scooping up forkfuls of what I assumed was mashed potatoes.

My eyes went to the time-stamp on the screen—which lined up with when Katelyn Willard was in the restaurant. No sooner had my eyes come back up to the image on the screen, than Katelyn appeared at the napkin dispenser, pulling out one after the other. I looked back at the man, seated just a table away from where she stood. He sat motionless—a chicken leg held before his mouth. He appeared to just be frozen, staring at her. A moment later, she walked off camera, back to the front counter. The man dropped the chicken leg to the box below it, lifted his tray by its edges, and stood. He walked straight to the trash bin and dumped everything in. Then he paused by the exit leading out to the parking lot.

"He looks like he's waiting," Beth said.

The man was staring back toward the front counter.

"And watching her. Can you switch it back to her at the counter?" I asked.

The kid did.

A second later, we saw her exit, and I made a note of the time.

"Put it back to where he was standing."

The kid did, and the man was gone.

I pulled my phone from my pocket and dialed Duffield.

CHAPTER THIRTY-FOUR

William neared his driveway and flicked on his blinker. He slowed to turn. William turned in, pulled up near the shed, and killed the motor. He stepped out and rounded the car. As he grasped the passenger door handle to open it and retrieve the bag of groceries, including the needed eyeliner sitting on the passenger seat, the sound of crunching gravel caught his ear. His head snapped to the left, and he stared down his driveway to see a dark sedan pulling up.

"Shit," William mumbled. He opened the passenger door, scooped the paper bag of groceries up into his arms, and then hip bumped the door closed.

The approaching car rolled to a stop, and two suited men stepped from the front car doors.

"Afternoon," the driver said.

William stared at the two men walking toward him over some celery poking from the top of the bag—the same two that had been outside his door earlier in the day. From what his neighbor Glen had said on the phone, they were feds.

"Can I help you?" William asked.

"Agents Tolman and Collette with the Louisville FBI," the man on the left said.

The agent pulled out a set of credentials from the inner pocket of his gray suit and held them up.

William spotted a shoulder-mounted firearm as the man went into his jacket. The two men stopped directly before him. William craned his neck closer to the outstretched ID to get a look. The agent's name was Rex Collette. The other agent produced a set of credentials from his jacket as well—his ID read Jerry Tolman.

"What, ah, what can I do for you, Agents?" William asked.

"Are you the homeowner here?" the man on the right, Agent Tolman, asked. He was a bit taller and heavier than the agent named Collette.

"I am."

"Your name?" he asked.

"William David."

The agent on the left, Collette, took a notepad from his pocket and wrote his name down.

"Can I ask what this is about?" William asked.

"We had an incident a few miles or so from here. We're checking with the locals to see if they've seen a police vehicle driving around here that seemed a little odd."

"How does a police vehicle driving around seem odd?" William asked.

"So you have or have not?" Agent Collette asked.

William's mind went to wondering how they knew about the car. He shrugged it off and put an elbow on the roof of his

Volkswagen. "Have not. What was the incident that occurred?"

They both ignored his question.

"Is this your only vehicle, sir?" the agent named Collette asked.

"Yes, it is. Can you guys just give me one second while I set these groceries in the house?"

"This shouldn't take too long," Agent Collette said.

"And I have a bag full of frozen foods that are in the process of melting. You guys can come in and ask whatever you need to ask while I'm putting this stuff in the freezer if you need to."

William walked to his side door, and the two agents followed. William rested the bag on his knee and stuck a key in the deadbolt to unlock the door. He paused for a moment, thinking of the state of the kitchen when he'd left. The mount had been moved to the back room before he'd gone for his groceries and eyeliner, the pot of wax emptied, cleaned, and replaced in the shed where it had come from. He continued to think but couldn't come up with anything that would seem off. He pushed the door open with the toe of his shoe and entered. The two agents entered behind him.

William's eyes immediately went to the hangers dangling from the bottom of the cupboard, with some wax still on them. He walked briskly to the area and set down the bag of groceries in an attempt to block them from view. He glanced toward the stairs leading to the basement and saw some red smears of blood on the floor. William looked back over his shoulder. The agents both stood just inside of the doorway, looking around.

"You guys can have a seat if you'd like." William nodded his head toward the kitchen table and rummaged through the bag.

The agents walked farther into the kitchen, nearer the table, but didn't sit.

"Okay. This will just take me a second to get the couple things into the freezer." He pulled some frozen fish from the bag and opened the freezer door.

"So what exactly do you guys need to know here?" William went back to the bag of groceries and rummaged around some more, removing a couple bags of frozen vegetables.

"We're just getting a list of registered vehicles in the area," Agent Collette said. "So, just to confirm. You have no other registered vehicles?"

"Nope. Just the VW," William said. He knew his answer would immediately be proven false if, or when, they ran him through the DMV.

"And that California plate," Agent Tolman asked. "Did you just move to the area?"

"A month or two ago, yes. I still have to get everything transferred over. I finally got my change-of-residence forms this week." He placed the vegetables in the freezer and walked back to the bag, where he put his back to the counter.

"Do you know the Emmerson family that lives in the area?" Agent Tolman asked. "Back out off of Flat Rock Road there. Beige brick single story?"

"The Emmersons? I don't believe I've met them. Did something happen to them or something?"

"They're fine," he said. "Someone we're after mailed something from their mailbox while they were out of town."

"Mailed something from their mailbox?" William asked.

"Correct. You didn't happen to see anyone near it, did you?"

"I'm not even sure I know what house you're referring to," William said. "You said they were out of town while this happened. Do they know this is going on?"

"They're back," Agent Tolman said. "They're aware."

"Okay," William said. "I guess I don't really have anything for you on that which could help. Like I said, I just moved to the area and haven't really met more than a handful of people around here."

"Sure. That shed out there"—Agent Tolman pointed—"anything in there?"

"No, just a garage space and my tools and that. Storage for stuff I don't want in the house. About it."

"Mind if we have a quick look?" the agent named Collette asked. "Then we'll get out of your hair."

"Don't know why you'd want to look in my shed, but sure, I guess." William walked to the sink, gave the agents his back, and flicked on the faucet. He hit the pump on the dispenser of dish soap and washed his hands. His eyes went down to the bottom of the sink, strewn with miscellaneous silverware that he'd yet to load into the dishwasher. His eyes came to rest on a paring knife.

"Just a quick look around if you don't mind," one of the agents said behind him.

William could see his fate unfolding—they would see the

car in the shed after he'd just told them he didn't own another vehicle. Even if they didn't put together that it was a former law-enforcement vehicle, they would question the lie. Their asking if they could have a look around without a doubt meant they suspected him. If William told them to get a warrant, they most certainly would, and they would be back with more men. William wasn't finished with Erin. He hadn't sent off what he needed to send off. He needed more time.

William used his elbow to bump off the running water and flicked his fingers down, shedding water from them into the sink. "I guess I could show you around."

He looked back over his shoulder and made eye contact with Agent Tolman, staring at him from a few feet away. The other agent, Collette, was looking out into the living room. William reached out with his left hand for a hand towel hanging from the handle of a cabinet door so his body would shield his right hand going into the sink for the knife. He pulled the towel from the cupboard door as he grasped the handle of the knife and lifted it from the sink. He used the towel over his hands to shield the knife.

"Let's head out there." William jerked his chin toward the door, hoping the two agents would lead the way out—they stood in place.

William tossed the towel onto the counter, causing both agents to look where the towel landed, near the corner on the counter by the refrigerator.

William took a single step, reached up with his right hand, and slashed the blade of the paring knife across the throat of the nearer agent—Tolman. The delivery of the strike was flawless. William saw a splash of red, and the agent's hands went for his own neck and, more importantly, not his weapon. With two lunging strides, William was on the other agent, who was going for his shoulder-holstered gun. William slammed the man chest- and face-first into the door leading outside, William's chest to Agent Collette's back. He could feel the agent's hand thrashing for his weapon inside his suit jacket. William did his best with his left hand to interfere with the agent's attempts to pull his gun while he plunged the knife repeatedly into the fed's lower back.

As William lifted the knife to wrap it around the agent's head and pull it across his throat, Agent Collette jerked his head back, making contact with William's nose. The impact stunned William, making his vision go black before the pain began. William's eyes welled with tears. Another blow from the agent came a split second later—a mule kick. The fed's heel caught William square in his manhood. William gasped and could feel his body wanting to drop and curl into a fetal position. His knees went weak. With his last bit of fight, William grabbed the agent's face with his left hand and yanked the fed's head to the side. William reached the knife around Collette's neck and pulled it from one side of his throat to the other.

The pair collapsed to the floor at the side door.

William squirmed in pain. Through teared eyes, he saw Agent Collette's left hand swiping the tile floor while his right held his throat. William watched blood pump through the fed's fingers until his hand went limp.

CHAPTER THIRTY-FIVE

The phone rang in my ear. Duffield answered just when I expected his voice mail to pick up.

"Duffield," he said.

"It's Hank. We have a tag number and vehicle."

I overheard the assistant manager tell Beth that he needed to attend to something and would be right back. He left the small office.

"You got the guy's car on video?" Duffield asked.

"It looks like it. Are you ready to take down the plate number?" I asked.

"One second—I need to get to a computer."

"Sure. Anything more on the missing mystery girl from California?" I asked.

"Not yet. We're doing what we can to look into it and still waiting on a couple of phone calls back."

"Well, we may have something more that ties in here. The tag on the car is a California plate."

"So things are starting to come together. Now, we just need to figure out how. All right, I'm at a desk. Give me the plate."

With the tip of my finger on my notepad, I followed the numbers and letters as I read them off, "6MHL880."

Duffield read the tag number back to me to confirm.

"That's correct," I said.

"Give me a second here. I'm just going to run it while we're on the phone."

I could hear him punching away at computer keys.

"It's coming up now. The plate comes back to a William Allen David. Age: fifty-two; height: five eleven; weight: one eighty-five. Address listed is in Sacramento."

"Height and weight fit with our guy on video taking Katelyn Willard. What's the make and model of vehicle that the tag comes back to? Not that it's a stolen plate."

"It says 2005 Chevy Impala. Color gray," Duffield said. "Also lists an older Volkswagen as a registered vehicle. Registration on the Impala is pretty recent."

"Okay. The Impala is the car we're looking at here, which also fits with what could have been used as an unmarked squad. What else does it say on him? Any priors?"

"Clean as a whistle. Nothing listed."

"Is there anything that links this guy to the Louisville area?" I asked.

"Nothing here on this, no. We'll have to start digging."

"There has to be a reason he picked the area."

"One would think," Duffield said. "We'll get going on the guy and see what we can find out. What does the video show, exactly?"

I gave him the highlights. "He was in the restaurant eating prior to her coming in. She walked inside the building and placed an order to go. As soon as he saw her, he dumped his food, waited around for her to leave, jogged out to his car, and went in pursuit."

"Are you dealing with a manager there, owner, employee, what?" Duffield asked.

"Assistant manager. Just a kid. Pretty sure the franchise is owned by the kid's family, though. He's been helpful so far."

"Can he make you a copy of the footage?" Duffield asked.

"I'll ask him when he comes back. He just left the office where Beth and I are sitting a second ago."

"Sure," Duffield said. "Just get something set on how we can get a copy if he doesn't have the ability to do it there."

"Yeah, I will."

"Okay, let me get on the phone. I need to get the ID, photo of this guy, and vehicle information out to everyone."

"Get someone going on banking, credit-card, and phone records right away. He has to be staying somewhere out here."

"Right," Duffield said. "I'm going to bring a few new people in to work on what we need. Also will have to get looking into if there's a way to connect this woman we have the print from and this William David."

The assistant manager appeared in the doorway.

"Okay," I said. "We'll see what we can do about the video and meet you back at the office."

"Are you guys coming straight back?"

"As of right now, yes."

"Okay. I'll see you in a bit," he said.

I clicked off and gave my attention to the assistant manager. "Any way we can get a copy of all that footage?" I asked.

"I actually don't know how to make copies of it, to tell you the truth. We never had to before."

"Is it your own system, or is it something that was set up from a security company?" Beth asked.

"It's all part of the whole franchise package. But the hard drive for it is located in the store here."

"Do you think we could just send one of our tech guys out, maybe?" Beth asked.

"I guess. I'd have to ask my dad to be sure, but I don't know why it would be a problem."

"Do you think we can maybe give him a call quick to check?" she asked.

The kid reached out for the telephone on the desk and paused. "You know, that will be fine." He rolled open a desk drawer and removed a card with his name on it. "Just have whoever needs to contact me give me a call when they are on their way, and I'll make sure they get whatever they need."

Beth took the card from the kid's hand. "I will. We appreciate all the help."

"Sure thing," he said.

Beth scooted her chair back, and I did the same.

We left the office and walked back through the kitchen and out from behind the counter. Beth made a left for the side exit. I followed her out to the car and got in on the passenger side.

"He didn't want to call his father and ask." Beth pulled

her seatbelt over her shoulder and started the rental.

"He was probably trying to show that he can make his own decisions on how to run the place is my guess," I said.

Beth backed from our parking spot, turned, and started forward to make a loop around the building and exit.

I pointed left at the giant cement chicken with the championship-title belt. "Pull through the drive-through so I can order."

"And here I thought you forgot about your chicken sandwich."

"I didn't forget."

Beth pulled into the lane, and I placed my order at the sign under the chicken's wing.

As I held my meal in a white paper bag on my lap, Beth drove for the interstate that would lead us back to the Bureau office. I stuffed my hand into the bag, pulled out a couple french fries, and jammed them into my mouth. I chewed the fries while I dug back into the bag for the sandwich. I took it from inside and held it up. The paper wrapping it was wet with grease or sauce or whatever it was. I peeled some of the paper away from one end to get a bite. As my teeth sank in, some peppers fell and some sauce dripped onto the bag on my lap.

Beth glanced over. "That thing looks like it's about fifteen hundred calories. If I ate that, I wouldn't have to eat again for a week."

I shrugged, licked some of the sauce running down the back of my hand, and took another bite. "It's delicious," I said through a mouthful of bread, cheese, peppers, and chicken. "You should try this." I held the sandwich out by her face.

"I'm not eating that," Beth said.

"You're missing out. But, speaking of eating, so what are these dinner plans that you have for the evening?"

"I guess I wouldn't really call them dinner plans," she said. "Nothing super important or anything."

"I believe *dinner plans* were the exact words that came out of your mouth earlier."

Beth remained quiet.

"So what you're saying is that you have a plan to go and do something for dinner but don't actually have dinner plans?"

"Right."

"That makes complete sense." I stopped chewing and looked over at her. "So, are you meeting someone for dinner later tonight?"

"No," Beth said. "Who would I be meeting?"

I sat in thought. Beth was playing the same kind of vague non-answer answer game that Karen had for years when she didn't want to tell me something—or did want to tell me something but needed a shove. I figured I'd try the same method of extraction that I used with Karen. "Oh. Okay. Well, have a good time." I said the words, went silent, and looked away.

Not fifteen seconds later, Beth broke the silence. "I'm going to dinner by myself."

"You're going out to eat by yourself? Those are your big plans?"

"Yes. It's kind of a long story, but basically when I was married to Scott, he'd never let me eat Indian food, which I absolutely love. He hated it, so that meant that I wasn't allowed to like it or eat it."

"Sounds real logical." I reached for my fountain drink in a cup holder. I took a big drink to wash down the food in my mouth and placed it back in the holder.

"Exactly. It was completely stupid. So when we got divorced, the first thing I did was go out to an Indian restaurant and gorge. I honestly ate like two years' worth of Indian food."

"Yeah, Indian food is good." I pulled the wrapper on my Philly chicken sandwich back farther and took another bite.

"I know. So that's what I'm doing tonight. Scott and I were back together, and I wasn't allowed. Now we're not, and I am."

I chewed and spoke. "Well, enjoy yourself. Bring me back some butter chicken."

"You can come if you'd like," Beth said.

"We'll figure it out later." I jammed the rest of the sandwich in my mouth.

CHAPTER THIRTY-SIX

Beth and I pulled into the parking lot of the Bureau office, parked, and headed inside. We entered serial crimes and walked straight to Duffield's office. He was sitting inside with the phone resting between his ear and shoulder. He pointed at Beth and me and then toward his guest chairs.

We sat. From the sounds of his phone call, he was speaking with someone regarding our possible suspect. Duffield continued his call for another minute or two, writing on a pad of paper as he talked. Then he clicked off and gave us his attention.

"Our guy, William Allen David, was a sports anchor at this television channel that Erin Cooper-Connelly, the woman we found the print from, worked at prior to her disappearance," he said. "She was also a sports anchor. Seemed she took the position after William Allen David was let go."

"The signature on the letters, The Sportsman, as in he was the sports man," I said.

Duffield nodded. "Yup."

"How did you find this out?" Beth asked.

"First thing one of my guys did—ran his name in a search

engine. He came up right away. That was an exec at the television channel that I was just on the phone with. Apparently, this Mr. David and the Cooper-Connelly woman weren't the best of friends. He didn't get into much detail but said that Mr. David had been asked to leave his position due to inappropriate behavior directed at Cooper-Connelly. This was a couple of years ago already, though."

"Her disappearance, what do we know there? Anything further?" Beth asked.

"Not really. I called the lieutenant that was on the scene of the suicide. He said that the man had been deceased for a week or so before he was found. From all accounts, it looked like a standard gunshot suicide."

"Was the letter in his handwriting?" I asked.

"Do you think our guy may have penned it?" Duffield asked.

"Even if he didn't, and it was in the deceased man's handwriting, we have experience with suspects forcing victims to write letters," Beth said. "It's definitely not out of the question."

"I'll see what we can do about looking into it," Duffield said.

"So where are we at now with locating this guy?" I asked.

"I put in for all the records. Shouldn't be too long. I pulled Houston and Braine off of their eyeball searching and stuck them on trying to get me a phone number on this guy so we can try to track it. Houston is contacting utility and cable providers in California. Braine is checking everything locally to see if anyone has his name on record."

"When do we circulate his name and photo?" Beth asked.

"We've already done it through law-enforcement branches," Duffield said. "The word is out on both vehicles as well. We'll have to get something set for the press yet this evening. I want this guy's face everywhere."

"We're going to need to get a tech guy out to that restaurant to get us the video they have," Beth said. "The assistant manager didn't know how to make a copy but said we're welcome to send someone over."

"I'll get someone sent out. Contact name there?" Duffield asked.

Beth pulled the kid's card from her bag and handed it to him.

"What about Collette and Tolman?" I asked. "Nothing out knocking on doors, hey?"

"Nope," Duffield said. "I actually tried both of them about twenty minutes ago and didn't get an answer from either. I imagine that they're conducting an interview. I left a message with the name, description, and vehicles that we're looking for. I'll try them again in a bit if I don't hear back from them."

"They've been out there for a while," Beth said. "I would think that they would have met with everyone local by now."

"Probably," Duffield said. "But they did say that they were going to try to stop back at the places where they didn't get answers at the door. Maybe they caught a couple of people home the second time around. Here, let me try them again." Duffield lifted his desk phone and punched in a number. He held the phone to his ear for a good thirty seconds before speaking up. "Tolman, it's Duffield, call in to report and confirm that you received my last message with the ID of our suspect." He reached out and pressed the button to disconnect from the call before dialing another number. Roughly thirty seconds later, he left a matching message for Collette on his voice mail. Duffield hung the phone back on its base. "Hmm." Duffield rubbed at his eye.

"What?" I asked.

He waved away my question. "Did you guys want to see the photos from the latest package? They have them downstairs."

"Same as before, you said?" Beth asked.

"Basically, though it looks like he did something different with the last woman. More wax museum than sideshow. That sounds awful, given the circumstances, but it's really about the most accurate description that I can come up with."

Beth glanced over at me. "I'm fine with not seeing them."

"Come on." I pushed myself up from the chair. "We need to put eyes on them." I paused. "Probably not the best choice of words, but we need to look. Maybe one of us will see something in the photos that can give us a lead."

Beth grumbled and stood.

Duffield remained at his desk. "I'm going to sit here and man the phone—I don't want to miss a call, and they've been coming in pretty much nonstop. Plus, seeing the photos once was about enough for me. Find Witting down there. He has everything."

"Will do," I said.

Beth and I left Duffield's office, took the elevator down,

and entered the forensics lab. I spotted Witting with another man in a white lab coat in one of the glassed-in cubicles on our right. Beth and I walked over, and I rapped on the door. Witting looked up from the file folder he held and handed it off to the man accompanying him. He walked toward us and opened the office door, closing it at his back.

"Did Duffield let you guys know that we had the IDs and photos?" he asked.

"We've been informed. The photos are what we're here to see," Beth said. "Unfortunately," she added.

"They're in my office." Witting waved over his shoulder for us to follow.

Beth and I walked into Witting's office behind him and took seats at his desk.

He sat and pushed a manila file folder toward us. "This is them."

I slid the file in front of Beth and myself and scooted up my chair. I flipped the cover and stared down. The page contained a photograph of an ID—Katelyn Willard. I flipped the page to see her alive, ball gag tied around her head and stuck in her mouth. I tried to make out anything at all other than her in the photo. The wall she stood against was white-painted cinderblock. I saw nothing else in the photo, other than a young woman with a look of fear on her face—probably within minutes of being murdered.

I flipped to the next page, where I knew what the photo would be. I stared down at the image of Katelyn Willard's head, minus her body. I glanced left toward Beth, seated beside me. She took her eyes away from the picture and looked at the ceiling. I took in what I could from the background of the photo—a white-plastic-covered table and a couple inches of a bloody reciprocating saw blade—nothing telling.

I let out a long breath and flipped the page. The mounted head looked similar to the others. Katelyn Willard's hair had been dyed and trimmed. Green glass eyes replaced her natural brown. The wood backing plate on the mount was identical to the photos of women past. The hands were positioned in the same fashion as the previous women as well. I saw nothing else in the background of the photo that could lead us in any direction. I turned the page to the next image, which was again of a driver's license.

They're arranged in there how they were contained on the film," Witting said.

I nodded and continued. By the fourth photo from the second woman, I'd realized what Duffield was talking about with his "more wax museum than sideshow" remark. The mount had a bit of a shine or gloss to it—as if covered in wax.

I looked up at Witting. "Is this mount covered in wax?"

"We believe it to be, yes. We have a blown-up image of the face. It appears as if the glass eyes are one with the eyelids, and the crease between the lips of the mouth is sealed."

"So that's what he was referring to as to perfecting his method," I said.

"Well, if his goal is to get them not to decompose, like the taxidermists or whoever were saying, I guess it's a better method than what he was doing," Beth said. "Sealed in wax can't decompose right?"

"I would think it would decompose internally, but am guessing the wax would hold form unless it came into contact with temperature," Witting said. "The hair still appears to just be glued, or really who knows how, attached to the head. I'd assume there is a scalp under there. I'd have to think that's going to shrink and pull back over time."

Beth squirmed in her chair with a disgusted look on her face. I imagined Witting's comments about interior decomposition and shrinking scalps weren't sitting right with her. I looked back at the photo. The hair, again trimmed and dyed, green eyes—a thought popped into my head. I pulled out my phone and brought up the Internet.

"What are you looking for?" Beth asked.

"One second." In my search bar, I typed the name of the girl we had the fingerprint for and then clicked for images. The results came up—rows and rows of photos containing a blond female sports anchor who bore an undeniable resemblance to the mounts our suspect was creating. "I just wanted to see how close these mounts look to the actual woman." I turned my phone so Beth could get a look at the screen.

Beth leaned in toward my phone for a better look. "They aren't that far off," she said. "It doesn't feel like an accident that her print was there," she said. "More like he wanted us to find it and make the connection. There isn't a single print from him on anything, and there just so happens to be one from this girl? Why?"

My phone buzzed in my pocket—I reached in, pulled it out, and glanced at the screen. "It's Duffield upstairs." I clicked the button to talk.

CHAPTER THIRTY-SEVEN

William had attached her hair and scraped the wax from around her eye sockets, exposing her green glass eyes. He'd painted the sealed nostril holes dark so they appeared open and had finished applying her makeup. The mount was done, aside from one final touch. William leaned back in his chair, gazing at a mission accomplished. He'd fulfilled his threat to the woman who had taken everything he'd worked for in life.

"Perfection," he said. "Just need to get the mic, and then it's on the wall for you."

William rolled his chair back and stood from the desk in the spare bedroom where he'd been working. He walked out to the kitchen and stopped just shy of the kitchen table. The floor from where he stood all the way to the door leading out was red. William stared down at the blood pool that had formed around the first agent he'd killed. He looked right to left—the blood started at the agent's throat, under his head, an almost three-foot-diameter puddle. From the pool, the blood had run across the tile, using the grout joints as a path to the base of the cabinets under the sink. William followed the blood with his eyes all the way down the baseboard of the cabinets to where it had puddled near the kitchen trash can. He noticed the lower and then the upper cabinets on the wall, speckled with more blood that had sprayed from the agent's throat while he was still vertical.

"What a mess," William said.

He looked past the first body on the floor to the other agent, who was blocking the doorway leading outside. William's gaze rose to the blood-covered white door. He walked directly toward the agent blocking his path outside, each footstep creating a void in the blood covering the kitchen tile.

William leaned down, flipped the agent's suit jacket to one side, took his weapon, and tucked it into his waistline. Then he stood and reached out for the bloody handle. William twisted the knob and pulled the door inward, which opened three inches before hitting the dead agent's shoulder and stopping. William yanked the door by the knob, slamming it into the dead man—the corpse slid an inch or two across the blood-covered tile. William yanked again, harder, and his hand slipped from the bloody knob. William placed his hands through the gap in the doorway and gripped the outside of the door with his bloody fingers. He pulled and yanked repeatedly, and each time, the agent's body slid a little farther back across the tile until William had enough room to squeeze through. He closed the door at his back and walked toward the shed.

William entered the shed and passed the front of the Impala parked inside. On a shelf attached to the wall, near the top, was a box marked Awards. William reached up and pulled it down. He set it on the bench in front of the car and opened the top. Inside were the miscellaneous accolades he'd won during his time in broadcasting. He pushed a few items to the sides and dug down into the box until the color gold flashed in his eyes. William grasped a gold-plated microphone and took it from the box—an engraved award he'd won, signifying twenty years of excellence. He left the box sitting open, stuffed the microphone into a pocket, and left the shed.

William entered the house through the kitchen again, slamming the door into the corpse of the agent and sliding him farther away from the doorway and nearer the cupboards beside the refrigerator. He stepped over the man's head and walked through the blood covering the floor. With another high step over Agent Tolman's body, William walked to the spare bedroom to get Erin's mount and then returned to the basement.

William stood, mount in hand, directly before his fireplace on the lower level. He stared Erin in the face as he hung the wooden base of the mount on the nail that awaited her. William stepped back, paused, and marveled at his achievement.

"Are you ready for our broadcast?" he asked.

His question didn't receive a response. William walked to the far corner of the room and picked up the makeshift cell-phone tripod he'd created. He carried it to the rear of the couch and set it up. William placed his cell phone in the cradle at the tripod's top, brought up the video-camera app, and centered the viewfinder on Erin's mount. He leaned over the couch, grabbed the remote control from the couch cushions, and clicked the television on. William went through his cable box's menus and clicked Play on the recorded sports highlights. He checked his cell phone's viewfinder to make sure the television was in full view and then paused the footage.

"Hang tight, Erin." William laughed at his own joke. "I'm going to go get dressed, clean up a bit, and do my hair. I have to look sharp for this one." He turned toward the stairs.

CHAPTER THIRTY-EIGHT

Beth and I walked through the open door of Duffield's office.

"You got a number?" I asked.

"Houston got one from the local cable and Internet provider in Sacramento," Duffield said. "I just got off the phone with the tech department. If we can get a GPS signal, we'll have his location within minutes."

"Provided it's the same phone he has on him right now," Beth said.

"Provided," Duffield said. When his phone rang at his desk, he snatched it from its base. "Duffield."

Beth and I sat in silence.

Duffield scribbled something on his pad of paper. "You're sure?"

I leaned forward in my chair to get a look at what Duffield had written down—an address.

"Thanks." Duffield hung the phone up. "We got a hit on the phone number. The coordinates say that it's in the area. Tech nailed it down to a home address."

"Let's get a warrant set," Beth said.

"I'll get someone on the warrant while we head out

there," Duffield said. "I'd rather have him trapped in the house, surrounded by law enforcement while we wait on the paperwork to enter, as opposed to waiting on the paperwork here while he slips away."

"Let's go." I slid my chair back as I stood.

Beth did the same. "Let's get the word out to local law enforcement for backup. Where is this address at?"

"One second." Duffield picked up the paper he'd written on and punched the address into his computer.

We waited a moment in silence.

"Shit. It's only a mile or two away from where the packages were sent from." Duffield scooped up his phone and started dialing. "I need to get the word to Tolman and Collette."

Beth and I waited at his office door.

"Tolman's voice mail," Duffield said. He tossed the phone back on its base and stood. He pulled his suit jacket from the back of his chair and jammed an arm through one of the sleeves, putting it on. "I'll call Collette on the way. Let's go. What the hell are these two doing?"

Neither Beth nor I responded.

Duffield grabbed the paper with the address from his desk, and Beth and I followed him from his office.

Duffield stopped at Agent Houston's desk in the main room of the serial crimes unit.

"What's going on?" Houston asked.

Duffield held the piece of paper out toward him. "We need a warrant for this address. As soon as you get it in hand, you and Braine come there."

"This is our guy?" Houston asked.

Duffield nodded. "We're leaving for the address now. Again, bring it the second it touches your hand."

"Got it. I'll call you when we're on our way." Houston lifted his desk phone to his ear and dialed.

"Let's go," Duffield said. "My truck is on the ground level of the secured structure."

We took the stairs down and entered the Bureau's parking garage.

Duffield walked a couple steps ahead of us, his phone pressed to his ear. I couldn't hear his entire conversation, but it sounded as though he was asking someone for coordinates. Beth and I piled into Duffield's truck, and we drove from the complex. Duffield made contact with the Louisville Metro Police Department within minutes of our departure—they would be sending units out to meet us.

I looked over at Duffield driving—he clutched his cell phone in his right hand, steering the truck with his left. Every couple of seconds, he stared down at his phone. His face said that he was bothered by something.

Duffield caught my glance. "Something isn't right," he said.

"Collette and Tolman?" I asked.

"I called the tech department to get me GPS locations on their phones," he said. "It's been too long without hearing back from them."

"The service might be spotty out there," Beth said. "It's pretty rural."

I figured Beth was trying to ease Duffield's mind.

"I spoke to them while they were out there," Duffield said. "They have coverage."

Beth didn't respond. We rode in silence another few miles before the sound of Duffield's phone chirping broke the silence in the cab of the truck.

He swiped the screen and held the phone to his ear. "Duffield," he said. "Where?" he asked a split second later. Then he clicked off from the call without saying another word and tossed the phone onto the truck's dash. He stared out the windshield and increased his speed.

"Location?" I asked.

Duffield didn't look at me to answer the question. "Same location as the suspect's."

We exited the interstate a few minutes later and drove zigzagging country roads farther east. I recognized the area from our visit to the Emmersons' house. Duffield slowed and made a right a mile away from their residence. We traveled a half mile and made a left down a road named Robin Lane. Four Louisville Metro patrol cars lined the right side of the road, parked with wheels in the grass. The officers stood outside their cars—each man had tan body armor over his patrol uniform. Duffield slowed near the car parked in the lead, where a group of six officers stood. One of the officers, six foot and wide shouldered, walked toward the passenger side of Duffield's Toyota. I dropped my window.

"Agent's Duffield, Rawlings, and Harper," Duffield said from the driver's seat.

"Sergeant Lucas Grainger," the officer said. He stuck his big hand through the window and shook our hands, Beth's coming up between the front seats of the truck.

"Did you pass the property?" Duffield asked.

"We did. It's a quarter mile up on the left. The road dead-ends, so he would have needed to drive past us if leaving by car. There's a Volkswagen and a government-issued vehicle in the driveway," Sergeant Grainger said. "What's the situation here? This is our guy making the headlines?"

"Yes," Duffield said.

"And the government-issued vehicle?" he asked.

"It's one of ours. I had two agents in the area going door-to-door. They haven't reported back in hours."

The sergeant remained silent.

"Let's get on that house and see what we have," Duffield said. "Make sure your guys are ready for anything."

"Do we have a warrant?" he asked.

"We have one coming, but if I think my guys are inside and in danger, we're going in regardless."

"Got it." Sergeant Grainger turned back toward his men. "We're rolling."

Duffield started forward, and I raised my window. A quarter mile up the road, Duffield veered to the left side of the road and parked in the grass. A tree line blocked our view of the home though I could see the base of a gravel driveway roughly ten car lengths in front of Duffield's truck. We stepped out as the patrol cars parked in a single file behind us. The officers exited their vehicles—eight men total—and two retrieved shotguns from their vehicles.

We gathered at Duffield's tailgate.

"We want this place locked down," Duffield said. "Let's

surround it and make sure we have eyes on any possible exit point. What's the layout of this place?"

"Single story house on a bit of a hill," one of the officers said. "This tree line breaks up about fifty feet up the driveway. The home faces the street, with the driveway splitting and passing the side of the house to the east. The driveway leads back to a big shed about the size of a three-car garage. There's a side entrance on the home that faces the driveway."

"Okay," Duffield said. "Let's take the driveway up and fan out as soon as we can. Whatever needs eyes on gets eyes on. We may have friendlies inside. Use your heads."

"Understood." The sergeant looked at his men. "Eggers, Dawson, you guys loop around to the back of the property." He looked at the officer that had mentioned the layout. "Young, you go with Brooks. Take a position behind that VW in the driveway. Keep a visual on that side of the home and the shed. The rest of you split between the main entrance and the other end of the home."

His men confirmed the instructions.

Our entire group started up the gravel driveway, weapons drawn. The Volkswagen was parked near the shed in front of Agents Tolman and Collette's vehicle. The thick trees opened up, and the officers split off to their respective positions. The jingling and clacking of items on the officers' utility belts faded as they jogged away. Duffield, Beth and I continued up the driveway with the sergeant and two of his officers following.

I looked at the home as we approached—the place appeared to have been built in the later seventies. The siding was dark blue, the shutters a shade lighter. The roof needed to be replaced. A large bay window sat to the right of the front doors, but the curtains were drawn, not allowing a visual inside. Past the solid front door to the left front side of the home, I spotted two more windows, which also had curtains drawn. I looked at the ground level and could see the tops of two low glass-block windows set inside window wells.

We approached the back of Tolman and Collette's car and rounded the side of it opposite the home. Duffield, who was leading, stopped to get a look into the vehicle. I passed him and walked toward the front of the car, staring at the side door of the home, and stopped at the front bumper.

I spoke over my shoulder to Beth. "There's blood on that side door."

CHAPTER THIRTY-NINE

We neared the side door of the home. My eyes were locked on the bloody handprint on the door's edge, which appeared to have been made by someone inside the house holding the edge of the door. Duffield was directly at my back, Beth behind him. The sergeant and another officer backed us up while one waited in the driveway.

Sergeant Grainger's radio came alive, and my head snapped back toward him. He jammed the palm of his hand over his shoulder radio to block the sound. The message that came through was that the home had a basement walk out on the back side of the property.

I took the right side of the door, with Beth behind me. Duffield, the sergeant, and his officer took the left side of the door. Duffield counted three on his fingers and reached for the doorknob. He gave it a twist and pushed it open. The door swung open a foot, hit something, and swung back. We remained quiet. I heard no footsteps or noises coming from inside. Duffield pushed the door again and poked his head and weapon into the opening to get a look inside the home.

"Son of a bitch," he said.

He motioned us into the house and entered through the gap between the doorjamb and whatever the door was hitting while the sergeant covered him.

Sergeant Grainger motioned Beth and me inside. We entered behind Duffield, who had moved further into the kitchen and was crouched near a body.

"What the hell," I mumbled. My eyes went from where Duffield was crouched back across the tile, which was covered in blood, to a man wearing a suit and lying on the floor to my right. The door blocked the upper torso and head of the man. I looked around the door to see Agent Collette's face. His eyes were open, staring at the ceiling. His mouth hung ajar, with his tongue protruding from one corner. His throat had been opened from ear to ear. Collette's jacket hung open, revealing that his service weapon was missing.

I turned my attention back to Duffield, who was looking back at Beth and me. Duffield stared downward, said the word *shit* in a hard whisper and shook his head. He rose, took a position against the wall in the dining room, and waved Beth and me over.

I turned back to the sergeant standing in the open doorway. "Make sure no one comes from here."

He confirmed.

Beth and I did our best to get to Duffield without stepping in any of the blood. I glanced down at Agent Tolman as we passed him—his throat had been cut just like Collette's. Beth and I met Duffield in the dining room and continued on. The living room was quickly cleared, and we made our way down a short hallway. I checked the first door to our left—a bedroom. I entered and cleared the closet before returning to Duffield and Beth in the hall. Duffield cleared a bathroom on our right. We continued. At the hallway's end was a pair of open doors—one left and one right. As we approached, I quickly glanced left—another bedroom. Beth dipped inside that bedroom, and Duffield and I entered the room on the right.

My eyes went left to right across the room, which from the size, I figured used to be the master bedroom. Tables and desks lined the wall in what appeared to be makeshift workstations. Wood bases and some kind of metal frames littered the table farthest left. The next desk contained pieces of brown clay and a pile of some kind of organic substance I couldn't make out. I took another step into the room, looking right to make sure the open closet area was clear—it was, and I saw no master bathroom. I continued scanning from one table to the next. The far right table contained a photo booth, and against the back wall were a mannequin head and hair trimmings on a table. A jar of green glass eyes caught my attention initially, followed by a bunch of different makeup products a moment later. Duffield stood near the pile of what I couldn't make out—he leaned in for a better view and yanked his head away.

I walked toward him to see what he was looking at. Duffield pointed at something protruding from the mound.

I spotted what looked like an eyeball mixed in with whatever the rest of the organic matter was.

I felt a momentary flutter in the back of my throat but swallowed it away.

"Other bedroom is clear," Beth said quietly, entering the room. Her eyes shot back and forth from one workstation to the next.

A sound caught my ear—faint talking. At first, I thought it was the sergeant and his men outside, but something didn't sound right about it. The voice was singular and not calls back and forth across a radio or someone giving orders.

"We need to clear that base—" Beth began.

I cut Beth off with my finger over my mouth and pointed down at my feet. "Listen," I said as quietly as I could.

We stood silent.

From directly below our feet, I could hear a low deep voice.

I pointed toward the room's doorway. We exited and made our way back down the hall and around to the kitchen.

"Are we clear?" Sergeant Grainger asked. He remained in his same position at the doorway leading out toward the driveway.

I pointed down and spoke quietly. "Talking coming from the basement."

The sergeant nodded and called to his men over his radio to stay sharp on the walkout door.

"Light under the door." Duffield pointed toward a closed door at the edge of the kitchen, where faint light came from the crack beneath it.

We approached and took the side of the door with the handle. Beth crouched nearest the door and held the door handle.

"I'll pull—you clear," she said.

“Got it.” I held my service weapon ready.

Beth twisted the knob and yanked the door. I rounded the doorway, pointing my gun down a yellow-linoleum-covered stairwell leading to the lower level. The murmur of voices I’d heard before increased in volume but I saw no one. At the bottom of the stairs was gray carpeting, and the lights were on. I couldn’t see the back wall at the base of the steps, and the room opened to the sides in both directions. I pulled back. The stairwell was about as dangerous as you could get for clearing, allowing a shooter from any direction.

I relayed the information. “Room opens up and goes in each direction at the base of the stairs.”

“We need to know where he is,” Duffield said, “or it’s a kill box.”

Beth turned and looked across the kitchen at the sergeant in the doorway. “You said that there was a walkout from the basement in the back?”

“Correct,” he said.

“Can we get a visual inside?” she asked.

“Hold on,” Sergeant Grainger said. He stepped from the doorway.

He made a call over his radio, but I couldn’t make out what exactly he was saying.

A moment later, the sergeant returned to the doorway. “The blinds are shut. We can’t see inside.”

I took a step down the stairwell, keeping my gun pointed downward. The voice I’d heard went silent.

“Hank,” Beth said softly. She turned into the doorway.

I motioned for her to wait.

I got as low as I could and took another step down. I still couldn't see the back wall. I took another step, keeping my gun pointed down, but still couldn't see. I took another step and put my knee down on the stairs to get lower. I followed the barrel of my gun left to right. I had a visual on the baseboard along the room's back wall. I motioned for Beth to come forward, and she stuck to the left wall and made her way down the four steps to me. I dropped another two steps and got as low as I could again, keeping my gun aimed in the direction I looked. I could see the left side of the room beyond the stairwell. The wall was solid aside from a single closed door. I swapped walls of the stairwell and looked to the right. The room continued in that direction. I pointed to the right, signaling which way I was headed at the base of the stairs.

A voice broke the silence. "I just need a couple of minutes here. I have a gun and suggest you let me finish my work. I won't hesitate to kill any of you if you try to impede what I'm doing. I'm sure the dead FBI agents up there can attest to that statement."

Duffield took two hard steps down the stairwell, but I held out my hand to stop him. Anger blazed in his face. I looked at Beth briefly and then turned my attention back to what I could see of the basement.

"I know that you're in the stairwell there," the voice continued. "I heard you come in and could hear you walking around upstairs. Now, if I wanted to take your life, I could just start firing into the wall and have a pretty damn good chance of killing you. I'm choosing not to do that, so I'll ask that you have the same professional courtesy and allow me the time that I need. I'll go out peacefully as soon as I'm finished."

"You're William Allen David?" I asked.

"That I am," he said.

"What can you tell me about Erin Cooper-Connelly?"

"You found her print on the film, hey? She's right here."

"Deceased?" I asked.

"Immortalized."

"I'd like to come down and talk."

"As soon as I tell you it's okay," he said. "Not before."

"What are you doing?"

"Uploading. It can't be interrupted."

I looked up the stairs at Beth. She was crouched, her gun held ready in both hands. Duffield stood behind her, a couple stairs up.

"Uploading what?" I asked.

"Oh, you'll see. Everyone will see," he said.

I heard a clank of what sounded like glass on glass.

"What was that?" I asked.

"Banged my glass of Scotch on the coaster. Ninety percent uploaded. Just a minute or two."

I heard a groan and then a squeak of what I figured to be a chair or old couch cushions. I took another step down the stairs and then another and another, moving as quietly as I could to the base of the stairwell. Beth did the same behind me. Duffield remained at the top of the stairs. I stood ready to round the corner into the room and fire if need be. Aside from the occasional sound of him rummaging around, I heard nothing. A noise caught my ear—liquid pouring. He was pouring himself another drink, and if he was doing that, he wouldn't be ready for me.

I gave a quick signal to Beth and rounded the corner, my gun out before me. I saw the left side of the room first with a closed door. Then my eyes shot right, to the backs of a couch and a lounge chair. Above the back of the chair, brown hair stuck up. Next to the chair was a rocks glass sitting next to a decanter of booze. The man's right hand, sticking out from the sleeve of a suit jacket, was wrapped around his drink. My eyes rose to a television mounted offset of center on the wall. Directly to the left of the television was the mantel of a fireplace and above it, a woman's mounted head, which had a waxy shine. Her hands, also mounted, held a golden microphone. I glanced farther right to see a glass sliding door that I figured to be the walkout. The seated man, presumably William David, was the only person in sight.

"Hands up where I can see them," I said, taking another step into the room.

Beth came to my shoulder, her weapon out before her. A moment later, I heard Duffield's footsteps coming down the stairs.

"Ninety-four percent. And you came before I said it was time." He took his right hand from his drink.

"Put your hands in the air!" Beth shouted.

Duffield appeared between Beth and me, his gun trained on William David. I jerked my head at Duffield to keep eyes on the room with the closed door at our backs. I wanted his gun off our suspect, who had just killed two of his agents. Duffield walked backward toward the door and out of my peripheral vision.

"Well, I suppose," William David said.

He leaned forward in the chair, stood and turned to face us.

His hair was parted on the left side, with not a single follicle out of place—the top was longer than the sides, which were mostly gray. A thick brown mustache sat on his upper lip, the rest of his face shaved clean. He appeared to be wearing makeup. His gray suit was pressed, with a blue handkerchief coming from the breast pocket. The tie hanging around his neck and lying against his white dress shirt matched the handkerchief's color. The high back of the chair that he had sat in blocked our view of his hands.

"Hands!" I shouted and motioned them up with the barrel of my gun.

He brought up his left hand, holding a cell phone, which he brought to his eye level. "Ninety-eight percent," he said.

"Drop the phone!" Beth ordered. "Other hand in the air! Walk around the chair slowly and drop to your knees!"

Sergeant Grainger and two additional officers came from the stairwell, guns drawn.

William David's eyes didn't leave the screen of his phone, and he didn't obey my command. A moment later, he tossed the phone to the couch and looked down at whatever was in his right hand.

Beth took a step farther to her right. "Gun!" she shouted.

He lifted his arm to take aim at us. I fired twice, as did

Beth. William David stumbled backward and hit the wall next to the fireplace with a thump. The impact sent him back toward us off the wall, and he dropped to the ground, the couch blocking my view of him. I kept my gun on where he'd dropped and heard him making noise. A second later, his head came into view as he used the couch to push himself back to his feet.

He took a wobbling step backward, swayed, and got his footing. He looked straight ahead, at the gap between Beth and me—no one was there. It was almost as if he was staring into a camera.

"And this is William Allen David," he said, "signing off."

In a single motion, he lifted the gun, placed it in his mouth, and pulled the trigger. I heard Beth shout the word *no* just as the shot echoed through the lower level of the house. A spray of red hit the back wall of the room, coating the television and the woman's mount hanging above the fireplace. His body fell backward, and his right arm flailed above his head to knock the mount from the wall. William David dropped to the ground. Pink mist hung in the air.

We rushed around the couch and chair—I one way, Beth the other. Duffield came from his spot at the back of the room and took a position at the rear of the couch. All of our guns aimed down toward the place William David had landed. I was first around.

I stared at him. He lay against a stack of logs in a bin to the right of the fireplace. The cheek of the mounted woman's head rested against his thigh. His right arm had come to rest in a position around the mount that almost made him look as though he was clutching it. I crouched at the man's side and looked him in his open eyes as I checked for a pulse—nothing. I holstered my weapon. The sound of footsteps pounding the stairs echoed through the lower level of the house. I looked over to see Duffield pointing to the other rooms that needed to be cleared.

CHAPTER FORTY

We waited outside of the house for the forensics team to give us the go-ahead to reenter and have a look around. Duffield, Beth, and I watched as one of the coroners and his assistant wheeled the bodies of Agents Collette and Tolman from the kitchen to a black van that had been pulled up near the side of the house.

None of us spoke a word. The deaths of the agents were the first I'd personally encountered while working with the Bureau. A few minutes later, the bodies were loaded, and the van pulled down the driveway, made a left, and disappeared from view. The local PD kept a presence on the scene but had been pushed back to handling traffic out front. I imagined a few local reporters and journalists had radios to their ears, waiting on any police radio transmissions regarding the case—a number of news vans had gathered farther down the road.

A man in a set of white coveralls came from the side of the home toward us. He dropped his hood from his head and pulled off the respirator covering his face—it was Witting from the forensics unit. "We're going to need a hazmat team in here to remove some of this stuff. Did you guys see everything in there?"

"There is a room or two in the basement that the locals cleared that we didn't see," I said. "I heard them talking and have a pretty good idea of what the rooms contain."

"Its hands down the worst thing that I've ever laid eyes on," Witting said. He let out a long breath. "I can give you guys a walk-through room-by-room and show you what we found."

I nodded.

We followed Witting back around the house in the direction he'd come from and entered the lower level of the home through the walkout patio doors. He stopped just inside the doorway and motioned to a large gray plastic box. "Gloves for hands, wraps for shoes. You'll want both, but I'll do my best to guide you away from anything you don't want to be in contact with."

We walked over, gloved up, and covered our shoes.

"You guys were a witness to what transpired there?" Witting motioned to where William David had taken his own life.

"Correct," I said.

"Let's start over here, then." Witting waved us to the doorway just off the main room.

We approached, and Witting stepped into the room a few feet. Duffield, Beth, and I gathered in the doorway for a look inside.

At my shoulder, Beth placed the sleeve of her blazer over her mouth and nose. The room was a small den with wood-paneled walls. The room smelled of decay. A single sofa sat against the left wall, above it, a single mounted head. Its waxy finish made me believe that it was more than likely the second-to-last victim that I'd seen photos of—Courtney Mouser. The right wall had a chair in the corner and a small table with a couple of books on it. The floor was littered with broken mounts of heads and hands. Decaying gray flesh hung from the bone, along with what looked like bits of clay still attached to the skulls.

"Geez," I said.

Beth took her sleeve from her face. "Looks to be four women on the floor, judging by what I can see here."

"That's the count in here," Witting said. "Aside from the one on the wall, we have four skulls, four mounts, eight hands. Looks like some of them were destroyed with that hammer there." He pointed to one of the mounts, which had a hammer embedded in it.

"What can you tell us about the mounts themselves?" I asked.

"Well, there is a skull and some spine underneath each. The skulls are clean and empty, meaning the brains and flesh had been removed prior to what you see here. Boiled, probably. We found some what I believe to be cooked brain matter upstairs." Witting paused as if waiting for a comment, but no one said anything. He continued, "The hands look like they were put into position with wire, prior to being dunked into wax and painted. There are a couple damaged ones that I had a look at. They are decomposing pretty bad under that wax. I doubt we'll be able to get any kind of prints from them. We have some clay molded to the bone of the skulls. The hair and facial skin look like they have been both glued and stitched on. That's all that I can really tell you just from the few minutes that I had in here. Obviously, I'll create a full write-up on everything back at the lab."

Witting motioned us out the doorway so he could exit the room.

"That it down here?" Duffield asked.

"We haven't even scratched the surface." Witting walked toward the wall nearest the stairwell that led up to the main level. He passed the stairwell and walked to an open doorway leading to another part of the basement.

We followed. I had a good idea what the room, cleared by the local law enforcement was—William David's kill room. In our brief time in the house, I'd yet to see the room that had the white cinderblock background in the photos—the room where he killed and decapitated the women.

"I'm going to have you watch your step, walking in." Witting pointed down. "Lots of blood in here, so try not to make contact with anything."

I was the first behind Witting entering the room. Bloody footprints covered a plastic-lined floor, but Witting's body blocked my view of the rest of the room. Then he moved to the left, and I got my first look. Blood-spattered plastic covered the entire floor and hung from the ceiling of every wall aside from a gap at the back wall of white cinderblock. Restraints hung from the ceiling near the gap in the plastic. In the center of the room was a large table, also covered in plastic. A naked, headless, and handless body lay on the table's surface. A blood-covered yellow reciprocating saw lay across the corpse's midsection. Behind the corpse were two men in head-to-toe clean suits—more of Witting's team having a look at another mounted head that seemed to be discarded in the corner of the room.

Beth groaned.

"I'll take you over to the woman on the table for a look in a second," Witting said. "There's more to see over here." He motioned to an open doorway off to the left and started in that direction.

Beth, Duffield, and I followed.

A smell filled my nose and began to grow in power with each step forward—the stink was that of an outhouse. I tried to limit my breathing. Witting stopped before entering the room. The plastic covering the wall near the door hung over something a couple of feet up from the ground. I looked back over my shoulder at the far wall, which looked the same.

Witting pulled the plastic back, exposing a chest freezer. "There's another two on the other side of the room as well. Same contents," he said.

Witting lifted the freezer's lid. I glanced inside to see two headless and handless female bodies stacked on top of each other. The skin color of the women was a pale blue—frozen solid.

"We have a count of six in the freezers," Witting said. "The one on the table makes seven."

"We only had six missing women," Beth said. "Erin

Cooper-Connelly would make seven if he actually had her."

"My hunch," I said, "she's the one on the table and the one that was above the fireplace."

"If she went missing in California, how did she end up here?" Beth asked.

"He may have gone and gotten her," Duffield said. "Kept her here while he perfected what he was doing."

"Hold that thought for a second." Witting closed the freezer lid and walked through the doorway into the next room. Beth, Duffield, and I followed Witting into the small room. The stink in the air increased.

Directly in front of us was a washer and dryer. To the right, tucked back into the corner of the room was a large cage, much larger than something for a house pet. A padlock lay on the floor next to it. I took in the seafoam-green cage. Each bar was steel bar stock an inch around. The edges and corners of the cage were double that in thickness. The cage stood three feet high by five feet long. Inside the cage were some stained blankets in a ball—they looked wet. I imagined the smell was coming from inside of the cage.

"No reason to have a cage like that unless you're keeping something in it that you don't want to get out," Witting said. "Probably from a zoo or something."

"Cooper-Connelly, perhaps," Duffield said.

"If that's the case, he would have had to have her in there for what, a month, two months?" I asked. "When did she go missing?"

"A month and a half or so ago." Duffield said.

"The thought of that is just terrifying," Beth said. "Think

about it—you have whatever was going on in the next room happening while you're locked in a cage in here."

"Well, it looks like he was trying to limit the sound coming from here or into here," Witting said. "The walls are covered with acoustic foam."

"If he had her in here for months, it was probably to keep her quiet." I felt myself getting light-headed—the tiny breaths I was taking to limit the smells coming into my airways were beginning to take their toll. "Anything else of interest in here?"

Witting shook his head and started for the door. "I'll show you the woman," he said.

We left the laundry room and walked back into the plastic-lined room.

"Watch your steps," Witting said.

I followed him toward the body, with Duffield and Beth following, being sure to watch my step as to not place a foot into a puddle of half-coagulated blood. I stood near the woman's foot, and Beth and Duffield came to my back.

"This woman died today. Looks like a knife wound to the heart." Witting pointed to the area above her left breast. "Which is the same with the bodies that we have in the freezers."

"We have a knife that probably matches up over here," one of Witting's guys said.

"Bag and tag," Witting said. He turned his attention back to us. "I'd say she was killed here." Witting walked to the small gap in the plastic on the wall. "We have restraints mounted into the floor and these here hanging from the I-beam. This pool of blood here is fairly fresh, and I have a blood trail from it back to the table. Guessing he carried her over there before he began with the saw."

I stood quiet for a moment, thinking about how the murders of these women had played out—how when he took what he wanted from their bodies, he prepared them in his work area upstairs.

"Do you think we can match up the cut marks from the saw? Place body with proper head and hands?" Duffield asked.

"I would think we should be able to," Witting said.

"It will help with getting complete remains back to the families," I said. "I suppose we could still get some DNA, but that depends as well. The saw marks might be our best way to match them up."

Witting nodded in agreement. "We'll make sure everything that matches stays together. Did you guys need to see the rooms upstairs? There's a bedroom that I'm sure will hold some interest for you."

"We saw it while we were clearing the home," I said. "Little workstations lining the walls."

"That would be the room I speak of," Witting said.

"It would have been good to get a heads-up before seeing any of this," a voice said at our backs.

I turned to see Aaron Koechner, the lead from the Louisville office's tech unit standing in the doorway, looking in. "Local PD showed me in through the back patio door there." He bobbed his head in that direction.

"Yeah, Aaron," Duffield said. "The phone is on the couch.

We haven't touched it." Duffield started toward Aaron at the door.

Beth and I followed. Witting stayed with his team in the room.

"You said that he was uploading something?" Aaron asked.

"That's what he said, yes," Duffield said.

We walked across the main room toward the couch.

"The phone is on the cushion there," Duffield said.

Aaron took a pair of gloves from his back pocket and pulled them over his hands. Looking at the couch, he leaned over and picked up the phone. He turned his back toward the fireplace. "I saw all of that over there once. I don't need to see it again, if possible." He held the phone in one hand and clicked on the screen. "No issues if I just dive into this phone here to see what he was doing?"

"That's why you're here," Duffield said.

"Sure. No screen lock," Aaron said. "That's a good start for us." He clicked at the phone's screen. "It looks like he uploaded a video. I have it here. Let's see what it was." Aaron clicked on the screen and placed the cell phone on the edge of the couch back so it would stand on its own and we could all watch.

The recording started. William David was standing directly between his television and the head mounted on the wall. He held the gold microphone in his left hand near his mouth. In his right hand was a television remote. He introduced himself and his coanchor, Erin Cooper-Connelly. He held the microphone up to her mouth. No sound came from the recording. Then the remote control came into frame as he played a clip and called the action of the sports highlights. He introduced the next clip, a local basketball game. He placed the mic in one hand beneath the mounted head of the woman and crossed his arms over his chest. The recording was silent. William David took the microphone from the hand on the mount and called the next sports clip—golf. He replaced the mic in her hand and repeated the process of the odd back-and-forth over and over. Finally, William took the mic, walked closer to the camera, and said, "I'm William Allen David"—he turned and pointed at the mounted head—"and *that* is Erin Cooper-Connelly. Enjoy your sports, America."

William reached over the camera and clicked off the recording.

"I don't even know what to call whatever that was I just watched," Beth said.

Aaron reached for the phone and lifted it back up. "Ah, when did this go up? Do we know?"

"An hour ago. Right around there," Duffield said.

"It's been viewed almost eight thousand times already," Aaron said. He clicked a couple more buttons on the phone. "It actually looks like this wasn't the only place he uploaded this to. I have five or six video-sharing sites in the recent memory here."

CHAPTER FORTY-ONE

We'd spent another two days at the Louisville Bureau field office—the Thursday had been filled with three separate press conferences and, between those, sorting through everything that had been found at the house. William David had not only uploaded the disturbing video of him anchoring sports with the mounted head, which we confirmed to be Erin Cooper-Connelly, but he'd also e-mailed countless digital photos of his acts to just about every national media outlet one could think of. Contained in the files included in his e-mails was the scan of another letter, which we'd found inside his home printer and scanner. The letter was short, and the basic idea of it was that he would become the best-known sports anchor of all time. Considering the amount of press he was generating, I didn't much doubt the claim.

We'd put in calls to each video-sharing website, trying to get the videos pulled, all of which agreed and took them down immediately. By the time they'd been removed, the clips had generated over a hundred thousand views. As Aaron from the tech department explained it, the videos were out there and had undoubtedly been copied and renamed countless times. He said that the companies would pull them upon them being reported or found, but basically if someone wanted to find the clip of William David coanchoring with a mounted head and watch it, they'd be able to somewhere without too much trouble.

Our Friday in Louisville was filled, morning until night, with compiling all our paperwork from the investigation and waiting on more things to trickle in. We had William David's bank records and found a flight to California along with numerous stops at gas stations that created a path back to Louisville. Videos were beginning to come back to us from local FBI field offices that were making trips out to the gas stations. Security videos showed William David in the Chevy Impala with a female locked in the back. The bodies from the freezers had thawed, and the forensics team was matching them via saw marks to the hands and spines at the points where the body parts were removed. While we were still waiting on confirmation for two of the women, April Backer and Jennifer Pasco, we had two bodies, two skulls, and four hands that remained—I imagined they would match up, and all of our women, as well as body parts, would be accounted for. The only thing we were really left wondering was if David was the person behind her husband's reported suicide. I was about ninety-nine percent sure that he was, but I'd placed a number of calls out to California to try to get more information on the subject and wasn't really coming up with anything new. I hoped more information would come in.

I sat at my dining-room table, looking over the Sunday

newspaper while being sure to avoid the paper's coverage of the murders, investigation, and details from the house, which were located on the front page, as well as continuing on multiple pages inside. I flipped another page of the newspaper, to the sports section, and folded the paper closed when I saw William David's face. I looked down at Porkchop, seated at my foot—more on my foot than at it.

I gave him a pat on the head. "I don't have any food for you, dummy."

"He thinks you do," Karen said.

I glanced over to the stairwell to see her putting on earrings and walking down toward me.

Her high heels hit the hardwood with a clack. Karen wore a gray blouse and long skirt, and her hair was pulled back in a ponytail. "Are you almost ready?"

I took a drink from my coffee and let out a breath. "Ready as I'll get, I guess."

She walked behind me, put her hands on my shoulders, and gave them a rub. "I'm telling you it's fate."

I craned my neck to look up at her. "Or just bad credit from the people who originally put in the offer," I said.

"Well, whatever the hell it is, we're getting another shot at the place."

"I want to give it a good look over again before making any decisions."

"I thought we had decided," Karen said.

"Actually, I said that I liked the place the last time we looked at it, and then you decided while I was gone at work. I mean, if you want to get all technical about it."

"I'm telling you, Hank. It's the one. Margie doesn't think it's going to last long. Lots of interest, she said."

"Mmm hmm. Isn't that Sales 101? Fear of loss? And 'Margie'? You're on a first name basis with the realtor that we've seen once and apparently you only communicated with via e-mail after that?"

"I may have gone and looked at it again this week," Karen said. "Twice."

I held up my palms. "You couldn't wait for me?"

"I'm sorry. I was excited. The place looks huge without all the previous owner's furniture in there. And it was actually three times I went and looked, but the last time, Margie wasn't there, and I just kind of parked and walked up and peeked into the windows."

I shook my head. "That's called trespassing. Or peeping. One of the two."

"She says it's a great buy," Karen said.

"Margie, I assume?"

"Yeah."

"The realtor thinks it's a great buy?" I asked sarcastically. "No shit."

"Okay, okay, she's probably not that impartial of a party. But it is appraised for higher than the asking price," Karen said.

"So I've been told."

"Why are you grumpy? This is supposed to be fun."

"I'm not grumpy," I said. "I just get a little antsy when the thought of spending hundreds of thousands of dollars comes up."

"I know, but we have to do something. We only have a few months left on the lease here. I think it's time we get a place.

Especially after the news of being accepted as an adoption family." Karen smiled. "Being settled into a nice house and welcoming in a child is kind of what we want, isn't it? Just think about it. A beautiful house, big yard, maybe a tire swing in the tree out front. The pitter patter of little feet."

"Now you're really laying it on thick. What time do we have to be there?"

"Noon. So if you want to stop and grab breakfast before, we should get our asses moving."

"Ten four," I said.

I grabbed my coffee, put the remaining half of a cup down in a big chug, and stood.

"Your Jeep or my truck?" Karen asked.

"You drive."

Karen scooped her keys from the breakfast bar separating the dining room and the kitchen and headed for the door. I followed her after I tossed Porkchop a treat from the container on the shelf and told him to be good. Karen drove us to a little diner down the street from our townhouse, and we shoveled down a quick breakfast. Twenty minutes, two coffees, and a giant bacon-egg-and-cheese sandwich that we split later, we were back on the road.

The house Karen was set on was located in Alexandria, fifteen minutes from our townhouse. The distance wouldn't really affect either of our commutes to work. Karen pointed out things that were cute and convenient around the neighborhood as we approached, casually putting a lot of effort into selling me. I didn't protest too much. We made a left on Leaf Lane and drove toward the address that, if I remembered correctly, would be approaching on our right after a small bend in the road. I looked left and right at the homes on the block. All looked ten to twenty years old, with mature trees and nice enough cars in the driveways. A guy going for his mailbox must have seen me staring at him, and he threw me a wave. I waved back.

"See how friendly they are around here?" Karen asked.

"Yeah, yeah."

"There it is." Karen bounced around in her seat. "It looks like Margie is already here."

The woman was standing at the end of the driveway waving at us.

Karen pulled to the side of the road, and we stepped out. I swung the passenger side door closed and watched Karen round the front of the truck and walk straight to the realtor. I stood at the edge of the driveway briefly while Karen and the realtor spoke—I heard the realtor woman make a joke about what time our moving truck was arriving.

I stared past a big tree in the front yard at the white two-story colonial. The place was exceptionally nice and a bit undervalued. The tree out front would definitely hold a swinging bench or tire swing—Karen's daydream. I went through a quick bit of rationalizing the cost and grumbled to myself. Karen was set on the place—really, really, set on it—and I'd be fine with calling it home.

"What the hell," I said. "May as well get this over with." I walked toward Karen and the realtor.

The End

For more books by E.H. Reinhard, please visit:
http://ehreinhard.com/

Made in United States
North Haven, CT
26 April 2023

35929749R00183